Common Grounds
Tabor Heights, Year 1, Book 3

By
Michelle Levigne

www.MtZionRidgePress.com

Mt Zion Ridge Press
295 Gum Springs Rd, NW
Georgetown, TN 37366

https://www.mtzionridgepress.com

Published in the United States of America
Publication Date: November 15, 2023

Editor-In-Chief: Michelle Levigne
Executive Editor: Tamera Lynn Kraft

Welcome to Tabor Heights:
A friendly little town on Ohio's North Coast, where sweet romance is always in the air.

Here you'll be able to explore the lives of the members of the congregation of Tabor Christian Church in the space of two years. The stories overlap, and there's no one right place to start.

Just like any small town, you come in, you meet someone, you hear their story and get to know them, and they introduce you to their friends, tell you something about them, and you learn those stories. As you get to know these new friends, they introduce you to other people, and tell you about other interesting stories in town.

It's the same way with Tabor Heights. Start with the story that interests you the most, and then branch out.

Settle back and enjoy your visit.
Welcome!

<u>Year One</u>

THE SECOND TIME AROUND
DETOURS
COMMON GROUNDS
WHITE ROSES
THE FAMILY WAY
FORGIVEN
FIRESONG
BEHIND THE SCENES
THE MISSION
ACCIDENTAL HEARTS
A QUIET PLACE

<u>Year Two</u>

COOKING UP TROUBLE
THE WRATH OF BUBBLES
INVITATION TO A WEDDING
TRUCK STOP ANGEL
A BOX OF PROMISES
WHEELS
THE TEDDY BEAR DANCER

Chapter One

Tuesday, December 10
Butler-Williams University
Tabor Heights, Ohio

"Hannah." The male voice came from the snowy darkness as she stepped through the side door of the university classroom building.

Hannah Blake swallowed a shriek and took a step backward, reaching for the pepper spray hanging from the strap of her purse. She listened for voices coming down the stairwell behind her, but her classmates and the professor had gone down the stairs at the other end of the building.

Then she recognized the voice and stopped the heavy, old-fashioned metal door from swinging closed.

"Chief?" Her voice wobbled a little and she grinned, feeling foolish as the lean, wide-shouldered figure of Chief Cooper stepped into the puddle of light in the doorway.

"Sorry." The head of the Tabor Police Department shrugged his broad shoulders and offered a crooked, weary smile that didn't reach his deep-set gray eyes. "I was on my way inside to meet you coming from class. Didn't mean to scare you."

"But you wanted to know how I did, talking with Arc's people today?" She took a deep breath, trying to calm her still-racing heart.

"Aren't you going the long way around to the parking lot?" He stepped back as she came outside.

"I didn't drive. It's just a short hop down the street to my apartment, so it practically takes more time to drive and park than—" She shook her head. The police chief had more important things on his mind than saving gas and getting some exercise after a long day sitting at her desk.

"I'll walk you home."

"I should be safe, shouldn't I? The White Rose prefers brunettes, not blondes, and he never stalks more than one girl at a time, right?"

"This is a college campus, going on nine p.m., and you're a pretty young woman walking alone. If you were my daughter, I'd ground you for taking risks like that, whether there was a serial killer on the loose or not." The very calmness of his voice sent chills up Hannah's spine. He let out a long, loud breath. "Sorry again. It's been a long day."

"I have messages waiting at three women's shelters that could meet your needs." Hannah fell into step with him and shrugged the strap of her book bag higher onto her shoulder. She flipped the collar of her long wool coat up around her neck as they stepped out from between the century-old sandstone university buildings, anticipating the gust of snowy wind that whipped around them. "I gave them my cell number, and I committed the unpardonable sin of leaving my phone on during Dr. Holwood's test review." That earned a soft chuckle from the chief, which had been her goal.

His humor faded quickly. "I want to get her out of town as soon as possible. Even if there's no place to send her."

"Who?" Hannah almost whispered. She had refused to ask when Chief Cooper met up with her at church Sunday morning to ask for her help, through Common Grounds legal clinic's many connections.

Common Grounds was sponsored by the Arc Foundation, which had battered women's shelters in four states, along with medical clinics, and other philanthropic outreaches. Chief Cooper wanted to get the latest target of the White Rose out of town before the stalker decided his "true love" had betrayed him. Before he killed her like he had the previous two girls he had terrorized.

"Annalee Gray," he murmured, so softly the rising wail of the wind almost wiped the words out of the air before they reached her ears.

Hannah muffled a moan. She knew Annalee. New to town, new to Tabor Christian Church, a quiet girl who lived with her elderly parents. Annalee fit the pattern of the White Rose's first two victims: dark-haired, dark-eyed, didn't socialize much, and lived at home. He had stalked them, demanded unconditional love, and murdered them when they betrayed his alleged love, Hannah wished she had encouraged Annalee to get more involved in the Singles group at church, made sure she was more socially active. Maybe the White Rose would have decided she wasn't the girl for him if she had been a social butterfly.

"If they don't call me before I go to bed, I'll call all three shelters again and reinforce how urgent the situation is," Hannah promised. They stopped at the intersection of Sackley and Main to wait for the light. A swirling gust of wind enfolded them in stinging white for a few seconds.

"Thanks. I'm sure Annalee and her parents will appreciate it."

He linked his arm through hers as they hurried across the street. Hannah was grateful for that support when her foot slipped just before stepping up onto the curb. They walked in silence down Main Street until they crossed Stephen, the intersecting side street. The Book Worm, situated on the corner, went dark. Hannah checked her watch—9:15 on the dot. She could set her watch by Dottie Wilkins, the owner of the new-and-used books store. A long row of Century houses stretched down this section of Main, all transformed into businesses on the ground floor and apartments on the upper floors. Hannah lived in the fourth house in the row. Chief Cooper pointed at the building next to the Book Worm, with the windows dark on the ground floor.

"How are things coming on setting up the branch office?" he asked as they started up the driveway of Hannah's apartment house.

"Someone from Arc was supposed to meet with Mandy today to inspect the office space and hand over the check. We're ready to start moving in."

"It'll be nice having Common Grounds right here in town. Nice for you, living so close to work."

"Definitely." Hannah muffled a squeak as her phone rang and she dropped her purse. Chief Cooper went to one knee as he dove to catch it before it landed in the pile of snow next to the driveway. "Thanks." She laughed as he handed her the phone. A silent plea raced through her heart, that this call would be the answer Chief Cooper wanted, and Annalee needed.

Ten minutes later, she stumbled up the old-fashioned iron fire escape that led to her second-floor apartment door, giddy from the good news and Chief Cooper's hard, quick hug of celebration. Annalee would be safe in Indiana before lunchtime tomorrow.

Then a new thought hit her. When the White Rose realized Annalee had escaped him, who would he target next?

~~~~~

"Don't worry, Annalee." Chief Cooper's voice vibrated through the wiretap. "By this time tomorrow, you'll be safe, a whole state away."

"I can't believe it's almost over." Annalee sighed, tears in her voice. "When will you come get me?"

"Tomorrow morning around nine."

No.

He cut the connection to the wiretap and fought the temptation to hurl the equipment across the cold, damp, dirty room full of shadows.

No, the police would not come get her. She wouldn't be there.

The time had come to punish her.

He couldn't sit still while fury and pain burned through his blood. He leaped to his feet to pace through the wreckage of the abandoned greenhouse. He couldn't decide who made him angrier. His angel, for betraying him just like the others had done? Or Chief Cooper, for helping his angel hide from him? He had to punish everyone who tried to steal his angel's love, or told her lies, or helped her to hide from him when she deserved to be punished.

This time, he had been so sure Annalee was the one. Wasn't three supposed to be the charm? After years of waiting, he was so sure she was
~~~~~

his angel, his reward for being patient, his recompense for the pain he had suffered when the first two had showed they were false, lying whores. He had thought they were his angel come back to life, but they revealed themselves as fallen angels. He thought the police wiretap on Annalee's home phone had been a sign. They made it so easy for him to listen to her phone calls and ensure no one tried to steal her love from him by telling her lies. He loved coming to his hiding place after work and listening to the tape recordings made of every phone call to and from the house, just to hear her voice. It was a gift. It was a sign. It was a promise that this time, he had found his angel.

"Fallen angel," he whispered, his heart breaking and shredding his voice.

Why had Chief Cooper believed her lies? Why was he helping her run away and hide from her punishment?

He shook his head and looked up at the grimy greenhouse roof. He could barely see the moonlight through the thick layer of snow clinging to the sloped surface. No, he couldn't really blame Chief Cooper, because hadn't he been deceived yet again, too? His angel wasn't sweetness and shy innocence. She had fooled them both. He couldn't blame Chief Cooper. The chief of police was his friend, after all.

But he had to punish his fallen angel.

Tonight.

~~~~~

"Why isn't Hannah eating with us?" Joan Archer asked, pausing midway through her first slice of pizza. She laughed when her question caught Xander Finley taking a big bite of pizza.

He grimaced and chewed. She would just have to wait until he finished. When Joan had called from the road, saying she wanted to meet with him before she headed home to Akron, Xander had chosen to work later than usual and picked up pizza from Mancuso's before he headed home. Mancuso's pizza was not to be hurried, even for an old friend.

The ringing phone stopped Xander in mid-chew. He rolled his eyes and stumbled away from the tiny bistro table set up on the plain hardwood floor in the middle of his echoing dining room. After three years in his condo, he still hadn't bought a dining room set. Or living room furniture. Or a frame for the mattress he slept on. He never thought about furniture until he had guests, like now.

Xander chewed and swallowed as he reached for the phone, and Joan's question finally registered.

Why *hadn't* he asked Hannah to join them? She would be in charge of the branch office of Common Grounds in Tabor. She liked Joan, and they got along great, like old friends. Inviting her to share in the brainstorming session tonight would have made sense.
~~~~~

Lately, he had daydreamed a little too often about how much nicer his condo would look and feel if she were there to light up the place with her bright smile, her chiming laughter echoing off the walls. Xander tried to keep his interest in Hannah just a little warmer than the long-term friendship he shared with Joan, the head of the Arc Foundation. He feared if he let their friendship grow into something closer, it might affect their working relationship.

When that happened, people might see how he felt about her, the images that filled his dreams. Xander knew how people gossiped, how a casual touch could be warped into sexual harassment. Hadn't he defended enough innocent bosses and schoolteachers since opening up Common Grounds? He knew what people's filthy imaginations could do to someone's reputation, and he had more than his own image to protect. Xander had no right to risk one fleck of dirt on his reputation, indirectly harming the Arc Foundation with his actions.

That resolve got harder to keep by the week, because sometimes he thought he would burst if he didn't tell Hannah how pretty she looked. How her presence brightened the office. How much better he felt when he had been sick last month, just because she touched his forehead and made him drink orange juice. Her voice soothed his headaches.

Hannah's slim, athletic build and strawberry-blonde hair were easy on the eyes after a long day digging for precedents and writing briefs and glaring across conference tables at opposing lawyers. She was paralegal, Gal Friday and den mother for the lawyers at Common Grounds Legal Clinic. Xander didn't know what he would do without her presence every day. Maybe he had put her in charge of the proposed Tabor branch office so her physical presence wouldn't torture him so much of every day?

You're in deep trouble, boy, he scolded himself, and shoved those forbidden daydreams back into the dark corner of his mind. He snatched up the phone just before the answering machine clicked on.

"Xander's shack," he said, before he quite had the phone to his mouth.

"Better be more than that," a lazy, rich voice drawled. "I don't do shacks."

"Tyler!" Xander laughed and turned to put his back to the corner where dining room wall met kitchen doorway. He slid down to the bare wood floor, his knees almost in his ears. "How are you doing, old man?"

"I'll remind you I'm three months younger than you, so who's the old man? Don't you lawyer types ever get details right?"

"Only when it pays. And since when do you artsy types care about reality?" Xander glanced around and saw Joan bending down to check on the chopped, leftover steak her big gray Akita, Ulysses, had for his dinner. "Hate to cut things short, but I'm having a business dinner. What's the news?"

Tyler knew when to keep things brief. In four minutes, Xander hung up the phone and shambled back across the scuffed hardwood floor to rejoin Joan. He finally loosened his tie and raked a hand through the tangle of his brown hair to get it out of his face. Why hadn't Hannah reminded him he needed a haircut? She had been unusually busy today, hadn't she?

"Business dinner? Two old study pals sharing a pizza?" Joan slouched in the chair, crossing her ankles with her jeans-clad legs stretched out in front of her. She wiggled her toes, making the red elves on her socks dance.

"Since when do we get together anymore unless we're talking about Arc or Common Grounds?" Xander shot back with a teasing grin.

There had once been three of them: Joan, Matt and Xander, kindred spirits who met during an evening class at Butler-Williams University and became study partners and an inseparable trio. Just before Joan connected with her long-missing father and joined the Arc Foundation, she and Matt had a disagreement that neither one would talk about, and their trio had lost some of its easy companionship. Whenever he thought long enough about it, Xander was convinced that a bungled attempt at romance had come between them, and still made them uncomfortable around each other.

"A friend from college," he said as he sat down. "Tyler Sloane. He's moving up here in a few weeks to take over the Royal Community Theater. Great guy. He's going to be my roommate. At least until we drive each other crazy." He snorted as he looked around his bare dining room. Tyler had an entire apartment's worth of furniture to fill in all the echoing spaces in the condo.

"Sounds good." Joan bit off half the crust of her second piece of pizza. "So, why didn't you ask Hannah?" she asked after chewing four times and swallowing. "You're moving her up to full partnership even before she passes the bar. Let her help carry some of the load now."

"She had an evening class. I couldn't ask her to skip. They're prepping for next week's finals." He shrugged and bit into his cooling pizza.

"Excuses, excuses. I think you just don't want me to spend time with Hannah. Maybe we'll trade nasty stories about you, or I'll hire her away to work for me at Arc."

"What?" Xander choked even before he saw the teasing grin brightening Joan's face.

"I really think you ought to pay better attention to her."

"Why?" He sat back and really looked at Joan. He was five years older than her and had counseled her through some rough spells when she discovered the father she had never known. How could Joan seem older than him, sometimes? Especially now, when he felt totally clueless and she wore that knowing little smirk?

"You know, when Anne was up here to help you guys, observing for the foundation, she thought there was something between you two."

"Really?" Xander's fingers slipped on the condensation coating his can of ginger ale.

"I'm thinking now it was just stress. On Anne's part." She took another bite of crust and chewed slowly, watching him with half-lidded eyes.

Yeah, Xander agreed silently. *It was all Anne's imagination. Stress.*

Anne had been accused of entrapment when she beat up a mugger who attacked her in the Metroparks. Then Bailiff Simons poisoned Hannah, trying to frame a crooked lawyer who opposed Xander's client. It had been a rough few weeks. Xander had been relieved when everything went back to normal.

What would he do without Hannah in his life? He didn't need her frightened off by more danger, death threats, or people trying to create an office romance.

He was lucky she hadn't hooked up with someone during her night classes at BWU. What if she met someone when she started working on her law degree at John Carroll University? What if she fell in love, and they had far more in common than he and Hannah had right now, and she left to set up practice with her husband?

Hannah was a smart girl. Lady, he corrected. A lady in every sense of the word. Tough and sensitive, common sense yet with a poetic side. She had a knack for getting abused children and battered wives to trust her when they would open up to no one else. She had to know that the next several years of study toward her law degree would be rough. No time for a boyfriend. Why waste her time on a relationship when every spare moment would be divided between work and studies? Even if Xander had promised to help her with every paper and loan her all his law books, it wouldn't be easy for her.

Please, God, don't let her quit on me.

"You okay?" Joan reached over the pizza box and rested her hand on his.

"A lot on my mind, I guess." He tried to smile.

"Worried about Hannah?"

"I try to take care of her. What would I do without her?" Xander shrugged and opened the box, even though his slice of pizza was only half-eaten. "More?"

"Xander..." Joan glared at him for several moments. Then she leaned forward to push the lid of the pizza box closed. "If you don't bring her down to Quarry Hall for one of our open houses this week or next week, I'm going to drive back up here, take Hannah out to lunch, and tell her all your dirty secrets."

"I don't have any."

"That's what you think." She waggled her eyebrows at him, earning a snort of laughter. "Besides, I can always make up some juicy stories about you."

"Blackmail!"

"Darn tootin'." Joan stuck her tongue out at him, then grinned and slouched a little more in her chair. "Your new office is in a great spot. I like your landlord, and she said she'll let you start the decorating and renovations even before the check clears."

"That's great." He pictured Hannah's delight when she got the news. Anything that made her happy made him happy.

Hannah enjoyed all the preparation work she had done; the file folders she had filled with floor plans and lists of wallpaper, paint, equipment and office furniture the new branch office would need. He would do anything to keep Hannah working alongside him. The new office had been her idea from the beginning. It was her pet project that gave her energy at the end of a long, rough day. He loved seeing how her eyes lit up when she worked on all the details. As long as Hannah was content to work with him, he was safe.

~~~~~

"I'm tempted." Hannah sighed in weary amusement and curled up a little tighter on the loveseat in her tiny living room. She switched the phone to her left ear, tucked a strand of hair behind her right ear, and pulled the rainbow-striped afghan a little closer around her.

"Just tempted?" Anne Hachworth's chuckle came through the phone loud and clear. "Even if I hadn't just ended a killer assignment, I'd want to be home, relaxing until the holidays are over. You have to come down for one of our open houses. The mansion is really something to see when it's all lit up. Especially when we have the school choirs come in to sing."

"I want to, but I'll need to talk Xander into taking an evening off. Maybe I should use the guilt factor on him."
~~~~~

Chapter Two

Hannah turned to look at the photo sitting on the bookshelf next to her, taken during the fourth anniversary celebration for Common Grounds Legal Clinic. At the oddest times, without warning, her heart still skipped a beat at the sight of Xander's comfortably ugly, grinning face. Hannah scolded herself for the reaction. She had sworn to give up on developing any kind of romantic relationship with Xander. Why couldn't she keep that vow?

He could never be called handsome, and he was as oblivious as a brick wall when it came to things like birthdays and new hairstyles. How could someone so homely trash all her good intentions and common sense? Xander's hair was a dull brown tangle that took on red highlights in the summer *if* he remembered to spend any time outdoors. His eyes were two different shades of muddy green-brown. His nose was too wide, and crooked to boot. His jaw was too square, making his face look like a squat pyramid. And it wasn't as if his voice made up for his physical defects, either. It was a rumble, at best. Like gravel tumbling in a barrel of oil. Though it was warm and kind and caring, even when he was tired.

Give up, Hannah Blake, she silently scolded for the thousandth time. But who was counting?

Maybe she should concentrate on her upcoming classes at John Carroll University and give up on Xander? Maybe she had to become a lawyer and his partner before he would get interested? It couldn't look good, could it, for a lawyer to become involved with his paralegal and office manager? It wasn't like she and Xander were committed to anyone else, after all. Still, if she had the status of a full-fledged lawyer, that would certainly tear down a wall or two that might be making Xander hesitate, even if unconsciously.

She had to ask herself, how could someone so brilliant and compassionate be so dense?

"Guilt factor?" Anne laughed. "What's that?"

"Our office is sponsored by Arc. He might be pals with the director of the foundation," Hannah said in pseudo-regal tones, "but missing a holiday function at Arc headquarters is a dire insult."

"Tell him we'll re-think your scholarship to law school if he messes up." A muted snicker came over the phone.

"I wonder if he even remembers I'm starting at JCU in January."

Hannah tried not to sigh.

"Are you having second thoughts?"

"A law degree is way down on my list of things to worry about and second guess." Hannah shivered when the wind moaned past the window behind her. "Hopefully, we're inspecting the new offices tomorrow." The door in the kitchen creaked and groaned open, and a breath of icy air swirled through the apartment. She didn't mind the cold, knowing her roommate, Rene Ackley, was finally home from work.

"New offices? What have I missed out on while I was on the road?"

"We're expanding, opening a branch office in Tabor. We're renting the downstairs in one of the big old houses on my street that got converted into stores and apartments. It's practically next door."

"That big old blue house with the deep windows you were talking about? Way cool, girlfriend," Anne drawled. "Think of all the time you'll save walking to work. It'll be your kingdom, your time to shine. You can handle it. Even starting law school in January. Heck, if you can keep Xander and four other lawyers in line, you can handle this, no problem."

"I keep telling myself that. But..." Hannah grinned and waved as Rene walked into the living room. Her slight, amber-haired roommate nodded and peeled out of her long coat as she crossed to her bedroom. "It's stupid — my whole fixation on Xander — and I know it's good to get out of the office and away from him. Get some distance and perspective. The man is a wonderful guy, intelligent, compassionate, dedicated — "

"So dedicated to helping the downtrodden, he still hasn't noticed that you're in love with him after working together for *years*. And you, being the disgustingly noble idiot you are, think it's wrong to go from paralegal to lawyer, just on the chance he'll see you as more than Gal Friday."

Long silence. Hannah held her breath and listened to the wind howling, louder and more mournful than just a few minutes ago. She finally released the breath and laughed.

"What, your guardian angel tells you what I'm *thinking*, now?"

"I spent enough time shadowing you and Xander for the foundation, I got a good view of the situation. You want to be his partner in every possible aspect of the word. Nothing wrong with that. And you're smart enough to know you can't push it. The guys who are worth the effort can't be hunted down and hogtied — they have to at least think it was all their idea. When he's ready to get his head out of his case files and start enjoying life, he'll realize you're a girl and more than just his best buddy and he'll..." Anne groaned. "Who am I to give lovelorn advice, anyway?"

"Smarter than me." Hannah wiped a tear from the corner of her eye.

She felt a twinge of guilt over going into the whole subject of romance and relationships with Anne. More than a year ago, Hannah had learned Anne had been raped as a child. No matter how whole and balanced she appeared, no matter how much she had healed, there still had to be scarring. As far as Hannah knew, Anne didn't go beyond casual friendship with men. Vincent, the head of security for Arc, was probably the closest male presence in Anne's life, and he was like a big brother to all the young women who worked for the foundation.

"There's a whole world of different definitions for 'smart,' girlfriend," Anne said with a weary chuckle that made Hannah wonder just how "killer" her last assignment had been. "Anyway, you two are officially invited to one of our holiday open houses. Anything going on in town that Joan should know about?"

"Well... Joan is meeting with Xander tonight, but I doubt he'd think to tell her about this. Chief Cooper asked us to help the White Rose's latest target get out of town. I made some calls today, arranging a place for her at one of your women's shelters. Out of state. Poor Annalee. She's so nice and quiet, and new to town. Until the police figure out who this guy is, when will it be safe for her to come home?"

"Maybe when the White Rose finally finds his true love."

"Yeah, a girl emotionally twisted enough to like being stalked by an anonymous sicko who demands she stay pure and faithful to him." Hannah shuddered. "The *Picayune* has been toning down the coverage, putting the stories on page three, to keep from encouraging him. The TV stations and *Plain Dealer* are actually following suit. It still worries me. I mean, so far he seems to only pick on dark-haired girls who live at home, but who knows if that's really his pattern? Any girl not in a serious relationship could be his next target."

"So, tell Xander to pretend to be your boyfriend so the creep ignores you," Anne offered. "I know. Bad joke. Hey, sometimes all we can do is pray. If you can't do anything about the problem, it won't do you any good to worry. We've got you and the entire town on our prayer list."

"Thanks." Hannah uncurled from the loveseat and got to her feet.

"But if Xander doesn't do something to protect you, he's more oblivious than I thought. If he doesn't straighten out, I'll send Vincent to either give him a lecture on treating a lady right or break something vital." She snickered. "Take care."

Hannah chuckled as she made her farewells and hung up.

~~~~~

He used to play in the old Shipley house when he was a boy and knew how to get inside without using the front or the back doors. The big old half-dead apple tree in the backyard offered thick, sturdy branches that went up to the roof like a natural stairway. The same pines that sheltered the tree from the snow so the wood was dry and safe for climbing also cast the entire backyard into shadow. No one could see him. Not even the police officer assigned to walk the neighborhood and keep
~~~~~

watch on the Gray house tonight.

When he could see all three members of the family in the front room, watching TV, he made his move. The volume was loud enough to be heard on the sidewalk. The noise would cover any sounds he made climbing up to Annalee's bedroom.

He stepped up onto the roof and climbed down the slope to the dormer window in a few heartbeats. The slimjim that let him open locked cars made it easy to unlock her old-fashioned sash window. He slipped inside and found a hiding place in her closet. He had the chloroform-soaked cloth in a plastic zipper bag, ready and waiting. When Annalee came upstairs, he would wait until she went to bed and fell asleep. She deserved no warning, no chance to plead for mercy. It wouldn't be nice to risk making noise to frighten her parents. They didn't deserve to be punished because their daughter was a lying slut.

She was so beautiful, and so faithless. Why hadn't she obeyed him? Why had she asked the police to help her run away from him? Why wouldn't she trust in his love? There was nothing to fear, because he loved her. He had the power and the knowledge to protect her, and he had promised to watch over her everywhere, because he loved her.

No, he *used to* love her. Not anymore. Not since he realized she was false, a liar, a deception, deliberately blinding him to the existence of his true angel. He had seen his angel, his true angel, his reward for patience and the pain he had suffered. When he had destroyed this liar who pretended to be his angel, he would contact his true angel. She had come back from the dead, just like she promised, and she would be delighted to know he had faithfully waited for her.

~~~~~

Xander stood at the door of his condo, ignoring the icy air wrapping around him as he watched Joan and Ulysses get into her Jeep to drive back to Quarry Hall. They had prayed together before she left, and the warmth of that special moment kept him from noticing the threat of another winter storm looming on the horizon. Xander remembered when he had prayed alone for Joan and Matt, and then prayed with Matt for Joan's salvation. His face warmed as he considered teasing them both about his suspicions and knew he didn't dare. Joan let him know she thought he was an idiot for not pursuing a closer relationship with Hannah. If he pestered her about a romance with Matt, then she would be justified in twitting him about Hannah.

"I don't know, Lord. What's it going to take for me to know if it's right?" he whispered and raised his hand a moment later to wave as Joan pulled out of the condo driveway onto Pearl Road, heading south to Route 18 and Akron.

~~~~~

He paused, adjusted the limp burden hanging over his shoulder, and listened to the muffled sound of voices coming from the old house two driveways away. He smiled when the two young women who lived upstairs laughed. He liked Hannah and Rene. They were both nice to him.

He could have loved them, either one of them, but he had already found his new angel, and he always stayed faithful to his angel. He always found his new angel when he learned the current one was false. When he had to punish her.

This new angel was the right one, this time. She would stay faithful. She was alone at school, far from home. That had been his mistake, he realized now. His angel had to be alone, waiting patiently for him to come for her. No family. No job to distract her. Hadn't he met his first angel, his true angel, when they were both in school? He should have known he would find his angel, returned from the dead, waiting at school. This angel was the right angel. She would love him and wait for him. She would stay pure. She wouldn't need to be punished, like all the others.

~~~~~

"Isn't that a little early?" Hannah stepped back and watched her roommate plug a two-foot-tall ceramic Christmas tree into the wall.

"Christmas should be kept in our hearts all year 'round." Rene slid backward from behind the combination bookshelf/entertainment center and raked pale curls off her sweaty forehead. "At least, that's what Pastor said on Sunday."

"I know, but—"

"Besides, it's two weeks until Christmas." She got to her feet and shifted the plywood cabinet back against the wall. Hannah hurried over to help her. "That's all I'm doing tonight. A little bit every day is about all I can handle, with the gym so busy." She flipped the little switch built into the electrical cord, lighting the bulb inside the tree's base. A rainbow of nearly one hundred plastic bulbs gleamed in the dim light of the tiny living room.

"Perfect," Hannah admitted with a smile. She dropped onto the loveseat, which was all that fit into that end of the room, and slouched down, messing the blue paisley throw while she toed off her shoes.

"Getting there." Rene sat on the other loveseat at the other end of the room, covered in a matching green paisley throw. If the roommates sat on the floor in front of the loveseats, their outstretched legs would have touched at the toes.

The tiny apartment on the second floor of the Century house on Main Street reminded Hannah of a doll's house. Rene always said there was more than enough room for two single girls, as long as they didn't gain weight. Three bedrooms barely long enough to accommodate a twin bed, a kitchen the size of a schooner's galley, a bathroom like a closet, and the
~~~~~

handkerchief-sized living room. Plenty of storage in the attic, parking on the street and walking-distance access to all the conveniences of downtown Tabor Heights. The rent was low enough to let them sock money away every month, and in another week, Hannah would have less than thirty yards to walk to get to work.

"So, what're your plans for Christmas?" Rene asked in the quiet that flowed like silk through their little apartment.

Hannah shrugged.

"Come on." She mock-glared through a mask of multicolored splotches of light. "With all those brothers, you must have a dozen invitations."

"Five. Four brothers and my parents equal five *demands*, not invitations." Hannah groaned. "I plan on a nice quiet Christmas Eve with you, your dad, Vic and Baxter. Your dad *is* coming for Christmas?"

"Believe it or not, he thinks they can survive at the rescue mission without him this year." Rene slid down to the floor and did a few lazy toe-touches as she talked. "What's Xander doing?"

"Heck if I know."

"No go with the dress?"

Rene had devoted an entire Sunday afternoon to helping Hannah make alterations in a silky wool, royal blue shirt-dress she had found just down the street at the Penny Pincher second-hand store. Hannah had worn it to the office today, positive it would catch Xander's attention. In the three hours he had spent at the office, he hadn't looked at her more than ten minutes total. Hannah had gone all the way through frustration to amusement and hung the dress at the back of her closet when she changed to go to class that evening.

Maybe she should just take it back to the store. Xander hadn't noticed, so why bother looking extra-special nice? Just like he hadn't noticed when she worked her way down to a size twelve and wore skirts every day instead of just on Sundays. He never noticed her appearance. Or if he did, he never let her know he noticed.

Was that too much to ask? Especially when she noticed every detail of his appearance, his health, his moods? No matter how hard she tried to treat him just like all the other men in the office, she noticed. She cared. She let him frustrate her.

"I don't know why I bother with the man. I mean, with all the pressure from my folks, you'd think I'd be allergic to the very idea of marriage. So what do I do? I dig my claws in harder and insist on trying to get some romance from a man who thinks I'm wonderful as long as we're at work and I keep the ten thousand strands of his life together. Once we leave the office, it's like I don't exist. What is wrong with me?"

"You're an extremely intelligent young woman who loves a

challenge."

"Xander Finley is more than a challenge, he's—" Hannah sighed and slid down so her neck rested against the back cushion. "For someone who's so smart, why can't I see it's a lost cause and concentrate on my law degree instead of my M.R.S. degree?"

"You love him. You're willing to wait a thousand years if you have to."

"Like you and Vic?" She immediately wished she could take back the words when Rene flinched and her smile stiffened. "Sorry."

A shadow in her roommate's past kept her from going beyond friendship with anything male. Hannah didn't know what or who had hurt Rene. She told herself she didn't want to know until her roommate was ready to tell her. With all her legal connections and access to police records across the nation, Hannah bet she could find out in less than a week's time. Of course, that assumed whatever happened to Rene had ever been reported. But she wouldn't do it. Rene meant too much to her to risk losing the closest thing she ever had to a sister.

"Vic and Baxter are my business partners. We like the same movies and the same stupid arcade games and we have season tickets for the Guardians." Rene's smile warmed again. "In a lot of ways, they're the best buddies anybody could ever ask for. I know better than to ruin it by wanting more than what God's given us."

"Like me?"

"You're not ruining anything. Xander's mind is so one-track, he's worn a groove through his entire life. He needs you. I bet if you started dating around, the shock would wake him up and he'd realize just what he feels about you and finally do something about it."

"Xander? Jealous?" Hannah shivered and wrapped her arms tight around herself. "That'd be the day, wouldn't it?" She decided to change the subject before she said anything stupid. But that didn't mean she couldn't enjoy the warm sensation that particular mental image created. "So, your dad's coming here. For how long?"

"Just through Friday morning," her roommate said with a sigh. "What are you doing Christmas day?"

"Making my command performance. What else? Buy me some earmuffs this year, would you?"

"Dare I ask why?"

"So I don't hear the same questions I get at Thanksgiving and Christmas every year: 'Why didn't you bring Xander?' and 'When are you going to give up on him and find a nice young man and give your mother some grandchildren?' As if she needs more!" Hannah thought of all the Christmas shopping she still had to do for her multitude of nephews. Maybe what her mother really wanted was grand*daughters*. Why did the

Blake family feel duty-bound to obey the biblical injunction to go forth and multiply?

"I saw some cute ones at Penny Pincher the other day. Bunny ears and little tiger ears and—"

A thud on the apartment door stopped her short. Hannah staggered to her feet to go to the kitchen to answer the door.

Mandy Gordon stood on the wide landing outside. The heavy-set, graying woman bent over a little, taking deep breaths and holding on for dear life to the iron railing of the fire escape. Snow swirled around her and flipped up the hem of her calf-length, neon-pink cape.

"Storm of the century!" Hannah reached out a hand to help her landlord in from the cold.

"Not quite," Mandy said with a breathless chuckle. She yanked her hood back off her spray-lacquered curls. "With all the climbing I do on all my rental properties, you'd think I'd be a size five, not twenty-five."

"Twenty," Rene said, coming into the kitchen. "Not an inch more. I brought some cookies home from Rick's. Care for some hot chocolate?"

"Thanks, lovey, but I haven't been home all evening. Just on my way back from the business meeting at church. Thought I'd stop and give you the good news." She nodded to Hannah, alerted by that wide, mischievous grin on the woman's cold-reddened face.

"Everything's cleared with Arc?" Hannah laughed and flung her arms around the hefty woman, uncaring of the snow that clung to her and soaked through her clothes. "When can we start remodeling?"

"Stop on over any time you want tomorrow and pick up your keys." She winked. "I told everybody at the meeting tonight. You'll get a lot of business once you're set up in town."

"Mr. Montgomery didn't happen to be attending that meeting, did he?" Rene asked with a sigh in her voice.

"Why... I believe he did. What a coincidence." Mandy widened her eyes in feigned innocence.

Chapter Three

"Dare we hope he was so upset at the news that our office has the green light, he didn't fight the prison ministry proposal this time?" Hannah made no effort to hide her glee at the idea.

It totally escaped her why a lawyer who claimed to be a Christian would oppose a church ministry to help newly released convicts re-enter society. Then again, there were quite a few things Arthur Montgomery did that Hannah didn't even try to understand. She was more grateful than she could express that she hadn't answered that want ad four years ago when Montgomery & Associates was looking for a paralegal. She had taken a chance on a new member of their church who was starting up a legal clinic in an abandoned furniture store twenty minutes away from Tabor Heights. She had never regretted that choice. When she could ignore the longing to be more than Xander's right-hand gal.

Mandy left a few moments later, after discussing the choir's Christmas Eve numbers with Rene. Hannah watched at the door, holding on to keep her balance against the gusting wind as her landlord tottered down the creaking, groaning, old-fashioned iron fire escape stairs. During the summer, the stairs were overgrown with flowering, climbing vines. Hannah adored the picturesque, quaint entrance to their little apartment, despite the bees that filled the air along with the heavenly perfume of the flowers. In the winter, however, she wished the previous owner of the old house hadn't torn out the inside staircase to create more floor space.

"Montgomery is going to be in a fury," Rene said, when Hannah had closed and locked the door.

"He's the only one who doesn't want the clinic to open a branch office in Tabor. What is wrong with the man?"

" Foggerty doesn't want Common Grounds around, either."

"Right." Hannah grinned as she reached for the refrigerator door to pull out the jug of milk to make their hot chocolate.

Xander had made a splash with his first appearance in Tabor Heights Municipal Court, in front of Judge Foggerty, less than six weeks after he opened Common Grounds. He successfully defended Curt Mehdlang, a reporter for the *Tabor Picayune*. It was common knowledge that Judge Foggerty loathed the local newspaper. Any time an employee of the *Picayune* stood before him, no matter how small the charges, they always came away paying the maximum fine or serving the longest community service sentence allowable.

Curt had been called into court to answer for unpaid parking tickets, and Xander had successfully proved that nine-tenths of those tickets had been falsified, using phone records to prove Curt had either been at work inside the *Picayune* office or working from home when those tickets were written, which meant he was legally parked. Rumors said the officer who forged the tickets had done so on Judge Foggerty's orders to harass Curt, when he quit the police department and left town with little warning, just after Xander won the case. Common Grounds had been on the judge's "blacklist" from that day onward.

"I wonder if Montgomery is afraid of losing the few church members who are his clients, once we open up," Hannah mused. She sat down at their tiny folding table tucked into the corner of the kitchen.

"Probably. The man has no compassion. I've helped a few people who went to him for bankruptcy help. They decided not to go that route because he was so self-righteous. Like, their mistakes were some huge flaw in their moral character, and not a lack of knowledge." Rene poured milk into the saucepan and turned on the gas for the burner. "I thought the whole 'misfortune is punishment from God' mentality went out when Job was written."

"That's why you're here. To give them the knowledge and keep them from going to him for help." Hannah shivered a little when the wind howled around the window frames and eaves of the old house. "I feel sorry for Lisa. Why she ever married Todd Montgomery, I'll never understand."

"What's wrong with Todd?"

"He takes after his father a little too much, if you ask me. Lisa is so quiet and she just keeps giving. Montgomery probably figured he had a guaranteed live-in slave for his old age with her. Heaven knows his own daughters want as little to do with him as possible. In-laws are a very good reason not to get married. Ever."

"Xander doesn't have any relatives within a thousand miles of here." Rene might have smiled as she poured the sugar into the warming milk.

"Maybe *my* humongous family is why Xander won't give *me* a second look." Hannah grinned, despite the sudden, sharp throb that went through her heart.

She really had to give up on Xander Finley. No matter how sweet and intelligent and just plain good, reliable, and devoted, no oblivious man was worth the bruises on her heart. Hannah had watched Lisa and Todd Montgomery's stormy courtship, and she had prayed Lisa would get the strength to send Todd away for good. He acted like the world revolved around him, just as oblivious as Xander but with none of the self-sacrificing generosity and charm. All four Montgomery daughters had moved out as soon as they turned eighteen. Hannah thought that said a great deal about what went on behind closed doors in that family. Was love reason enough for Lisa to put up with emotional abuse from her father-in-law, and neglect from her husband?

Hannah didn't think so. She silently scolded herself yet again to forget about Xander, concentrate on getting her law degree, and let God take care of bringing some romance into her life. Maybe she was never meant to have someone special, her completion and the one she completed.

Wednesday, December 11

Xander's day started early. Vic Thomas wanted to talk with him about some paperwork covering Gold Tone Gym, the business he, Rene Ackley, and Baxter Stemple operated. That meant coming in to work more than an hour early, so he would be ready to go when Hannah showed up to head Downtown to the Justice Center.

Vic waited by the back entrance of the furniture-store-turned-office, leaning against the side of his dark green Oldsmobile, hidden in the shadows of the other buildings. Xander mentally shook his head, like he always did when he saw the other man. Something about Vic made him think he belonged in a late model Corvette, wearing black leather and mirror sunglasses, with a suspicious bulge from a shoulder holster under his jacket. Maybe it was Vic's dark Italian features. Maybe it was the way he always checked out newcomers, to their church or Tabor Heights in general, as if he thought they might explode or turn into axe murderers. Vic didn't quite trust or open up to anyone until he knew their backgrounds, making Xander think he had a number of dark secrets in his past. Whatever they were, Vic had obviously grown past them, because he was an active, giving member of their church and someone Xander knew he could go to with any kind of trouble.

"Isn't it kind of cold to be waiting out here like that?" Xander called, as he got out of his car and headed for the back door of the building. He shifted his bulging portfolio case under his arm, held out one hand to shake Vic's in greeting, and dug for the office keys in his pocket with the other hand. It was far too cold this morning to stand outside socializing even for a few moments.

"I wasn't waiting long enough to get cold," Vic said with a shrug. For once, that mischievous sparkle was missing from his big, dark eyes. Xander hoped whatever Vic wanted to discuss wasn't too serious.

Once inside the building, Xander fumbled his way to the breaker box, leaving Vic standing in the weak puddle of the red emergency lights. A moment later, accompanied by a series of stiff clicks, lights came on all through the unit that was one enormous room, divided by cubicles. Xander didn't take his coat off until after they walked up front and he had filled the coffee machine and started a carafe brewing.

"What did you want to talk about?" He turned around from the coat rack and held out a hand for Vic's black pea coat.

"I need something that will put everything in Rene's hands if I — well, if Baxter and I vanish." Vic didn't look at Xander, but concentrated on the stream of glistening black trickling into the coffee pot.

"Vanish." Xander took a deep breath. Held it. Exhaled slowly. "Are you in some kind of trouble?"

"Not yet. And I hope never." He jammed his hands into the pockets of his black jeans and shrugged. "Don't take this the wrong way, Xander, but are we on the clock?"

"Lawyer-client confidentiality started the moment you walked through the door." Xander gestured toward the chairs on the other side of the reception area and didn't wait for Vic to move before throwing himself into one. "What's up?"

"I'm living — Baxter, too — under a false identity. Our third." He grimaced when Xander whistled softly at the implications that raced through his mind. "Basically, we turned state's witness against organized crime. Very organized, very loyal, and very intent on punishing disloyalty. Our cover got blown twice, so we struck out on our own."

"So if you think you're in danger and you have to run, you don't want Rene to lose the gym." He nodded. "Makes sense."

"You're taking it pretty calmly." Vic managed a thin smile. "I hope Rene takes it this well, if we have to vanish."

"Then let's pray you don't have to." He thought for a moment. "You've been in Tabor — what? — going on three years now. How long did it take for trouble to catch up with you the last two times?"

"Eight months and eleven. We're gearing up for the holidays, and I realized that we have traditions now. It struck me, there's a whole lot more to leave behind this time." He shrugged and looked away, through the big plate glass window that looked over Pearl Road and the slushy, shadowy, early morning traffic.

"A whole lot more people, too?" Xander murmured.

Joan's comments last night had influenced his dreams, and now Vic's sudden revelation got him wondering. What if he had to take off suddenly, to save his life? What would he leave behind? Not much in the way of personal items; just his clothes and books and his condo in Medina. The clinic belonged to the Arc Foundation, and Xander was happy to have it that way.

He would leave a lot behind in terms of people, though, and that idea hurt. Did Vic intend to just take off, with no word of warning or explanation for Rene? Xander wondered if he could do the same thing to Hannah, if he had to.

He shivered, feeling the ache from a possible, unwelcome future. The thought of never seeing Hannah again threatened to steal his breath. Thank goodness his only enemies were lawyers and corporations he had defeated in court, or the con artists whose frivolous lawsuits he refused to represent.

"I have a template for that kind of document," he said, to break that chain of thought. "Come on back, and we'll start punching in the details." He stood and led the way.

Xander felt like the floor had shifted to a slightly off angle. Was he really that emotionally tied to Hannah? All right, he had cried when she was poisoned. At the time, Xander thought it was just guilt that made him want to carry her away somewhere safe. When all the fuss had settled down, Xander thought everything had gone back to normal between him and Hannah.

So he had been wrong. But what was he supposed to do about it?

He couldn't let his feelings interfere with the smooth running of the clinic. Especially when he didn't understand what was going on inside his own head.

Bottom line: he could not afford to scare Hannah away. He needed her too badly to take any chances.

~~~~~

The pre-trial meeting with Judge McGonahoy ended almost before it began. The plaintiff, for some reason no one could or would explain, had vanished two days earlier. His lawyer obviously didn't want to be there and did a slipshod job. Xander presented the facts of his case. Halfway through he fully expected the judge to throw the whole thing out. That had never happened before, but there was always a first time, wasn't there?

"Something odd's going on," Hannah agreed, as they headed up East 9th toward the I-71 entrance ramp two hours earlier than expected. Rush hour traffic had barely begun to ease up for the day.

"We can either go back to the office and get involved in something we'll have to put aside in an hour, or we can go over to the new office early. What'll it be?" He grinned and reached into his pocket to pull out his cell phone. He handed it to Hannah before she could open her mouth to answer. As if there was any question.

In moments, she had made the call and determined it would be fine to show up at Mandy Gordon's house early.

Mandy lived on the corner of Stephen and Coast, across the street from the BWU pool complex. When Xander turned off Sackley onto Coast,
~~~~~

he found the pavement hadn't been plowed yet from last night's mini-blizzard. There were empty, clean blocks of pavement all up and down the street where residents' cars had parked overnight. Stephen had been plowed, so Xander decided to park on that street instead of risking getting stuck if a plow came and left a hill of snow alongside his car. He parked halfway to Church Street, by a clear path to the sidewalk so Hannah wouldn't have to struggle through calf-high snow once she got out of the car. Movement caught his attention as he got out of the car, and Xander looked down Church Street, to a big, white, three-story Century house. Two children built a snowman, and another child and an adult sat on the front steps, watching them. How long had it been since he had taken the time to play in the snow? Since he was a child himself? It looked like fun. He envied Doria Holwood, who could take the time to play with her foster children today.

"Did you ever think of fostering?" spilled out of his mouth as he hurried around to the passenger door to offer Hannah a hand.

"What?" Hannah glanced down the street where he had been looking. "Oh—what's everybody doing home at the Holwoods'? Was school cancelled?"

"No idea." He waited until she had exited the car and slammed the door. "Well, would you?"

"I... I'm not quite sure why you're asking." She didn't look at him, but fussed with tugging her long, gray wool coat straight.

"Sometimes, you just wonder if you're going to spend the rest of your life alone." He shrugged and forced a chuckle. "Got to admit, they're doing a great thing, fostering kids like they've been."

"Considering that we've profited, I'd agree." She hurried up the gravel driveway. Someone had been out already, scraping snow away and sprinkling salt.

Xander frowned after her, caught between wondering why Hannah's voice sounded so jittery for a moment, and what she had been talking about. Then he remembered—the Holwoods' oldest foster daughter, Nikki, was the reason Joan Archer had first come to Tabor Heights. They were sisters, separated when their mother abandoned Nikki as an infant. If Joan hadn't come to town to find her sister, she wouldn't have become friends with Xander and wouldn't have eventually offered Common Grounds the Arc Foundation's backing.

Where would they be right this minute if Dr. Holwood and his wife hadn't agreed to take in a baby abandoned in a storm, and then kept her against all odds? Without Arc's money, he might be working for another law firm, and might never have met Hannah.

When they knocked on her door, Mandy Gordon appeared to be working on several projects at once, with papers spread out on two folding tables and the sofas, swishing around her living room in a psychedelic rainbow caftan that threatened to give Xander a headache from eyestrain. She welcomed them in, fluttered past her TV set to turn down the volume, then yanked open the doors of an armoire-style computer cabinet. One door had pegs on the inside, holding dozens of sets of keys. Xander didn't see a single label or marker of any kind on the sets or the pegs. He could only imagine the trouble that could result from those keys getting scrambled. Mandy was the queen of organization, though. She could always be depended on.

"Here you go," she said with a bubbling chuckle, as she swept back across the room to where he and Hannah waited and melted on the welcome mat. "Oh, almost forgot." She took a half-step to the right and swept up a handful of slips of notebook paper. "If you need any help with decorating and moving. These last three, with stars, are people who want to make appointments."

"Uh, Mandy—" Xander wasn't quite sure if he should laugh or be embarrassed.

"How much commission are we paying you?" Hannah chuckled.

"I'm not asking for anything, sweetie." Mandy giggled in return and fluttered her eyelashes.

That wicked sparkle of delight in her eyes warned Xander. Hannah had told him about the prison ministry proposal, and Montgomery's continued campaign to keep it off the church budget. Add to that the man's opposition to Common Grounds expanding into Tabor Heights, it had probably been a very interesting church board meeting last night. Thank goodness Joan had come through town on her way home from a business trip. He wasn't a coward, but he preferred to keep business battles and church separate whenever possible.

"What exactly happened at the meeting?" he had to ask.

"Vengeance is God's playground." She winked. "Xander, do you have any idea how many people are delighted you're standing up to Self-Appointed Saint Arthur?"

"Yes, and so does he. Did he demand you rent the property to him again?"

"Better than that. He sent his gang of yes-men to talk to me last night before the meeting. They cornered me in a very public, busy intersection at church, and made the mistake of bringing a lot of witnesses with them. No one embarrasses *me* into giving them their way. Then they tried to tag-team me, insisting it was a lot smarter to support an *established institution* rather than help an *upstart newcomer*. You're a newcomer, after four years?

"I reminded them that the *institution* told me to take a hike when the tenant in your spot violated the lease, vandalized the building, and had the gall to accuse me of driving away customers. The *institution* had the nerve to scold me, in front of witnesses, for bringing up 'sordid business matters' in church when he heard me telling someone I was getting legal advice on the problem. Then he got upset when he told me to go through proper channels to make an appointment with his office, and I reminded him, in front of those same witnesses, that he had refused to help me months ago and I had retained other legal counsel already." Mandy huffed, shaking her head for punctuation without dislodging a single glossy curl. "Can you believe that woman at Kiddie-Time, insulting everyone in Tabor Heights, then accusing me of telling people not to shop at her overpriced store, and then suing me for evicting her when she refused to pay her rent on 'ethical grounds'? It was the *upstart newcomer* who defended me in court."

"And will again, if they win that motion for an appeal," Hannah offered.

"Honey, I've got people lined up around the block to testify in court that arrogant twit ruined her own business without any help from me." Mandy's eyes twinkled brighter, if that was possible. "Then Saint Arthur had the gall to offer me fifty dollars less per month than the last time he tried to 'talk sense' into me. I pointed it out, too. He didn't like that. You'd think I set out to make him look like a fool in front of his friends." She snorted. "Don't you worry your head about that old Pharisee. The entire church is behind you. Go on over and start looking around. I can't wait to see what you two do with the place." She caught hold of Xander's overcoat by the left sleeve and turned him to the door.

He had learned long ago to grin and accept her affectionate bossiness. What was the use of resenting it, when she was a loving, fun woman without a vicious bone in her generous body? Granted, she loved to tweak noses and knock self-righteous hardheads back down to size, but Xander knew she included them in her prayers every night.

He and Hannah chose to walk to the new office site. It would take them less time than getting back in the car and looking for a parking spot on Main Street. The row of old renovated houses the Gordons owned were only two blocks away, with their backs to Church Street.

Chapter Four

"How about we stop at my place for an early lunch when we get finished?" Hannah said as they came down the sidewalk and turned right on Main.

"Sounds good. Is that peanut butter and honey still available?" Xander gave himself points for remembering the lunch Hannah had offered to share with him yesterday, when he had been running late and couldn't take a break between meetings.

"I think I can spring for something a little more upscale, to celebrate." She shrugged and looked away, and for a moment her cheeks seemed a little pinker than could be blamed on the brisk wind that stirred up particles of last night's snow.

"I happen to adore peanut butter, in any form."

"Oh, come on."

"I never got to eat it when I was a kid." Xander raised his gloved hand as if taking an oath. "Swear."

"What planet did you grow up on?"

"My parents didn't believe in grocery stores. Anything they couldn't grow and either can, dry, or freeze, we usually didn't taste unless we visited friends' houses."

"Sounds... boring?" She winked as they started up the steps to the sprawling, wooden porch.

Painted dark, dull royal blue and trimmed in navy, the deep wooden porch spread across the entire front of the building. It had been converted to apartments on the top two floors, and the previous troublesome tenant on the bottom floor had been a children's clothing store. The Penny Pincher and Book Worm, also on Main, were long-established fixtures in the Tabor Heights shopping scene. Newcomers like Kiddie-Time didn't do well unless Tabor residents owned them. It was also part of a chain based in another county, The unfriendly owners refused to hire Tabor residents, which added to its demise.

"First order of business," Xander said, as they reached the top of the steps. "Clean the windows."

Hannah muffled a chuckle into a snort and nodded. Pictures of children at play had been painted on all the windows in tempera paints, in what could only be called "primitive style." Xander took a few steps closer to study the children on a teeter-totter and revised his assessment.

"Primitive" was too flattering a description. He wondered if the owners' grandchildren had done the painting. He was no art critic, but he suspected simply using the primary colors would have made the paintings more acceptable. This hodge-podge looked like someone cared more about using up all the paints, rather than how the color combinations worked together.

"Do you want to do the honors?" Hannah gestured at the door.

"Madam, this is your castle." Xander bowed and held out the keys. "Besides, Dad always said ladies first."

Hannah blushed, but she smiled and her eyes sparkled the way he liked to see. She nearly dropped the keys but got the right one in place on the second try.

The door creaked only a little, and warm, dusty air filtered out to meet them, displaced by the icy air trying to get inside.

"Definitely a bell. Maybe a couple. Instead of chimes," Xander added, when Hannah gave him a questioning look. "You know, like in those old-time country stores." He gestured up at the doorway as they stepped inside.

"Oh. Right. That sounds good." She pulled her ever-present steno pad from her briefcase and set the case down so she could make a note. Xander shut the door and waited until she finished.

"They did a good job cleaning up when they left. I expected trash to be all over the place."

"It was. Mandy hired half the senior high Sunday school class and had them in here sweeping and scrubbing two hours after Kiddie-Time moved out."

"They missed the windows."

"Mandy's still waiting for Kiddie-Time to ante up and bring in a professional cleaner. I think she'd be better off accepting their offer to pay for the cleaning solution and I'll do it myself. They violated their contract by painting on the windows and then sealing it with a spray polymer." Hannah sighed. "Rene heard some people at the gym say Kiddie-Time is trying to hire some troublemakers to say Mandy told people not to shop here, since the judge told her he couldn't accept her allegations without witnesses."

"Hey, even I heard what snots the clerks were to everybody. Besides, Maggie wouldn't have anything to do with them. If Maggie doesn't like a place, it's condemned."

"Let's hope she comes to visit us before the grand opening, then."

If the threatened appeal in court did become reality, Xander planned on representing Mandy Gordon *pro bono*, instead of at a reduced rate like last time. He agreed with Hannah in hoping Maggie visited them. An eccentric old woman, Maggie was Tabor's resident street person, and wandered the town in all weather. No one was sure where she lived, but she was a fixture in Tabor Heights like the gazebo by the lake, or City Hall, or Tabor Christian Church. Everyone loved her, especially the children, and the entire town would rise up in a fury if anything happened to the ragged old woman. The Kiddie-Time clerks had chased her away the day they opened for business, and all Maggie had done was sit on the bottom step to eat an ice cream bar.

That, in Xander's opinion, had condemned the business. Their high prices and snippy attitude toward customers finished the job. Their feud with Mandy didn't start until they realized they were in trouble, with only non-residents of Tabor Heights patronizing them.

Tabor Heights took care of their own.

"Where's your office?"

"Right up front, of course." Hannah gestured toward the left-hand room that opened off the entryway.

It had no door, just a wide archway with carved woodwork around it. Xander was pleased to see the dark grain had been left alone, not hidden under fluorescent paint.

He listened and nodded approval as Hannah pointed out where she intended to put her desk, filing cabinets and bookshelves. It would give her plenty of floor space and put the desk in the corner between the bay windows that opened onto the front sidewalk and the side windows that looked over the driveway next door. She would be able to see everything on Main Street, and everybody who entered the office. Very necessary for an office manager. And necessary for security, too, Xander noted, with a slight dropping in his good spirits.

Well, danger from disgruntled clients, rejected would-be clients, and lunatics with causes was part of the territory for lawyers.

"And over here?" Xander asked, gesturing at the room to the right of the doorway.

He had a good idea of what went where, but he asked because he liked seeing Hannah so excited, so caught up in her work. He could almost see everything materializing and taking on warmth and color as she spoke.

This would be the conference room, and Hannah already had permission from Mandy to install sliding pocket doors for privacy. They would have a long table to accommodate meetings, and a few easy chairs in the nook in the back of the room for smaller, more intimate conferences. Xander nodded and let his imagination fill in the details as Hannah described the hanging plants she wanted to put in the windows, and the art prints, the lamps, the runners and throw rugs, and the cabinet for the coffee machine and their half-size refrigerator.

"We're going to look pretty classy in no time at all. You're doing a fantastic job, Hannah." Xander muffled a chuckle when she shrugged a little and her lips twitched as she fought a grin.

It took so little to make her happy, so why couldn't he remember to do it more often? Xander wanted to tell Hannah regularly just how important she was to him, to his sanity and the efficiency of the clinic. And keeping warmth, color, and music in his life. He had wanted to tell her yesterday, especially, how pretty she looked in that blue dress, but he had two sexual harassment suits on his mind and that stopped him. The wrong words might drive her away or give her the wrong idea. How could he give her the right idea when he wasn't sure himself?

"Okay, now what's back here?" he asked, as he stepped over the ornate metal grid in the floor that was part of the heating system.

Xander liked those old-fashioned touches. They brought back memories of boring, rainy childhood afternoons, crouching on the floor and dropping things through the holes in the grids. At least, until his father caught him and made him help clean out all the heating ducts.

He frowned at a whiff of something odd in the air. Hannah continued down the wide, dark hallway to the back of the building, but he stepped back to the warm air vent.

"Something... sweet." He swallowed hard, suddenly glad he had passed up his usual apple fritter at that bakery on Superior Avenue before they left Downtown. "Hannah, do you smell something... odd?"

Xander hoped something hadn't crawled into the old-fashioned heating system and died. He wouldn't put it past that vindictive woman who ran Kiddie-Time to have done something nasty, like leaving a caged animal hidden somewhere, left to die slowly and then rot.

The world was full of sick people. He was just grateful he had chosen a field of legal practice where he could speak for the innocent and downtrodden most of the time, instead of having to defend the deranged and cruel.

"Odd?" Hannah came back to where he stood, and turned in a slow circle, sniffing. "No. Nothing. What does it smell like?"

"I don't know." He shrugged and gestured for her to lead the way. "Maybe it's just from this place being shut up for so long."

"Probably." She headed down the hall and reached for the light switch.

Xander didn't like admitting, even to himself, how much comfort that spill of light down the hallway gave him. What was wrong with him? Not enough sleep last night? Or was something gnawing at his subconscious, trying to break through with a warning or an answer that might just come too late?

"The bathroom," Hannah said, tapping on the first door they passed. "Convenient, having a shower available. To spiff up before that important court case."

"I always sweat buckets in front of Foggerty," he muttered. That earned a muffled snort of laughter, and he grinned, glad he could get that response from her.

"The rest of these rooms are pretty much still up in the air. Storage for records, and we could even leave them empty against the time we bring more people on full-time." She walked to the last room at the end of the hall and opened the door as she continued. "I assume you're going to basically use the conference room as your office when you're out here, so it'd be a waste of time to set aside an entire room just for—"

Hannah didn't gasp, didn't flinch, didn't even blink. Her utter stillness frightened Xander more than any other reaction could have.

The light through the naked window washed her face in snow-bright white. Her eyes grew wider with every passing second. Hannah swallowed hard as Xander stepped up next to her.

A young woman lay on a white sheet on the floor. Her long, blue-black hair spread out around her head like the corona of the sun. She wore a long white robe, like a baptismal robe that covered her down to her ankles, with her bare feet showing. She held a single white rose in her pale hands, which were folded across her chest. The petals were crushed, some of them scattered across her robe, and the head was nearly snapped off the stem.

There were no clothes in the room. No furniture. Nothing but the sheet and the girl in the robe.

The sweet smell Xander had caught in the hall lingered a little more strongly in this room.

"Chloroform," he whispered, glad to have that particular mystery solved. Then a chill washed over him at the realization that the answer just made the situation here worse.

Why was this girl here? How she had gotten here and who had put her here?

"The White Rose," Hannah whispered.

Her voice sounded like a shout, emphasizing the lack of other sounds in the building. Nothing from the tenants upstairs. Not even the hum and rumble of the furnace or the whisper of the ventilation system. Maybe not even the sound of breathing.

"What about the rose?" He took a step into the room, intending to go to the girl and shake her awake.

What kind of a sicko made a girl sleep in that kind of getup in an empty office? Probably she had been put to sleep and brought here. That snowstorm last night would have covered up any odd activity and made footprints invisible in minutes.

"No!" She grabbed him by the arm and held on tight. "It's the White

Rose Killer, Xander. She's victim three," Hannah whispered, and tears made her eyes glisten.

~~~~~

Hannah didn't want to talk after Xander made the call to the police. They sat in the wide window ledge of the room that would be Hannah's domain, as far as possible from the body in the back room, and waited in silence. It gave Xander time to think.

Had he been that busy lately, that he barely paid attention to what had been going on in town? Yes, he had heard about the White Rose murders. So called because the victims had been sent white roses by a man who watched them, stalked them, and sent them furious letters because they weren't "faithful" to him. After weeks of terror, threats, and roses and photos left in their homes and locked cars, proving he could see them and get to them anywhere, the girls vanished. They were found a day or two later with a single, mangled white rose in their hands.

Dead.

Hannah probably thought him the densest, most oblivious idiot to ever walk the planet. Xander knew he should have been concerned just because it was happening in Tabor Heights. Hannah lived here. Tabor was one of those towns where the old-timers still left their doors unlocked at night, half the town shut down on Sundays, and the Sandstone Festival was the highlight of the summer, a month before the Cuyahoga County Fair took over the fairgrounds. Murder didn't belong in Tabor Heights any more than it belonged in Mayberry.

Especially not when pretty young women were terrorized by a man who demanded purity, faithfulness, love, and never identified himself to his victims.

"Number three. I didn't know he'd gone after his third victim." Xander flinched when his voice cracked. It sounded too loud in the echoing room.

"They kept it quiet. At church, Chief Cooper—" Hannah's voice broke. "He asked me about the women's shelters Arc has outside the state. He wanted to send—her—there." She gestured down the hallway.

"Do you know her?"

"Annalee Gray. She's new in town. Just a couple months. She's only been going to our church about four weeks now. I sat next to her in church on Sunday and we talked about the New Year's Eve party for the Singles class." Hannah shook her head and knuckled her eyes, driving away the hints of tears. "It's just her and her parents. They're retired. Her father inherited the Shipley house. Remember Mrs. Shipley?"

Xander nodded. He knew the name, but his mind had gone completely blank under the enormity of what had happened. He had probably passed Annalee or her parents in church and didn't do more than
~~~~~

smile, nod, and mutter meaningless pleasantries.

"If she's new in town, she probably didn't know—"

A hard rap on the glass of the door cut him off, just before the latch clicked and the door creaked open. Chief Cooper walked in, followed by Officer Mark Donovan. Both men carried ominous-looking black bags of official police equipment. They paused just a moment in the doorway, nodded to Hannah and Xander, and headed down the hall. Xander was grateful. He just wasn't up to answering questions. Not yet. He was impressed and grateful that Cooper himself got involved. The man had impressed him from the beginning with his quiet concern for the entire town, and the fact that he didn't fit into the stereotype of a smalltown police chief. Tall and angular, with graying temples and close-cropped sandy hair, Chief Cooper inspired confidence.

The door didn't quite close when Donovan shoved it. Xander got up to latch it before another gust of icy wind caught it. Movement through the garish paint filling the glass made him pause, then swing the door open.

"Sorry," Curt Mehdlang gasped as his tall, lean frame vaulted the steps. "I hope you guys don't mind, but I was picking up the Police Blotter news at the station when the call came in and..." He waved his reporter's notepad with the *Tabor Picayune* pen-and-scroll logo on it. "It's my job." He raked a gloved hand through his sloppy mop of white-blond hair and offered them an uneasy grin that didn't light up his long face like it usually did.

Xander managed a half-hearted smile and stood back, gesturing for the reporter to come in. Curt nodded to Hannah before looking down the hall. A flash of light indicated the two officers had started their work.

"Maybe if I get the questions out of the way, you won't have to repeat yourselves too much." Curt settled down in the wide window seat with his back to the alley. He pulled out a miniature tape recorder to accompany his notepad. "Coroner'll be here in maybe half an hour. They can't move the body until then."

"I can't believe she's dead," Hannah whispered, and shuddered slightly.

Xander slid back onto the seat next to her and wrapped his arm tight around her shoulders. Hannah needed him. That was the important thing to remember here.

"Annalee's the sweetest kid I ever met. She tried answering the phones for us for about two weeks, but the crazies we get on delivery day were too much for her. We switched her over to getting the Police Blotter news, and she got along great with everybody at the station. She left a message on Angela's phone last night, saying she was leaving town this morning. Some of us at the paper knew about the White Rose, and we were taking turns looking after her while she was at work." Curt swallowed hard. "I thought the Chief found a safe place for her. Then I was at the station and Mark gave me the news." His usually gentle eyes grew hard. "She just vanished from her room last night. Her folks didn't hear a thing.

"Sometimes I really hate this job. Just imagine how the Chief and Mark feel right now. The whole station'll probably be in shock when they hear." Curt raked his fingers through his tangled hair again. "I'd swear half the guys on the force were in love with her. The Chief was hoping if there wasn't a fuss this time, she'd be safe. Who knows? Maybe we should have put it on the front page after all."

"What do you mean, if there wasn't a fuss?" Xander asked. The lawyer in him insisted that if they concentrated on details, the personal horror of all this would stay away for a little while longer.

"The first victim went to the police to complain about the crazy who seemed to think he owned her. Nobody paid much attention. Another psycho stalker. We wrote up a piece, warning girls to be careful, then ran another story asking for help in identifying this guy."

"I remember," Hannah murmured, nodding. "Gretchen McKenzie."

"The notes got worse, the police tightened up their precautions, and they suggested she get out of town for a while. Then the White Rose got her. Just slipped past the officers watching her house like he was smoke. He left a love note for his second victim, Katrina Harper, before anybody found Gretchen's body." Curt swallowed hard. "Chief Cooper asked us to make a big fuss, run a full story about Gretchen and Katrina, asking for help. Then that moron, Sam Conrad, decided to play hero. He convinced Katrina to pretend he was her boyfriend, on the theory that a boyfriend or a rival would either drive the White Rose away or make him show his face. Sam got ambushed with a baseball bat and left hanging by his ankles in the park." Curt swallowed, his expression going hard for a few moments.

Chapter Five

"Katrina got two really vicious letters," Curt continued after a few moments, "calling her a whore because she let Sam pick her up from work a few times. They found her body at that cabin in the Metroparks where they rent out roller skates and cross-country ski equipment. This time, with Annalee, Angela didn't want anybody to even know the new target's name. The Chief figured, if nobody knew about the White Rose's third victim, nobody would get hurt and maybe she'd last longer because nobody was a threat to his ownership."

"That's sick," Xander growled.

"Hey, a guy who demands a girl love him and stay faithful to him, but won't tell her who he is, and gets mad when she's terrified of him... *that's* sick."

"Her parents couldn't believe she was in any danger. Nobody ever does, but then it happens right under their noses—" Hannah's voice cracked.

Her face didn't change, but under his protective arm, Xander felt the sudden ice-fragile tension whip through her body. He pulled her close.

"Hannah?" he whispered, while Curt's face shifted through guilt, horror and discomfort, and the lanky reporter settled back against the window frame to wait.

"I was asleep, only two doors away, while this happened. It happened last night, didn't it? I mean, Mandy said she was over here last night, doing a last check after she showed Joan the place. And with all the traffic of people coming in and out, with the shops, and the theater across the street, and nobody could have gotten in here until after dark and..." She closed her eyes and went limp against him.

"Well, knowing that saves a few steps," Chief Cooper said from the opening into the hallway. He looked at the three of them. "You two didn't touch anything? Didn't think so." He offered a thin smile when Xander shook his head. Hannah didn't move. "So, we have a pretty narrow time frame for all this to happen. That helps a little."

"Not much," Curt offered.

"Every new clue helps."

"But how long do you have to gather clues from dead girls before you catch this guy?" Hannah's voice vibrated against Xander's shoulder. She finally raised her head. Her eyes glimmered a little, but he could tell she refused to cry.

"Hopefully, not much longer. Curt, I'll be talking to Angela. With the cooperation of the paper, we're going to make sure every potential victim knows what to do to stay safe. Maybe we'll even frustrate this monster so he doesn't pick a new target for a long time."

"He sent his first letters to Katrina before they found Gretchen's body," Curt said.

Hannah flinched. Xander wished Curt hadn't said that, even though they needed to know all the details to help the next girl the White Rose Killer targeted.

The last thing he wanted was for Hannah to spend another moment thinking about what had happened, only two doors down from her apartment.

Maybe he should invite her—and Rene, of course—to stay with him until the culprit was found?

Xander almost laughed aloud. What was he thinking? What would the people at church think, to have two single girls living in his tiny Medina condominium? This would be the perfect opening for Arthur Montgomery to haul him before the deacons on charges of immorality.

Stop it, Xander scolded himself. Viciously swirling thoughts were the first sign of panic. *Focus. Think about helping the police and Hannah and stay on track.*

"We're going to have to talk to everybody on the street," the police chief said slowly. "Do you mind if we start with you, Hannah?" He offered a tiny twitch of his lips as an apologetic smile.

"No. The sooner we get this over with, the better." A rusty chuckle shook her whole body and made Xander flinch. "This isn't going to slow down our moving in here, is it? I mean—will you listen to me?" She nearly twisted free of Xander's arm around her, but he held on tight. Now the shaking started. "Annalee's dead and I'm thinking about work instead of—Oh, her poor parents. This is going to kill them."

"It's a natural reaction. You want to think about anything but this." He pulled a police radio from his pocket. "We'll have to talk to Rene, too. Do you know where she is?"

"Wednesdays, she spends most of the day at the gym, then goes straight to church for choir practice."

Chief Cooper contacted the dispatcher and asked the woman to send an officer to Gold Tone Gym to ask Rene Ackley to meet him at her apartment or wait for him at the gym, whichever was more convenient.

Xander kept his arm around Hannah and held both her hands clasped in his free hand while Chief Cooper questioned her. He had been through so many police interrogations in his time, he had lost count, but Xander was once again impressed with the Tabor police chief. How Chief

Cooper managed to do his job so well without growing callous or cold or treating the witnesses like potential criminals, he didn't know. He admired the man as he took Hannah through her memories of last night before going to bed, if she heard anything and woke briefly, and what she noticed when she left the apartment this morning.

Then they were both questioned, repeatedly and from different angles, about what they noticed when they came into the building and found the body. Curt took notes and turned on his recorder. Xander didn't begrudge the man. As the reporter had said, the fewer times they had to go over this, the better.

"Found out a few things," Donovan announced as he rejoined them. He finished putting his camera away in its case as he talked. "The murder took place someplace else. Someplace wet, judging by the condition of her hair. She has the same kind of abrasions on her throat as Gretchen and Katrina, meaning she was strangled with some thick wire. The skin was broken and bled in several places, and it was still fresh and smeared when he put her in the robe. And," he paused dramatically, "he broke a window to get in here last night."

"How do you know that?" Curt offered a sheepish smile when both police officers frowned at him.

"The killer took the time to replace the window he broke with a plastic pane, meaning he was prepared. Meaning he planned to dump her here, it wasn't just spur of the moment. He cleaned up after himself, but not good enough." Donovan nodded and held out a few evidence bags. Shards of glass glinted in one of them when Chief Cooper took them. "I found spots on the floor where snow melted on the dust and then dried. Probably someone can calculate how long ago that was, factoring in the inside temperature and the dimensions of the puddle marks. But not me. I wouldn't have known the pane was plastic, but the wind's strong enough to knock a tree branch against the windows. You can hear the difference between wood on plastic and wood on glass."

"But it's good enough to fool the eye," Xander said. "Who has the money for that kind of plastic?"

"Another clue," Chief Cooper said, nodding.

"One that doesn't go in the paper?" Curt asked, before the man could turn to him and open his mouth. "You forget that I have a stake in finding out who this guy is."

"What's that supposed to mean?" Hannah asked, her voice breaking again.

"I have a theory, that's all. Somebody I knew, who was killed when I was a kid, was probably the first real victim. Kind of personal," he added with a shrug.

~~~~~
~~~~~

"This feels a little personal." Rene wrapped her arms around herself when another shiver took her.

She had elected to meet Chief Cooper at their apartment, to Hannah's relief. The sooner Hannah could get out of that building, the better. She couldn't sit still in the front room, knowing that someone she had laughed with just last week lay dead in another room.

Chief Cooper had been thorough and patient and gentle as he explained to Rene what had happened, and then questioned her about anything she might have seen the night before. Hannah was able to sit back now and listen, and truly appreciate the man's technique.

It helped to have Xander right there, perched on the arm of the loveseat, his hand on her shoulder. She would have preferred he kept one arm around her and held onto her hand, but it was hard to walk up the sidewalk from the office to her apartment in that position. He had to let go of her anyway, to remove their coats.

Amusing, really, how easily he kept up that physical contact. Was he suddenly afraid someone would snatch her away and harm her? Or was he simply unnerved by what had happened, and this was his way of steadying himself?

Somehow, Hannah couldn't make herself believe that, even for a few seconds. Xander touched her shoulder, held her hand, hovered close to offer comfort and shelter. She drank up his concern like a drought-stricken flower drank up rain.

If only it would last.

"Personal?" Chief Cooper echoed.

"It happened practically under our bedroom windows. That makes it kind of personal." Rene shuddered dramatically, and a moment later popped up out of the loveseat. "Anybody hungry? I was just starting to take orders for lunch when you called."

Rene never thought of food during times like this, Hannah knew. She always worried about feeding other people, though. That meant her roommate was getting ready to start smother-loving her.

That mental image started up a train of associations Hannah didn't particularly care to allow into her mental depot.

Chief Cooper and Donovan declined. She didn't really expect them to accept, since they had reports to file, other authorities to notify, and the coroner to check with. Somewhere out there, if the White Rose Killer followed his pattern, victim number four had already received her first "love note." Some frightened girl had just discovered someone she didn't even know had claimed her as his personal property. She had to stay faithful and pure, and she would be punished if she did not display love for this stranger who terrified her.

Didn't he know that love and fear couldn't exist in the same place?

"I guess we won't be decorating for a while, huh?" Xander said, almost mumbling.

After the officers left, there had been silence among the four of them: Rene, Curt, Xander and Hannah. She glanced over at her boss now and felt a smile touch her lips. Any break in the waiting, tense quiet was a relief. Even if it did remind them of the poor dead girl lying in the back room of their office.

If it would ever be their office. Would Xander decide not to move in?

Hannah felt a flicker of irritation as she realized that would please Mr. Montgomery. She didn't want to do anything that would make him happy, but where did propriety and common sense meet and guide their actions?

"Don't see why not." Curt stood in the tiny kitchen, leaning against the narrow window that looked down Main Street. "Coroner's van is pulling away. They wouldn't move the body until they had all the evidence. If Donovan thinks she was murdered somewhere else and brought in... I think the sooner that place is put to use and changed around, the better."

"Sounds good to me," Xander said, nodding. "Not that we could contribute to preventing —" He closed his eyes and shook his head.

"We're going to tiptoe around the subject for hours, maybe days," Rene said. She pushed herself off the tall stool in the niche between the stove and the cabinets, and reached for the refrigerator. "Everybody for lunch?" She shook her head when no one responded and looked around the cramped kitchen. "Let me tell you something, folks, it's either stay here and eat and talk things through or get out. And if you're outside, you know you're going to be bombarded with questions and voyeurs and... people who have a lot better things to do with their time and their itsy bitsy excuses for brains."

"Sounds like you've gone through something like this before," Curt said with a crooked smile.

"Something like." Rene busied herself with unloading the refrigerator of anything that could be used to make sandwiches.

But not before Hannah saw that flicker of darkness in her roommate's eyes. Like some painful memory had risen up to her consciousness.

Hannah guessed something had happened to Rene that put her in the spotlight of attention once. She had faced questions and thrill-seekers, and people who intruded where they didn't belong. Maybe she knew from experience they needed to talk about this; knew from experience it would turn to poison if allowed to sit and fester in their minds.

"I heard some interesting news," Curt offered. He unburied the plates Hannah put on the table, just before Rene's second armload of lunch supplies, and took two slices of bread from the wrapper. "Montgomery's trying to ram through a charter amendment."

"Having to do with us?" Hannah blurted. She pulled out a chair from the tiny table and sank down into it. Curt nodded. "What's wrong with him that he can't allow a speck of competition?"

"What's the amendment about?" Rene asked as she opened up the jar of dill pickles.

"Something to supposedly preserve the character of Tabor Heights by limiting multiplication of businesses." Curt snorted. "What he's saying is, Tabor's such a one-horse town, we can't afford to have more than one florist, one grocery store, one restaurant—see where I'm going with this?"

"Whatever happened to free enterprise and the power of competition to keep the market fair?" Xander cast a lopsided grin at Hannah. "I'm surprised he's trying it at this late date. Even if he gets the legislation rammed through, to be put on the next ballot in May, he won't be able to do anything about us. Charter changes won't affect existing conditions. Especially businesses."

"If it did, you can expect the town to split down the middle over who to throw out and who to keep," Rene added. "Does it extend to churches? Only one Christian church, one Buddhist shrine—"

"We don't have any," Curt said.

"You know what I mean." She slapped at him with a wrapped cheese slice.

"The man's sick." Hannah punctuated her words by slapping a scoop of cottage cheese down onto her plate.

"Self-righteous and so sure that he's the center of the universe, his feelings are hurt when people disagree with him," Xander added.

Hannah welcomed the chance to down-talk their mutual nemesis, even though she knew it wasn't very mature. All four of them had endured unpleasant run-ins with the man. Curt kept them laughing with his own stories, including the time Mr. Montgomery wanted Curt to personally ensure the delivery of his paper. A newspaper not printed by the *Tabor Picayune*, which he refused to subscribe to. Still, he insisted Curt be responsible for the other newspaper, simply because he was a reporter and "part of the media."

Hannah had worked the switchboard at the *Picayune* during two high school summers, and she had her own tales of lunatic customers to share. The four were soon laughing and trying to top each other, sharing horrendous experiences from their days of working their way through college.

"People basically think that if you're answering the phone, you're not a human being anymore. You don't have any rights, and your sole reason for living is to let them kick you in the teeth," Curt said with a sigh. He looked down into his mug that had held chocolate milk a moment ago.

"I've even gotten death threats because somebody didn't like an article that ran in *People,* and he expected us to fix it. Every member of the media is guilty and responsible."

As quickly as if someone had flipped a switch, the warmth and lightness that had filled the room drained away.

"I wish there was something we could do to help catch that creep," Hannah whispered.

"The best thing to do is get the news out," Rene said. She reached across the table, picked up Curt's empty plate and stood. Her movements were just brisk enough to make Hannah notice and wonder about her roommate. "With something like this, your first reaction is to keep quiet, to hide it, to protect everybody else from the ugliness of it all. Maybe Annalee would still be alive if they had made more of a fuss over Gretchen and Katrina. We need to work even harder to get the news out, get people involved, not cover it up like it's something to be ashamed of. If you hide something like this, the next victims don't know what the warning signs are."

Hannah shivered, knowing this harkened back to whatever had happened to Rene. Something had happened to other people — other girls, maybe? — and nobody had talked about it, so she had been hurt, with no warning. Hannah was sure of it. She wished she could press her roommate for details but knew Rene wouldn't open up to her until she was ready. Pressure could only harm their relationship, not help it.

"I'll do everything I can," Curt said. "Mr. Coffelt and Angela will print every word I write. This kind of thing shouldn't happen here."

"It shouldn't happen anywhere," Rene said, talking to the refrigerator instead of them. "But it does."

Thursday, December 12

Non Nobis Solum.
Not For Us Alone.

Hannah thought the Latin motto, carved into the stone archway above the entrance of Quarry Hall, to be thoroughly fitting for the Arc Foundation's headquarters. It explained why Arc existed, the many philanthropic and ministry outreaches it supported, and the reason for the series of open houses through the holiday season.

The long, curving, quarter-mile driveway leading from the gatehouse to the main house was bright with tiny golden lights decorating each of the two dozen apple trees that lined it. The Tudor-revival style house was gold and white with lights along every peak and seam of the roof, framing all the leaded glass windows, trimming the foundations and entrances, and even strung among the ivy climbing the stone walls. Lights spread out in all directions, green and gold to outline the multitude of theme gardens that went in stair-step fashion down the slopes, even to the valley far below the house, where the Summit County Metroparks began. Hannah glimpsed a splash of purple and green far to the right, where the grape arbor led to the summerhouse and the string of interconnected ponds that provided swimming in the summer and ice-skating now.

Instrumental Christmas carols rang softly through the frosty night air from hidden speakers. Glimpses of movement in all the downstairs windows, shadows and flashes of color in the gaps in the curtains, showed the house was alive with guests.

It had taken some doing to get Xander to come all the way down to Akron tonight. She suspected he had agreed out of concern for her and the shock they had both had, finding a dead body in their new office. Hannah swallowed a sudden thickness in her throat and blinked away tears for Annalee's parents. Murder was horrible at any season, but why Christmas? Maybe it was selfish to try to push those thoughts out of her mind for tonight, but she was determined to leave all those problems and questions and grieving behind in Tabor.

"Merry Christmas, Madam. Sir." The tuxedo-clad woman who opened the door wasn't familiar to Hannah.

Usually, one of the young women who worked for Arc and lived at Quarry Hall played the part of butler at the holidays. Last year it had been Su-Ma, with her kinky red hair tamed by a gallon of gel, clad in a tuxedo, with a fake moustache and goatee bristling under her mischievous blue eyes. This slim brunette stranger was dressed as a butler from the time the original owners of Quarry Hall had entertained the local gentry, opera stars, and presidents. A radio clipped to her belt was visible when she turned to hold the door open for Hannah and Xander. That bulge at her waist under the back of her coat looked suspiciously like a gun.

Chapter Six

"Security?" Xander murmured, when he caught Hannah studying the stranger. She shrugged and let him take her arm and guide her down the hall to the formal greeting room, where another tuxedo-clad stranger, an Asian man this time, took their coats. They stepped through a doorway into the main hall that ran the length of the first floor of the house, intending to go to the Great Hall and check out the two-story-tall Christmas tree.

"You made it!" a familiar young female voice crowed. A flash of green warned them just before Nikki flung her arms around Hannah. Joan's younger half-sister laughed as she gave Xander his hug. "I bet Sophie and Vincent that you'd make it. They thought for sure you'd be too busy. Joan didn't say a thing, so I was pretty sure I was right."

"What did you win?" Xander asked, as she hooked her arms through theirs and led them into the Great Hall.

The wood-paneled walls glowed softly in the green, crimson and gold lights of the massive tree. The scent of pine made the air sweet and spicy. The room was oddly empty of guests. A burst of sound came down the hall from the left. The open houses always featured local school and church choirs, orchestras and ensembles. This evening's children's choir was performing, keeping most of the guests in the music room for now. When the music ended, the children would be set loose on a scavenger hunt through all the public downstairs rooms, to find treats hidden inside fist-sized, hollow ornaments. Hannah had enjoyed helping to fill ornaments last year. It had been a relaxing weekend, chatting and laughing with the "daughters" of Quarry Hall, watching movies, eating far too much chocolate and pizza, and basically having a two-day pajama party.

"She didn't *win* anything," a mellow, lazy voice answered. The speaker appeared in the doorway from the dining room.

From his shaved, glistening ebony head to his boot-clad feet, Vincent exuded efficiency and danger, slim and elegant even in a bulky pine-green sweater and matching slacks. He tipped his head to one side, crossed his arms, and gave Nikki a look that Hannah could only describe as fond exasperation.

"I did so. Two whole days without you beating me black and blue," Nikki retorted. She winked at Hannah. "What's the use of learning self-defense if I'm so sore I can't move to defend myself?"

"You'll be soorrrrry," Anne half-sang as she stepped into the room from behind Vincent. She wore crimson in Empire style and tonight she wore her long, dark blond hair pulled up in a stylish chignon.

Argus, Anne's big German shepherd, darted out past her to demand a greeting from Hannah and Xander. Like all the companion dogs trained by Vincent, Argus was very well-behaved. He sat up and held out a paw to shake, instead of jumping up and trying to lick their faces.

Anne's elegant look, however, was slightly ruined by the cast— painted red and gold and decorated with green beads—on her left wrist. Hannah winced when she saw the cast. Anne hadn't been joking when she said her last assignment had been a killer. She said a silent prayer of gratitude that Argus had been there to protect Anne.

"And when you start up your lessons again, and you've forgotten a dozen moves in two days, who's going to mop the floor with your sorry little butt?" Vincent said to Nikki, when they had all exchanged greetings. His slow smile held teasing threat.

Then again, Hannah supposed it wasn't really a threat. Vincent taught self-defense to all the members of the foundation. With Arc's hands-on policy and employees traveling all over the country to investigate worthy causes and problems, including rescuing women and children from abusive situations, they needed to know self-defense.

Hannah had been present at a memorial service for Kathryn, one of the first members of Arc and a cousin of Joan, who was buried on the estate grounds. She had been gunned down during an attempt to rescue Nikki from kidnappers several years ago. The Arc Foundation didn't believe in guns, but they did believe in precautions. The trained dogs assigned to each mobile agent, and Vincent's self-defense lessons, were just the tip of that iceberg.

She wondered if the security people lightly disguised as hired help tonight were there because of another threat against Arc.

"Maybe Uncle Harrison will give me a new assignment for Christmas, and I'll get away from you for good," Nikki said with a touch of sauciness. Hannah wondered if she had just realized that winning her bet hadn't been such a good thing.

"In your dreams, short-stuff." Vincent winked at Hannah. "Good to see you two. If things get tight up in Tabor, give me a call. I'll come look over the place, give you some suggestions for security, that sort of thing."

Xander thanked him, and a few moments later, Vincent continued down the hall to the music room while Nikki led them to the refreshments laid out in the dining room. Tapestries depicting Chaucer's Canterbury Tales, original to the house, decorated the walls and added an old-fashioned touch to the candlelit buffet on the long, U-shaped table. Anne excused herself to go upstairs and take a tray of refreshments to Sophie, who was on duty in the communications center. Brooklyn, who presided over the kitchen at Quarry Hall, was just bringing in a tray of cookies that smelled of cinnamon, fresh from the oven. She chatted with them for a little while, then hurried back to the kitchen when the timer attached to her belt went off.

Gray, Nikki's gun-metal gray Akita, appeared in the doorway from the Great Hall. He sat with his enormous paws right on the edge of the threshold and gave Nikki a pitiful look. Hannah laughed, seeing him. The dogs of Quarry Hall were indeed very well trained. They stayed away from the formal dining room and the kitchen, but went into the breakfast room without hesitating. It escaped her how they could be so big and fierce-looking, yet manage to look like pleading, starving puppies when they wanted a treat.

"Beggar," Nikki muttered. She picked up a single shrimp by the bit of shell still on its tail and dipped it in the crimson bowl of cocktail sauce, then walked over to the doorway with her hand under the treat to catch drippings. "Look pretty."

Gray tipped his head back, his ears went up, he threw out his chest and raised one paw, striking a dignified pose. Hannah tried not to laugh, and nearly got her first mouthful of spiced cranberry punch up her nose. Nikki went down on her knees and popped the shrimp into the dog's mouth, then hugged him.

"I can't believe you fed a dog shrimp," Xander said.

"He earned it. And he likes it." Nikki shrugged.

"But—shrimp? That can't be good for him, can it?"

"You wouldn't believe what this glutton would eat if I let him. Thank goodness he's trained not to take anything from anyone but me, or he'd be the size of the house. Kids just love him when we're out on courier runs."

Nikki went to take care of new guests at the door, accompanied by Gray. Hannah and Xander went to the music room. The children performing tonight ranged between seven and twelve years old, wearing white shirts and dark pants or skirts. Their voices nicely showed the intense devotion and effort put into their training by the tiny Black woman who directed them. Her face gleamed with sweat and her hands drew out subtle nuances from the children, whose gazes never left her face, even during the short breaks between songs. Hannah imagined that intense concentration shattering into glee as the children scattered through the house, looking for their treats.

Joan sat in the window alcove. She wore a long, black velvet dress, simple and sleek, and not a single piece of jewelry beyond her silver stud earrings. Her dog, Ulysses, sat on the floor at her feet. Joan perched on the deep, cushioned windowsill and one hand rested on the shoulder of the man with her.

Harrison Carter, Joan's father, sat in a wheelchair. Hannah couldn't remember a time she hadn't seen him in his wheelchair, though Joan and Xander both said sometimes his health improved enough to let him walk on his own. Neither Hannah nor Xander had been to Quarry Hall since the charity baseball game on the lawn last June, and Hannah felt a jolt of pity when she saw the changes in the man. His jowls sagged a little more, revealing additional weight lost to the disease that sapped his strength. His square shoulders slumped now, and his steely gray hair had gone pure white. His black tuxedo looked elegant and sleek but couldn't hide the frailty in the wide hands that rested on the padded leather arms of the chair, or the thinness of his wrists.

Hannah wasn't sure of all the details. She only knew the disease that ate at Carter had been a cruel gift from a powerful, technically sophisticated enemy he had made during his deep, dark past. The millions that funded the Arc Foundation had come from what Carter referred to as "unkind, heartless means, if not quite unethical." Somewhere in his dark past, he had been involved in international affairs and what Joan referred to as the "information underground." The adulterous affair that produced Joan had occurred during those years. How Elizabeth, Carter's wife, had stayed with him through those years, Hannah didn't know. She studied the serene blonde woman dressed in silvery-gray, sitting next to Carter, and wondered if she would ever have the strength and love to stick with a man who betrayed her, even if just temporarily, for another woman. Whatever had happened, Carter and Elizabeth had certainly put it behind them. They were visibly devoted to each other, and Joan seemed to be good friends with her stepmother. Hannah was happy for her, for all of them.

Maybe even envious? She gave Xander a sideways look while he laughed at the silly song the children currently sang. If something didn't change and grow in their relationship soon, maybe she should give up and look for someone else? Hannah wanted someone whom she could sit with forty years from now, serenely looking back on a long, good life together.

~~~~~

Xander and Hannah ended up with the Carters and Joan when the happy ruckus of the children's treasure hunt began. The five found seats in the Great Hall in front of the massive fireplace, where the children would eventually settle down for a story, read by Elizabeth, before going home. It was tradition, along with the enormous Christmas tree cookies decorated with thick icing and pieces of candy, that Brooklyn would hand each child before they left. Xander appreciated all the traditions. Except for one.

Mistletoe hung in every doorway. He wondered how Hannah
~~~~~

managed to miss it, like little landmines placed so people couldn't go anywhere without taking a big risk. Last year, he had tried to joke about the sudden leap in colds during the mistletoe season, but Xander decided not to even try this year. Not when he kept looking at Hannah and wishing he dared kiss her. She would probably laugh and not make anything more of it, excusing the liberty as a holiday tradition. Xander didn't know if it would hurt more for Hannah to be offended, frightened, or dismiss a kiss from him as nothing. He wanted their first kiss, if there ever was a first kiss, to be something special.

You're a hopeless idiot, he scolded himself, and tried to concentrate on what Harrison Carter was saying about the children's treasure hunt. Joan had once told Xander, she suspected her father had instituted the tradition just to make up for all the gifts and fun times he hadn't been able to give her when she was growing up.

It's just not fair, Xander mused. *Joan finally found her father and he's been dying since the day they met.*

Then again, who ever promised life would be fair?

His fixation on mistletoe tonight was probably just a reaction to what happened yesterday, anyway. He was glad Hannah had talked him into getting out of Tabor for a few hours, away from phone calls from TV stations and newspapers. Xander didn't mind the phone calls — that was what answering machines and the new receptionist at Common Grounds were for. What mattered to him was making sure Hannah had something fun to distract her and help her get over the shock from seeing Annalee's dead body in their office.

"You're doing it all by yourself?" Joan leaned around Hannah to glare teasingly at Xander. "Then what good is this big ape if he can't slap around a paintbrush and put up a couple shelves?"

"I swear, I told her we could wait and just do the remodeling on the weekends," Xander said, holding up his hands. "When I have plenty of time, and when we can ask for some help from the guys who don't have families, you know?" He grinned when Carter and Elizabeth both seemed amused by the tone of the conversation. When had the topic slipped around to the new office again? He should have paid better attention and spent less time mooning over Hannah.

"And I told him, if we have to wait for weekends, we won't be set up for business until February," Hannah said. "I honestly think it'll get done faster if I do it by myself. The workload has slowed down with the holidays coming, and this way... well, there's no one to complain to but myself if something doesn't work out the way I wanted it."

"You just send the word, and I'm sure a couple of the girls will gladly drive up to Tabor to help out," Joan said.

"Me, too," Vincent said, appearing out of the shadows. "I was pretty handy with a paintbrush and screwdriver, back in the bad old days." He winked at Hannah and she laughed. "Besides, I don't like the idea of you being alone in that place."

"The police are checking everything over to make sure it's completely safe before we go in," Xander hurried to say.

"Okay. Don't ever let it be said I wouldn't cooperate with the local police." Vincent settled down on a hassock next to Elizabeth. It was short, probably made for a child, but he didn't look ridiculous.

Xander sighed. Whatever Vincent had been, whatever he had done before he joined the Arc Foundation, he still carried that air about him that prevented him from ever looking ridiculous. Xander was jealous.

"But you promise me, Hannah," Vincent continued. "You feel even the tiniest bit creepy, being there alone, you call me. I'll keep an eye on the place."

"Oh, thanks." Hannah traded grins with Joan. "I wasn't worried until you said that." She laughed, and the others laughed with her. Xander hoped this was the last time they had to think about such considerations.

Friday, December 13

"It's not that I'm superstitious or anything..."

Hannah cast a sideways glance at Xander as they walked up the steps of the old house. Officer Donovan and Mandy Gordon walked behind them. Only two days after the body had been found, everything inside the house that could be tied to Annalee's death had been examined. All that remained was the final inspection and walk-through, and to officially clear the house for use again. Hannah had volunteered not to do anything with the back room. Chief Cooper had thanked her, even though he said it wasn't necessary.

"Superstitious?" Xander asked.

"Friday the thirteenth," Donovan muttered.

"It's only bad luck if we let it be." He reached the top step and crossed the porch. Xander allowed himself a moment to pause and look around the old-fashioned porch on both sides of the big doorway. He imagined putting some benches out there, sitting outside with friends, clients, townspeople on fine, warm summer evenings. Becoming a part of the town's traffic and lifeblood.

Maybe Arthur Montgomery was so dead set against him opening the branch office here in Tabor Heights because Common Grounds and its employees could become an integral part of Tabor in ways and depths that the older law firm never would. Xander smiled and silently admitted he was pleased with the contrast between their two legal firms. Montgomery

& Associates would never be a part of the heart of Tabor Heights, where people turned in good times as well as bad. They were necessary, but they didn't exist to help people through good will and the simple desire to help. Who would be grateful to turn to high-priced lawyers who treated their clients as stepping-stones to a grander reputation?

Montgomery had turned down his share of questionable cases, but Xander knew many people shared an opinion he had never voiced: Montgomery's office turned down a case because his firm couldn't win, it wouldn't have paid well, or it simply wasn't big enough to suit their standards and reputation. Montgomery and his people might sneer at Common Grounds because the only condition was that the clients honestly needed help. Xander could smile under that scorn because he knew his conscience was unscarred, and he could face himself in the mirror every morning.

"Okay, let's get the show on the road," he muttered as he unlocked the door and pushed it open.

He bowed with a flourish to let the other three go in ahead of him. Donovan nodded and Mandy winked at him. Hannah just gave him that slightly fond, slightly exasperated little smile and shake of the head that a best friend would give him when he was being just a little ridiculous.

Her golden-red hair caught the light for a moment, and Xander caught his breath as a totally unexpected thought hit him from out of left field. The relief he felt at that sudden bit of insight shocked him.

Hannah would never be the White Rose's target.

Xander examined the thought as he followed the other three indoors and pushed the door closed. Hannah would never be a target. She didn't fit the profile. She was a strawberry blonde, and all three murdered girls were brunettes. She had a roommate and worked, and the victims had all lived at home with their parents or other relatives.

The sense of relief that made him feel a little giddy also made him wonder if he had been pushing himself just a little too hard the last few weeks. What was wrong with him, lately, that his mind kept wandering back to imagining Hannah becoming a part of his life outside the office, not just inside?

"Looks good," Donovan called down the hall.

Xander shook his head and hurried to join the others. What was he doing, standing there in the entryway and woolgathering? He had work to do.

He entered the back room where the body had waited for him and Hannah just two days ago. Donovan was wrapping Tabor last of the yellow and black crime scene tape around his hand. A piece of plywood covered the window the murderer had entered through. The plastic pane had been removed to check for fingerprints and to analyze it. Something like that wasn't an ordinary, everyday item. Once they figured out what that sheet of plastic was used for, if it had been cut down or taken out of something larger, if it was new or used, they might be able to narrow down who had bought it, or at least where it came from.

If it had been stolen, it was unusual enough, big enough, somebody would notice and report it stolen, at the very least.

Xander silently scolded himself to stop worrying about things like that. He had enough on his plate today and for the next few months without trying to do the police department's job, too.

The walk-through of the office rooms went without a hitch. Xander didn't catch a whiff of anything even remotely reminiscent of chloroform. He tried to jerk his thoughts away from the very idea of someone so twisted he would kill an innocent girl to punish her for imagined infidelity, and yet show mercy by rendering her unconscious before strangling her. He supposed it had something to do with the White Rose Killer's professed love for the girls whom he believed had betrayed him.

He tried to concentrate on the rooms and on the discussion between Mandy and Hannah over what would be done with each room. Wouldn't it bother her to work in a place where a dead body had been left? Annalee hadn't been killed there, and Xander supposed that made a big difference. He knew Hannah wasn't one of those people who could shrug off such a disruption, a violation of life and safety. He was glad she was so sensitive. It made her the perfect front-line person for Common Grounds. Would the memory of it eat at her? Maybe it wasn't too late to get out of the lease?

He almost laughed aloud at that thought, as their little foursome headed for the door to leave. All the unpleasantness at church instigated by Arthur Montgomery hadn't made him back down one inch from his plans to establish the branch office in Tabor Heights. But he *would* turn his back on the place in a heartbeat, if it bothered Hannah to be there.

Chapter Seven

Mandy and Donovan went their separate ways. Xander wanted to discuss his theories with Hannah but couldn't right away. They walked sidewalks messy with melting snow, heading down Main toward the sprawling complex of connected buildings that housed City Hall, the police station, and the Municipal Court facilities. People around them took advantage of the pleasant weather to be outdoors, Christmas shopping or just traveling through Downtown Tabor Heights. They didn't have the privacy he wanted until they reached the steps of the main entrance, tucked behind the library. Hannah listened to him all the way through the front doors, then stopped six feet inside the lobby.

"You're kidding, right?" She grinned, took a step backward out of the traffic flow around them, and jammed her fists into her hips as she looked Xander up and down.

"No, I'm not kidding. Stop looking at me like I've lost my mind." He couldn't help grinning back, even as he suspected they might create a scene in another moment or two.

"I don't know if I should be flattered or insulted." She still smiled, so Xander didn't think he was in too much trouble. "You think it would bother me, working in there?"

"You're not the kind of girl—lady who can shrug off something like that. I don't want you uncomfortable."

"Thanks. That's really sweet." Hannah brushed his cheek with the tips of her gloved fingers.

Just for a moment, Xander wondered if she would lean forward and kiss him. Just brush her lips against his cheek, like his mother when she said he was being sweet.

His face warmed as an image filled his head: Hannah kissing him on the lips, instead.

"I'm not being sweet." He forced a chuckle that sounded half-strangled. A few heads turned in their direction. "I'm just desperate not to frighten away the best office manager I could ever get my hands on."

"Oooh, now that sounds compromising," a raspy, young female voice called out behind them.

Xander swallowed a groan and turned. Then relieved, he laughed with Hannah. Melissa Donovan, Mark's twin sister and a reporter for the *Picayune*, leaned against the counter where court visitors signed in and asked questions.

She had her brother's reddish-brown hair and pug nose. On him it looked tough, no-nonsense, but gave Melissa a mischievous, tomboy look. She yanked out a tissue and blew her nose as she left the counter to cross the lobby to them. Her cold explained her raspy voice.

"What sort of trouble are you two up to today?" she asked as she joined them.

"Nothing good whatsoever, obviously," a chill, thin baritone voice answered, coming from the doorway leading to the court's offices.

The voice twisted a knot in Xander's gut, even as he mentally struggled yet again to classify the slight hint of accent. Something he could only label "Ivy League Snob."

Xander turned and swallowed a groan yet again. The last two people he wanted to see in Tabor Heights — no, make that the entire state of Ohio — stood together. Judging by their black overcoats, leather gloves and hats, they were likely heading out for an early lunch and conference. Arthur Montgomery and Judge Foggerty.

Xander wanted to ask if they didn't think they violated ethical guidelines by socializing during working hours. Not that it would matter to them. Judge Foggerty had already proven he considered the law a tool to wield as he chose, not something to defend. As for Mr. Montgomery, Xander speculated he socialized with the leading judge of the Tabor Municipal Court because nobody else in town would eat with him.

Not a very Christian attitude, but Xander didn't feel particularly repentant right now.

"Carrying on with your assistant isn't going to help your reputation in this town," Montgomery continued.

How could he talk with his upper lip curling back in disdain the way it did?

"Carrying on?" Melissa echoed. "People who work together aren't allowed to share a few laughs?"

"It seems to me there's some sort of emotional attachment on display here." Judge Foggerty's rumbling voice didn't belong with a man of his vicious reputation. Xander always thought such a warm, genial, chocolate-and-whipped-cream voice belonged to Santa Claus, or Tabor Christian's senior minister, Pastor Glenn.

"Neither dignified nor ethical," Montgomery said, shaking his head. He looked down his nose at Xander, as if he were ten years old and had been caught tracking mud into the church.

"Emotional?" Hannah laughed. Xander detected a slight strain in her voice, but he thought nobody else did. "We're not allowed to be friends? Is that what you're saying? At Common Grounds, we like to let the people we represent know we care. It makes our job much easier if they trust us and work with us, instead of expecting us to condemn them for their problems and then charge them for the privilege."

Mr. Montgomery drew back as if he had been snapped at by a snake. A glacial chill filled the lobby.

"Fine talk for someone who likely slept with her employer to get and keep her job," Judge Foggerty murmured.

"Xander doesn't sleep, didn't you know that?" Melissa snapped back, and laughed until she broke into jagged coughs a moment later.

"Yes, the vigilante." He swept his cold, expressionless gaze over Xander. "I wonder what your hidden agenda is, Mr. Finley, that you so eagerly defend the indigent."

"If you mean people who can't pay their legal defense bills half the time... that's why Common Grounds exists. To help the helpless. I believe it's even commanded in Scripture," Xander responded. He kept his mouth in a thin smile, his tone warm, when he actually wanted to slap that satisfied little sneer from the judge's face.

The gall of the man, implying Hannah used sex to keep her job! She was the finest assistant anyone could ever hope for. Sure, Xander wondered sometimes what it would be like to kiss her or see her face from across the breakfast table for the rest of his life, but that was a far cry from having a sexual relationship.

Judge Foggerty was a fine one to talk. Rumors said he was having problems with his third wife, who had married him only four weeks after his divorce from wife number two had finalized. Xander hadn't been in town long enough to know all the dirty gossip, but it was common knowledge in the legal community that Mrs. Foggerty number two had engaged in an affair with the judge five years before his first wife found out. What amazed him was that she expected the man to stay faithful once she married him.

Fighting a verbal battle with hypocrites would do no good. Xander had to keep his nose clean and never lower himself to the same tactics.

"Scripture," Judge Foggerty said with a snort, while Xander's last few words still seemed to ring through the lobby. "I've heard about your precious Arc Foundation. There's something very wrong with a group that uses the Bible to justify their actions. The harder you try to appear upright and spotless, the easier it is to have the entire facade torn away."

"The voice of experience," Melissa muttered. Xander prayed neither man heard her.

"Let me save you some time, Judge." Hannah's voice was gentle, but Xander recognized that sharp glint in her eyes. He silently applauded her self-control. "When you investigate the Arc Foundation, you'll learn that they don't use the Bible to justify their actions. They do what the Bible tells them to do. That simple. You won't find them hiding anything because

51

there is nothing to hide."

"I should apologize, Alex, for her disrespect. I'm ashamed to admit she attends my church," Montgomery growled. He wouldn't look at Hannah. "I'm proud to say most of our congregation still shows proper respect for public officials. Most of them." He glared at Xander.

"Respect has to be earned," Melissa muttered, even softer than last time. Her eyes sparkled with malicious humor.

"It's not disrespect, Arthur," Judge Foggerty said with a sneering little smile Xander wanted to wipe off his face with a brick. "It's refreshing optimism, even if it is misguided. It will be a very sad day when her eyes are opened to the real world." He nodded toward the door. "Our table is waiting." He walked away. As if the other three weren't there at all.

"You'd better be careful, Finley, what you do around here. Small towns aren't as likely to forgive... indiscretions." Montgomery turned sharply on one heel and hurried out after the judge.

"The nerve of that creep," Melissa rasped.

"Sums up a lot of what I've heard about him," Hannah muttered. Then her gaze met Xander's and she sighed. The extra color left her cheeks and she looked tired. "Sorry. Guess we have to be a lot more careful about what we say and do around here, with enemies watching everything we do."

"Isn't there something in the Bible about being surrounded by witnesses?" he quipped.

"That's dealing with angels." She frowned. "Isn't it?"

"Yeah, well, there's angels and there's fallen angels," Melissa said. "Curt told us about that proposed charter change. It won't fly for a second. People like to be able to choose, and once word gets around that the amendment was started just to keep *you* out of town, well..."

"You have to have proof before you can say that in the paper." Xander hated having to point that out.

"Not if we quote people who are just airing their opinions and beliefs." She jerked her chin toward the two men who had left. It was a far more effective gesture of derision than anything filthy. "We don't fight dirty over at the *Picayune,* which makes a lot of slime bags a little angry. I mean, they can't accuse us if we don't play by their rules, can they? Don't worry about those two teaming up against you. I can't say anything because that would be scooping somebody who could break my fingers." From the sparkle of mischief in her reddened eyes, Xander could guess she meant Curt. "But I *can* say you won't be a topic of conversation for long. Some nice, warm friendships are going to get pretty cold soon, and some people who would like to shoot at you are going to be too busy dodging bullets to do you any harm."

"You think he wasn't making an idle threat, to have Arc

investigated?" Hannah asked.

"Hey, Mendoza tried to dig up dirt on Arc, and he couldn't find anything," Xander said. He tried to sound unconcerned, but something heavy dropped into his stomach. Even if he had the time to devote to a deeper relationship with Hannah, now was definitely the wrong time to pursue it. Especially if Foggerty and his cronies were going to put him and Hannah and Arc under a microscope.

"What are you doing, hassling these nice people?" Mark Donovan called as he strode across the lobby. He winked at Xander and wrapped an arm around his sister's shoulders to shake her. "How's the cold?"

"It was fine until you started rattling me around," Melissa squeaked. She pushed herself free. "We're going to lunch. Want to come along?"

"Thanks," Hannah said, shaking her head. "We have some work to do, then we have to head back to the office."

"Maybe next time."

Xander and Hannah headed down the hall to the clerk's office to take care of their paperwork for an upcoming case.

"We don't have that much to do," he said.

"I know." Hannah looked in both directions, then lowered her voice as she continued. "But I figure, Foggerty hates the *Picayune* enough as it is. If Mel was hinting at a story that could embarrass him, the less time we spend with her, the safer she's going to be. What if he thinks we gave her the story, or she's siding with us?"

"She is. From what Curt said, most of the town will side with us."

"But he has power. The less we tempt him to use it against us and our friends, the better I'll sleep at night."

"Yeah." He jammed his hands into his pockets. "Sorry. You have to live here, don't you?"

He shivered, despite the warmth of the building. It was all too easy to imagine someone coming after Hannah to punish her for embarrassing or simply standing up to Judge Foggerty. Despite the fact that the man seemed universally disliked, he did have supporters, and they were the type who found justification for every cruel thing they did and said, no matter what innocent people were hurt.

Tuesday, December 17

Hannah woke Tuesday morning in a better mood than she had known in nearly a week. She supposed part of it could be blamed on the weather, with hints of a brilliant day streaking the sky with blue and gold and scarlet, and the sound of snow melting and dripping off the eaves just above her tiny bedroom window. Or the fact she would spend the day at the new office, free from worry about clothes or makeup or styling her hair. Why look fancy to paint walls and scrape windows?

On Friday, Kiddie-Time's corporate office agreed to settle out of court. Curt had promised the write-up would be in the paper that morning, so Hannah left a message on Xander's answering machine, asking him to pick up a copy of the *Picayune* on his way out to visit that afternoon. Kiddie-Time had agreed to buy buckets of solvent and hired college students to spread it on the lease-violating window decorations yesterday. The solution had had all night to work. Hannah looked forward to scraping off the ugly paint and seeing clear glass today.

This office was her domain now, and the sooner it looked like a legal clinic where people could get help, the better.

She whistled a few notes from the new praise song the choir had introduced on Sunday as she strolled down the sidewalk from her apartment. There was something especially grand about wearing sneakers outdoors in December.

Then she opened the door and the near-toxic smell of the solvent rushed out to slap her in the face. Hannah coughed, stepped back to fill her lungs with clean air, then braced herself and dashed inside. She opened two windows in front, then one on each side, filled her lungs with more clean air, and ran to the back of the office to open a window in what would be the kitchen. She wore a sweatshirt, so what was a little shivering compared to suffocating at nine in the morning? Or worse yet, feeling her brains dissolving and running out her ears.

Rene stopped over to check on her progress after her weekly morning business clinic, sponsored by the Chamber of Commerce and held in a conference room in the Tabor Heights Library. She brought along her fellow teacher, Bailey Malone.

"What a difference!" Rene called, pausing in the doorway. "We came to see if you could use some muscle, but..." She gestured at the clear, clean windows and laughed.

"It's a hundred percent improved already," Bailey said. "This old house deserves some dignity."

"True." Hannah paused and set her roller on the edge of the tray filled with dusty blue paint for the walls. The baseboards would be a darker blue, and she intended to paper with a deep maroon and muted gold pinstripe between the floor and chair rail.

"What can we do to help?" Rene asked. "I called the gym, and Baxter says things are dead, what with all the BWU students suffering through exams and going home for break."

"And Jayne is playing Scrooge, so there's no way I'm heading back to the office until I have to," Bailey added with a dramatic shudder that loosened some of her ebony curls from under her white stocking cap.

Hannah laughed, despite a throb of pity for Bailey. Her father had died a year or so before. She had to sell some of his shares in SafetyNet, the company he had created, to help pay the hospital bills not covered by insurance. Mr. Malone had been the majority shareholder, but Bailey was now the minority shareholder. It hadn't been so bad when Mr. Carpenter, his partner, had still been alive. He had appreciated Bailey's business talent and put her in charge of all SafetyNet's dealings with customers and suppliers. But he died before Bailey's father, and his widow, Jayne, inherited his shares. According to Bailey, Jayne hadn't cared about the company except for how much money it generated so she could go shopping. Then about ten minutes after Mr. Malone's funeral, she made a complete about-face and wanted to run everything. Hannah wished there was something she could do to help, but it wasn't against the law to be nasty and pig-headed, so she couldn't take Jayne to court.

Between the three of them, they had Hannah's work area, the entryway and the conference room painted by noon. The floors were scrubbed and ready for a one-step stain to be applied at the end of the day. They had just started to strip what looked like five layers of wallpaper from the kitchen when Xander arrived. Hannah heard the door creak open and stomping footsteps. Her first thought was relief that she had thought to put the thick rubber mat in the doorway to catch the snow and grit that came in on shoes. Her second was that she should have hung that bell she had purchased yesterday for the door, to warn when people came in. A bell was dignified and added to the atmosphere. A creaky door did not.

Frankly, creaky doors made her think of haunted houses she visited during Halloween in her teens. She didn't want anyone reminded that a dead body had been found in her back room.

"This place looks like a law office," Xander called. "Is it safe to walk on the floor? Looks too shiny and clean to me." He laughed.

"Safe." Hannah straightened from kneeling to peel up the fourth layer of wallpaper at the floor. She was grateful for the solution she bought at Floor-to-Ceiling that soaked through the paper and loosened the ancient paste. Especially since it didn't stink and give her a sinus headache.

She hoped it was just hunger and not fumes that made her head light as she stood.

"I brought lunch. Good thing I planned on an army," Xander added with a chuckle as he came into the room and found Bailey and Rene hard at work. "Anybody for pizza?"

"You're an angel," Bailey said, accenting her words with a groan as she pried herself up from her knees. She tugged her oversized sweatshirt straight and staggered against the first wall they had stripped clean. "I tell you, Hannah, if you don't marry him, I'll take him. Men who bring pizza and *ask* if it's safe to walk on the floor are few and far between."

"Xander's married to the office." Hannah kept tugging on the old paper, keeping her back to him until the warmth in her face cooled a few degrees.

"Does that make me a bigamist, since we have two?" Xander retorted. "Hey, these boxes are getting heavy. Where do I put them?"

She turned, just as the heavenly aroma of tomato sauce, pepperoni and onions wrapped around her in a stomach-rumbling cloud. Hannah groaned, then smiled at the sight of Xander with his long coat hanging open, holding two extra-large pizza boxes from Mancuso's Emporium. Side salads sat on top of the boxes, sharing space with a tray of sealed cups from Stay-A-While. Above all that, Xander's homely face grinned at them.

"What happened?" Even pizza from Mancuso's wouldn't make Xander glow like that in the middle of the day.

"Let me put down our lunch before I lose it."

They settled in Hannah's office space, since they had moved the two new-used desks and five chairs into that spot when the floor was done. Xander had brought a large ginger ale, large cream soda, large vanilla cappuccino and large chai from Stay-A-While, so there was plenty for everyone to drink. Friends had dropped off a crate of paper plates, cups and bowls and plastic tableware as an office-warming gift the day before. They divided up the salads and drinks, then Xander held up a hand.

"I think we should bless this feast, since it's the first meal in our new office." He winked at Hannah, reinforcing her suspicion that he had received some very good news. She barely bowed her head and closed her eyes in time before he started praying. "And Lord, thank You for reminding us that Your timing is best, and we should learn to wait for You to shame our enemies instead of taking up the fight ourselves. Amen," he finished.

Chapter Eight

Rene slapped her hand down on the lid of the top pizza box when Xander reached for it.

"Spill," she demanded, eyes sparkling.

"Nobody read the *Picayune* this morning?" he asked in a deceptively innocent tone.

One thing about Xander's homely face. It was made for playing poker or working a jury to either indignation or pity. Now, he sat close enough he couldn't hide the mischievous twinkle in his eyes.

"Too busy," Hannah said. "Melissa did warn us." A giggle escaped her. She blamed her hunger and the remaining fumes in the office for her suddenly giddy feeling. "Where is it?"

Xander reached back behind himself for the overcoat he had tossed across the spare desk. He gestured for them to start eating, then made a laborious production out of snapping the paper open and tilting back in his chair, propped up against the desk behind him. It reminded Hannah of old Andy Griffith episodes where the town gossips rocked on the front porch of the general store. She had to smother a chuckle.

Xander regaled them with the short story about Kiddie-Time withdrawing their lawsuit against Mandy Gordon. It was only one column wide, just long enough to fit in the top half of the second page next to the Police Blotter. Curt had quoted several prominent residents of Tabor, expressing their distaste for how Kiddie-Time treated their customers and defaced the Century house. He added their declining sales figures. Where he had obtained those, Hannah didn't know, but Kiddie-Time wouldn't have released that information voluntarily. They wanted everybody to think Mandy had forced them out, not that they had retreated in disgrace. Interspersed with the facts, Xander added his own comments and imitated some voices of those quoted.

"Very nice," Bailey said, "but I doubt that's what made you so happy. If anything, I'd think you'd be disappointed they dropped their suit because it meant one less job for you."

"Hey, five new clients have approached us about working on retainer just since we signed the lease." Xander winked at Hannah.

"Business is busy." Hannah deliberately took a big bite of her pizza to keep from grinning back at him.

Where did this sudden closeness come from? This sense that in another few moments, she could read his mind? They worked well together. They shared common tastes in books, movies and sports, and their passion for helping those who truly needed justice. Why did she feel something had changed in the last few days, and nobody had notified her?

Hannah glanced over at the deep windowsill as memory sprang up full-blown. Xander had kept his arm around her while they waited for the verdict from Chief Cooper and Donovan. He had been protective of her, more than he had been when she was sweating, vomiting and miserable in the hospital after being poisoned. It hadn't felt awkward to lean into the support of his arm around her, and Xander hadn't shown any discomfort the entire time. He hadn't even been uneasy about Curt seeing them in that intimate posture.

Was the change in Xander?

Hannah nearly choked on her mouthful of pizza. Was he starting to see her as more than his right hand? Did he see her as a woman, rather than just a co-worker, someone to yell and scream with him at the stupid umpires on TV during the World Series office parties?

"More information has come to light," Xander said, putting on that stuffy tone of voice he used to mock pompous windbag judges.

The paper crinkled loudly as he snapped it stiff and straight. Hannah turned back to see him reading from the front page.

"Fourteen months ago, Tabor residents were upset when Municipal Court Judge Alexander Foggerty supported the attempts of an abortion clinic to purchase and rezone property adjacent to the Mission, a community outreach center of Tabor Christian Church, housed in the former Eloise Elementary School," Xander read.

The three women sat up straight and put down their paper cups. The air in the office rang with their suddenly rapt attention.

Xander read straight through the next four paragraphs, which summarized allegations and investigations. The judge had stepped over the line supporting the proposed legislation. He didn't live in Tabor Heights, leading many citizens to protest his interference in what was strictly Tabor business. Anonymous tips poured into the *Tabor Picayune's* office, which were passed on to various watchdog groups, and revealed that the judge had made offers to purchase three of the five properties adjacent to the Mission. The other two properties, already on the market, were considering offers from an alleged women's health corporation. Further investigation revealed Foggerty was acting as a go-between for the corporation, to hide their connection to the proposed rezoning of the property. The clincher to the story came when Curt dug up documentation showing their purpose was to provide abortions on an assembly line basis. Despite their claims to be a holistic women's health service, they provided no health screenings, counseling or prescriptions, and no options or alternatives. Tabor Christian Church headed the movement to stop such a business from moving into Tabor and next to the Mission.

At the same time, the police received numerous complaints about excessive traffic and noise at the Mission. Yet when they were investigated, no one within five blocks of the property had complained. Rumors said Judge Foggerty was behind the false complaints to cause trouble for the Mission. The feud between Judge Foggerty and the church started at that time. He sent letters to the editor on a weekly basis, expounding on women's health and reproductive rights. Pastor Glenn wrote letters rebutting him, emphasizing the lack of any services other than abortion at the site, and pointing out the paradox of having a place that promoted the death of the unborn, next door to one that offered shelter and comfort in crises and support to families, and taught the sanctity of life.

The three homeowners approached by Foggerty banded together to announce they would not sell their homes. Two publicly established trusts, leaving their property to the Mission when they died. The two homeowners who were in negotiation with the corporation stopped the proceedings. Judge Foggerty made thinly veiled threats about business obligations. However, no contracts had been signed, and when he pushed the issue, several watchdog groups and the Ohio Bar Association handed down a rebuke.

Today's story, which took up nearly the entire top half of the paper and continued on page three, revealed that Judge Foggerty was a shareholder in the falsely labeled women's health corporation. Hannah held her breath when Xander read that part of the story. It put a whole new twist on last year's events. She wondered what the judiciary ethics board in Columbus would say about such an affiliation. It had to be a violation of ethics as well as a conflict of interest for Foggerty to be a shareholder, considering the volatility of the abortion issue. Almost the moment that thought came clear, Xander read a quote from the head of the board, requesting an investigation into the ethics of the situation.

"Well, that's interesting," Rene said on a sigh as Xander finished reading.

"I want to know if Curt was working on this before we had that run-in with Foggerty last week," Hannah murmured.

"From what Melissa said, yes. It's a good thing she didn't write it, since she was there at the time." Xander folded up the paper and tossed it over his shoulder onto his coat. He picked up his now-cool chai and saluted them with the cup before drinking. "Here's to God's timing."

"I don't understand," Bailey said, frowning.

"Montgomery's friendship with Foggerty cooled a lot during that investigation. He's an upstanding leader in our church. No way he can show his support, even by having dinner with a shareholder in such a business. He was probably counting on Foggerty making things unpleasant for us, so we'd give up and leave town." Hannah shared a grin with Xander. "With all this coming back into public scrutiny, he's lost a valuable ally."

"Publicly, at least." Xander's smile faded a little. "On the downside of all this, we've definitely been pushed into the enemy camp. A story this big has been in the works for a long time, but after that showdown the other day, he's going to think we nudged Curt into writing it. That's just the way his mind works."

Xander had to get back to the main office in Padua, but he promised to stop by before the end of the day and help move furniture. Hannah lost Rene and Bailey soon after Xander left, so they could get back to their own jobs. She continued stripping wallpaper and painting in silence, welcoming the quiet and grateful for all their help and the progress in the renovations.

Her mind kept going back to her memories of those tense times more than a year ago. Rumors circulated that either couldn't be substantiated or had a grain of truth so buried in allegations and prejudice, no one could dig down to it. Hannah believed the rumors that Judge Foggerty wanted to force the Mission out of the neighborhood entirely.

After the false complaints about noise and traffic at the Mission had been lodged, the *Picayune* had run a survey of the affected neighborhoods. Nearly ninety-seven percent of the Mission's neighbors enjoyed having children playing in the fenced meadow and the playground behind the former elementary school. Many of them had attended Eloise Elementary, and their children had as well. They liked the work the Mission was doing, the expanding services provided to the community. The alleged excessive traffic and noise were actually less than when the building was used as a school.

The newspaper had then researched and reported on all the corporations that had wanted to buy the old school building and their proposed uses for it before Tabor Christian bought it. They included a fitness center and a mini-mall, both of which would have brought totally different clientele and traffic patterns to the neighborhood. No one would support any action to force the Mission out, if something like that was possible or legal, while those options were clear in people's minds.

Hannah hoped Curt's story had helped Common Grounds by driving a wedge between Foggerty and Montgomery. She hoped the help outweighed the negative impact, because there was definitely no way to ever return to neutral ground. She prayed Xander never again had to take a sensitive case before Judge Foggerty. The man was vindictive enough to decide against Xander's client and ignore justice.

Wednesday, December 18

"What's up for tonight?" Xander asked as he stepped into the front reception area of the Common Grounds Padua office. Hannah was still hard at work at her desk.

It was past six and everyone else had gone home. She had put in a half-day at the Padua office, trying to make up for all the work she didn't do on Tuesday. Xander liked knowing she was there, hearing her voice drift to him at the back of the building as she directed their clerks or talked with potential clients. Common Grounds just didn't feel right without Hannah there.

"Class." She sighed and stretched her arms toward the ceiling and then slouched in her desk chair.

"I thought you had your finals last night." He tugged a chair over from in front of the coffee table and turned it around so the back faced Hannah, then sat, straddling the back.

"We should have, but there was a power outage in the building last night, so it got rescheduled for tonight."

"Oh. I was thinking maybe we could pick up some sandwiches and I could get those brackets hung for the shades since they came in this afternoon." Xander hooked his thumb over his shoulder at the pile of long, narrow brown shipping cartons sitting in the corner next to the copy machine.

"Wish I could. I barely have time to run home and change. It's a good thing the building is just around the corner, or I'd never make it. Speaking of which..." She stood and crossed the office to the coat rack.

Xander watched her, appreciating once again her athletic grace. The contrast struck him full force, between Hannah in her slim, professional clothes and Hannah with paint spatter on her nose and fingers, dressed in jeans and sweatshirt. Xander hadn't really noticed how graceful she was until they were moving furniture last night. She was strong, but not muscle-bound. She lifted boxes and stacked chairs with a smooth economy of motion that made him wonder if she had studied dance, maybe ballet, before she went into law.

Get your eyeballs back into your head, Xander silently scolded himself as his gaze traveled down Hannah's back to her legs.

In penance, he hurried over to the pile of boxes and picked up three-quarters of them before she could get there. Then he offered to take them to the Tabor office himself to save her time.

"Not that much time, but thanks. Umm, I know it's warmed up a little, but shouldn't you put your coat on?" she added, laughing as they headed out the door with their arms full.

"Too late." Xander shrugged and tried not to wince as the icy, damp wind slapped at his shirtsleeves.

He got the idea as he fished out his car keys and handed them to Hannah, to unlock the back door.

"How about we meet for dessert after your class?" he said once everything was loaded in his back seat. "We can celebrate your acing the exam. It's Dr. Holwood and you love his classes, so you're sure to pass."

"I know." Between the shadows of the parking lot and the chill wind, it was hard to tell if she was blushing or her cheeks were just cold. "I didn't think you paid that much attention."

"Everything you do is important, Hannah. Don't sell yourself short. My entire life would be in ruins if you walked out." Xander forced a chuckle. His lips felt slightly scalded from letting out that confession. What had possessed him to say that? "So," he continued, trying for a light tone, "that's your official notice that you are stuck working at Common Grounds for the rest of your life. Got it?"

"Got it." Her nod was a little jerky, along with her voice. She definitely blushed now.

Xander didn't know why that made him feel so good. What was wrong with him? He could read juries and witnesses with a skill that might have come directly from God, but he couldn't understand himself or someone who was increasingly important to him.

"So, what about dessert?"

"Can't." She took a few steps backward toward her car. "I'm—ah— well, I actually have a date."

"A date?" He winced, hating the shock in his voice.

Of course she had a date. Hannah probably had offers to go out three or four times a week. She was beautiful, she was smart, she had a good sense of humor, and she was "real," as his mother would say.

Xander's stomach dropped down to his shoes. Maybe this was what the blind man felt like when Jesus smeared mud on his eyes and told him to wash. A little ridiculous and blinded by the sudden brilliance that filled his head.

"Anybody I know?" he continued, and coughed to cover the break in his voice.

"I don't know. Al Colson? He's in my class. We were going to go out for dinner tonight to celebrate surviving, but since the class was postponed until tonight, it'll probably be just coffee somewhere."

"Colson." Xander started to shake his head.

An image flashed into his mind: a long, golden-tanned face and hard planes that gave new definition to "chiseled features." Granite-gray eyes, movie star perfect golden hair that never mussed even when it dripped with sweat after a hard game of basketball. He had played Colson more times than he could count in the basketball league formed of young lawyers and paralegals throughout the county. Colson stood five inches taller than Xander, and sometimes it seemed like the ball was attached to his hands with invisible elastic rope.

"Umm, Hannah? He works for Montgomery."

Hannah busied herself with unlocking her car door. "I know. I didn't think that mattered." She directed a crooked smile over her shoulder at him.

For a moment, Xander felt like he had been thrown a dry turkey leg while someone else got to enjoy the whole Thanksgiving feast. He didn't like that feeling. Mostly because he knew it was stupid.

"I don't hold that against him," she continued, "and if nobody tells Montgomery, Al won't get in trouble for taking me out. I mean, it's not like we're on opposite sides of a case, right?"

"Right." Xander swallowed hard and had to consciously unclench his fists. "First date?" Why were these words coming out of his mouth? That was the exactly wrong question to ask.

"Actually, yes." Hannah slid into the driver's seat. "Are you sure you don't want help unloading all that stuff?"

"Positive. Do good on your exam."

He refused to tell her to have a good time on her date.

Hannah nodded. Her smile seemed a little warmer, more relaxed, and she waved as she pulled out of the parking lot.

"You're jealous," he growled to himself, and a slap of icy wind touched with snow answered him. "You've got no right to be jealous, so just stop it right here." He hunched his shoulders and hurried for the back door to close up the office and get his coat.

Still, the image of Hannah on a date with Al Colson ate through Xander's thoughts like drain cleaner as he drove to Tabor. He imagined them sitting at a window table at Stay-A-While, laughing over coffee and one of those gooey desserts the cafe specialized in. The ones full of fruit and icing that were big enough for two to share. Xander could just imagine Colson being slimy enough to try to feed Hannah with his own fork. Maybe he would walk her home and try to steal a kiss at the top of that creaky old iron fire escape.

Hannah wouldn't let him, would she? She wasn't the kind of girl to allow anything physical on the first date. But if Colson was charming enough, good enough company, wouldn't she let him come back? Work his way up to kisses? Maybe even propose marriage? They would have beautiful children, with their golden coloring and athletic grace and—

"Don't be stupid. He works for the enemy and he's ten times better than you on the court. That's the only reason you hate his guts." A bark of harsh laughter escaped him. He hoped nobody was next to him in traffic, to see him talking to himself. Xander wasn't about to look. *You're still worried about Hannah after finding Annalee, and you're still scared she'll leave once she gets her degree and... you're a pathetic excuse for a man, and a liar.*

Xander would have lowered his head and banged it against the steering wheel a few dozen times until he knocked some sense into himself, but the light changed to green.

When he got to the new office, he was tempted to put up all the window shades, but Xander gave in to common sense. The walls weren't ready anywhere except in Hannah's office and the conference room. He could do that much tonight, but anything more would be a waste of effort. Besides, it would be a blatant attempt to hang around until Hannah's class let out and he could watch her walk down Main with Colson. What did he think he was going to do? Run out and play father figure, demanding to know the other lawyer's intentions toward her?

Yeah, just fatherly interest. Got to protect her, Xander told himself as he closed up his toolbox and stepped back to examine the last set of brackets he had put up. *She's too important to me to let anybody steal her, to work at another office. Maybe that's what's happening — Colson's trying to recruit her to work for Montgomery.*

That last idea struck him as so ridiculous, Xander burst out laughing at himself. He settled on Hannah's desk and didn't care if anyone happened to be walking past the building and saw him.

"You're hungry and you're tired and you're neurotic. That's what happens when you miss working out too many nights in a row."

Xander stopped at Mancuso's for a sandwich after he left the new office, dropped off his dry cleaning at Daisy Fresh a block later, and headed for Gold Tone Gym. After pushing himself to a sweaty, achy, glorious exhaustion, his head felt clearer and he could laugh at himself. He took a shower at the gym, so when he got home he dove directly into bed, read his devotional book, and turned out the light. He smiled into the darkness as sleep crept over him almost immediately.

"Lord, please take care of her," he whispered. "I don't know what I'd do without her in my life."

Chapter Nine

Thursday, December 19

Ten minutes before nine, and the coffee hadn't finished brewing yet at the Padua office of Common Grounds. The phone rang. Xander dove for the phone.

"Xander?" Hannah said, before he could finish saying hello.

"Hey, hard at work already? How did the date go? What do you think of the job I did last night?" he hurried on, before she could answer.

"Date?" Hannah's voice cracked and sounded thin.

"Hannah—"

"Xander, can you get over here? Right now? I—I can't talk about it on the phone, but I really need you here."

"Sure. Ten minutes."

It usually took twenty minutes to get from Padua to Tabor, but Xander prayed for green lights the whole way as he grabbed up his coat and ran for the back door. Nelson and Walter were just coming in from the back parking lot. Xander told them he had to run help Hannah with something and left them to finish opening up the office for the day.

He reached the border between Tabor and Hyburg in a record eleven minutes. The school zone sign started flashing just after he passed through, going forty-one in a thirty-five zone. Xander didn't even look for a black-and-white or listen for a siren, his mind too full of that strange note in Hannah's voice. Something had hurt or frightened her. The idea twisted his insides and made him feel like he couldn't get enough air. He gripped the steering wheel hard enough to turn his fingers white and then prickle with the threat of numbness.

He reached the corner of Sackley and Main and turned left on the yellow arrow. Xander caught a glimpse of a delivery truck edging forward, to turn right on red, and half-braced himself for a crash. Nothing happened and he glanced back to see the truck sitting still. Maybe he had scared the driver?

Then he didn't have time to think of that. He intended to park in front of the office, but just as he reached Hannah's apartment he saw there were no lights on in the new office, so he slammed the car into park just past her building. Xander flung the driver's side door open without looking to see if another car was coming up behind him on the left. Someone was, but the woman driving the van swerved slightly to the left without honking her horn or even looking at him. He finished turning off the ignition after he had one leg out of the car.

The old fire escape rattled and clanged as he ran up the iron steps, three at a time. The door hung open and Xander nearly stumbled on the landing. Terror for Hannah knifed through his gut. Then he realized Rene stood there, zipping up her parka, obviously ready to step out. She held the door for him.

"Thanks," she said as she stepped past him. "There's an emergency at the gym, otherwise I'd stay." A shaky little smile didn't do anything to relieve the tension lines and pallor of her face. "I think she'd rather you were here, anyway. She didn't want to call the police until you got here."

"Hannah?" Xander stumbled through the door into the kitchen. Rene shut the door behind him.

She waited for him, perched on a tall stool, arms wrapped around herself, tucked into the niche between the window and the stove. Hannah wore jeans and sweatshirt, but her hair was tangled and she wore slippers. Whatever happened had interrupted her halfway through getting ready to go work on the office.

"What's—" He stopped as she held out a piece of heavy white paper.

Stationery, he realized a moment later, as he saw the ragged edge and the line of gold embossing down one side. Hannah's hand didn't shake as she held it out to him, but her fingers looked white and the paper was dented and damp from the pressure of her skin.

"I found this when I went for the newspaper," she said. Her voice was only a few steps above a whisper, but it didn't sound cracked and weak like it had on the phone. "Read it."

My angel of mercy. My guardian of justice. I have searched long and diligently for you, and I have found you because you are pure and worthy. You have returned from the grave to me. Stay faithful to me. Give your love to no one but me, and you will be rewarded with joy beyond your wildest dreams. Remember that you are mine, I have claimed you, and betrayal will be punished with misery that will follow you beyond the grave.

"What kind of a crazy—" He closed his eyes, feeling his sausage biscuit try to come up his throat as memory slammed through his mind, recalling other notes full of similar words.

Promises of joy. Demands for fidelity. Threats of punishment. This note was nearly a perfect match with others he had read, even discounting flaws in his memory. And Xander's memory was too perfect when it came to things like this.

He opened his eyes, swallowed hard and turned back to Hannah. The floor tilted under his feet for a heartbeat.

She held a white rose in her other hand, and now her hand did shake.

"Nothing's going to happen," Xander vowed, and reached out to wrap his arms tight around Hannah.

She slid off the stool and clung to him, shaking just enough for him to feel it. Or was that the terrified racing of her heart? Xander tightened his arms around her until he could feel her ribs bending under the pressure. She didn't protest the squeezing and that portion of his mind that always looked at life with humor told him her silence was a sure sign of how much all this had knocked her for a loop.

The phone rang, startling a yelp out of her. Xander ground his teeth. His throat ached with curses he hadn't used since high school. He kept one arm around her and reached for the phone hanging on the wall. Hopefully, it was the police. No, she hadn't called the police yet, had she? Should he be glad she had waited for him, or shake her until her teeth rattled?

"Hello," he barked.

Silence. Hannah flinched. She probably thought it was the White Rose. What if it was? What if he had broken his pattern, calling to make contact instead of limiting himself to leaving notes? He had broken his pattern already by choosing strawberry blond Hannah as his target, instead of a brunette. Xander felt sick at that speculation. Had he condemned Hannah to death just by being in her apartment?

"Sorry, I think I've got—no, wait. Are you an officer?" The man's voice sounded strained and harsh with an effort to whisper.

"No. If you're looking for Hannah Blake, this is her boss."

"Finley. Am I glad you're there. Is Hannah okay?"

"Who is—Colson?"

"Al?" Hannah whispered. "What does he want?" She lost what little color had remained in her face. "He got a note, too?"

Xander understood immediately. Sam Conrad, who had pretended to be Katrina Harper's boyfriend, had received threatening notes from the White Rose Killer, warning him to stay away from her or suffer the consequences for trying to "pollute" and "steal" her.

"Finley? You still there?" Colson said, his voice rising.

"Yeah, we're both here. Let's meet at the police station," Xander said.

"She got it, didn't she?" The other man groaned softly before Xander could answer. "I was praying this was some kind of stupid prank. The guys were ragging on me because I had plans with Hannah last night. The half-wits claimed I was dating the enemy. I thought they were just being sick, but... I'll meet you there. Neutral ground."

"Sounds good."

Xander hung up and wrapped both arms around Hannah again and held on tight. He couldn't think straight for all the emotions boiling through him. He wished he could just turn off his feelings like Mr. Spock, so he could analyze and figure out what to do.

Worst of all, guilt cut through his fury for Hannah's sake, his fear for her, as he tried to imagine what she had felt and thought when she saw that rose. Guilt, because he actually enjoyed the feel of her in his arms, pressed tight against him, her fingers digging into his shoulders, so he would probably find bruises there tomorrow. She had called *him* before she called the police, when she was frightened.

Battlefield romance, he silently scolded himself. *Foxhole religion. When this all calms down, we'll go back to normal.*

Xander wondered if "this" would ever calm down. There were only two endings, weren't there? Either they would catch the White Rose this time, or Hannah would vanish in the night and her dead body would be found somewhere a day or two later, laid out in a white robe with a mangled rose in her cold hands.

~~~~~

"Sure you don't want anything?" Taylor Dunlop said, her rich voice muted.

"I would love a box of chocolate covered cherries right now, but there's this dress I want to fit into for Christmas..." Hannah trailed off with a breathy, ragged little chuckle.

Xander, Hannah, Colson, and Taylor sat in Chief Cooper's conference room. He had left them twenty minutes ago to confer with the two officers he had sent out to check on the area around Hannah's apartment house and the Montgomery & Associates building. Thanks to the fresh snow and hard winds last night, lasting until nearly five this morning, there was very little chance of finding any clues, such as footprints or fibers caught on fences or other sharp edges, or even anyone who would remember seeing a mysterious figure skulking around. They still had to check.

Taylor worked for the Tabor Heights Police Department as a combination dispatcher, counselor and jail attendant when the occasional female prisoner was brought in. Chief Cooper called her into the office as soon as Xander pulled the white rose from his briefcase.

The twenty minutes became half an hour, then fifty minutes while the four sat and Taylor tried to guide the conversation into innocuous territory. Xander wondered how that was helping Hannah, until he realized some of the comments and questions Taylor brought up offered her a chance to speak about what had happened, what she felt, even offer some strength with faint parallels with other similar cases.

Maybe he should take Hannah to Dr. Harris over at church when they were done with this. The silver-haired, elegant woman had counseled dozens of people.
~~~~~

At least it was something he could do. After all, it wasn't like there was a strong enough emotional bond between him and Hannah for her to rest completely on him. He could physically protect her and even talk her into going to one of the battered women shelters the Arc Foundation sponsored, but he wasn't close enough to her heart to be her rock.

He wanted to be her rock.

Foxhole religion, Xander reminded himself. When this was over, Hannah would not appreciate it if he tricked her into opening her heart to him. There had to be a foundation there before she exposed all her hurt and fear, or she would resent him for a long time. Maybe years. Maybe the rest of her life. Bad enough to prompt her to leave Common Grounds? Xander swore he wouldn't let that happen.

"What's taking him so long?" Colson grumbled.

"This is a police station," Taylor said with that lazy smile that lit her olive-toned face at the oddest times. As if she found something bitterly amusing in every situation.

Working at the police department, doing the many things she did, Xander supposed she had to use humor as a shield or else fall victim to the nasty, dark side of life she was exposed to every day.

"This feels like the crisis of the year," the woman continued, focused on Hannah, "but there are other crimes being committed and the chief is a busy man. If the field officers aren't checking with him on something, there are politicians and school officials and trouble at the university and... need I elaborate?"

"Seems like a heavy price to pay for cappuccino and French silk pie," Hannah murmured. "I'm sorry you got dragged into this, Al."

"Hey, don't let this jerk start you thinking you're at fault. You're the victim here and he's the criminal." Colson reached across Taylor to clasp Hannah's hand, resting on the arm of her sturdy, institutional green upholstered chair. "We didn't do anything wrong last night." When Hannah raised her eyes to meet his gaze, he offered that grin Xander had seen him use on the basketball court when he scored a seemingly impossible three-point shot.

Xander wondered what would have happened to Colson if he had tried to kiss Hannah good night last night, and the White Rose had been around to see it.

Thank goodness she's not that kind of girl.

Chief Cooper swung the door open hard and strode into the room. The pneumatic hinge pulled it closed again with a soft sigh. "Sorry about that. Something rather odd has come up. I wanted to tie up a few loose ends first, so I could give you a complete story instead of just pieces."

"Involving us?" Xander asked.

Hannah flashed him a confused look for a moment, and that hurt.

Didn't she think he cared enough to include himself in her problems? What was wrong with their friendship, their partnership, that she would doubt him?

"Very much so." The police chief sighed as he sank down into the fifth seat at the table. "The short of it is, either the White Rose is changing his pattern, or we have a copycat on our hands."

Silence rang through the office for five painfully long seconds.

"Someone else got a rose last night?" Hannah's hands slid off the arms of her chair, where she had been bracing herself. She clasped them in her lap. Without thinking, Xander reached over and caught up one hand to hold between both of his.

"Actually, the new target got her first communication the night Annalee died." Cooper's jaw muscles tightened. The weathered lines bracketing his mouth and the squint lines around his eyes deepened.

After a moment's pause to let that statement sink in, he continued. The other target of the White Rose was a sophomore Butler-Williams student living in a dormitory across the street from the Mission. She didn't usually read the local papers and hadn't realized what the white rose meant. She even accused a former boyfriend of trying to make up with her. He took the credit. More notes appeared after they had a date, ordering her to stay pure, scolding her for betraying him so quickly. If the former boyfriend received a note warning him to stay away, he never told her. He also hadn't made contact with her since their date, but the girl had blamed final exams and the rush to Christmas break. She blamed the note on a jealous classmate who wanted her boyfriend.

Then her roommate brought some older newspapers to their room on Sunday to wrap some presents to ship home for Christmas. The new victim, Tracy Brickman, read the story about Annalee and realized what was happening.

"Why did she wait so long to report it?" Taylor asked.

"She was terrified. Three girls had died already, so what hope did she have? She took her final exam Tuesday afternoon, emptied out her dormitory room that night and left. She swore her roommate to secrecy. Nobody else knew she wasn't planning on coming back after Christmas break until her parents started making a lot of angry phone calls. The White Rose even left a Christmas present in her car while she was packing it."

"What was it?" Hannah asked in a harsh whisper.

"A glass angel. I've made arrangements for the authorities there to take it for testing. Fingerprints, whatever they can find. Donovan is checking the stores to find out where it was bought." He sighed and rubbed at his eyes, looking so weary Xander suspected the man had been up all night.

"If he gave her a gift, then he didn't know she was leaving for good. Or he guessed..." Xander shook his head. "Something just doesn't feel right. If he's jealous enough to threaten someone who makes a move on the girl he wants, and to follow through when the guy doesn't listen... he wouldn't give up so easily when his target leaves town."

"So you think I'm the copycat's victim?" Hannah asked.

"Let's hope so," Taylor said.

"I'll second that," Colson said.

"His pattern is to contact his next target before anyone knows the previous one is dead," Chief Cooper said, nodding. "But we can't afford to be wrong about this, Hannah. What if this poor college student is the copycat's victim? What if the White Rose didn't contact you before he killed Annalee because he hadn't picked you as his new target, or the girl he did pick left town unexpectedly and threw him off his pattern? You are an aberration from the pattern. Tracy Brickman from Pennsylvania fits the physical profile." He sighed, looking like he hated the things he had to say. "We have to consider that if *your* stalker is the copycat, you could be in even more danger, because we don't have a pattern to give us at least some sense of security. Do you see where I'm headed?"

"You're not being very encouraging," she whispered. "But I know you have to do this. So, what do I do?"

"There's the shelter you were talking about for Annalee," Xander began. He didn't like the frown that darkened the chief's face, nor the sharp way the man shook his head.

"Why not?" Colson said. "That sounds like a good idea. Get Hannah out of danger before he realizes we're onto him."

"He already knows that," Hannah snapped. "If he's watching me like he seemed to watch the other girls, he knows we came here. He saw Xander walk in with his arm around me, and he saw you come in. He knew Annalee was planning to leave town to hide from him. That means he's smart enough to put things together and guess what we're talking about and doing right now."

"Exactly," Chief Cooper whispered. "Hannah, a lot of this is going to depend on you. Can you work with us to catch this guy?"

"Did you ever consider we're going at this from the wrong angle? What if the White Rose is a lesbian?" Taylor offered. "Much as the homosexual community would like us to believe them to be peaceful and loving, they are just as prone to violence and the stalker mentality as the rest of the population. We're looking for a man, but there could be a woman walking the streets of Tabor, picking her next love interest and turning vicious when the sweet little girl she wants won't respond."

Hannah's frown changed, growing more thoughtful as she visibly considered the idea. It sickened Xander, but he had to agree Taylor might be right. Stalkers weren't limited to men preying on women. He had enough evidence from past cases to prove that.

"You know, if a woman made a pass at me, I might never realize it," Hannah continued after a few seconds. "I'm just not geared to think that way, to recognize a come-on from someone of my own gender. It could be someone we've all known for years but would never suspect because we just don't think that way. We don't recognize the signs."

"How long have you had this theory, Taylor?" Cooper asked with a nod of approval.

"I'm sorry to say, I didn't start thinking about it until yesterday. I helped question a little girl who finally told her mother about some strange games she plays with her babysitter. The tame ones involve taking off her clothes for her babysitter and her female friends." Taylor's usually warm eyes took on a cold hardness that made Xander wince in pity for her. And for the child who hadn't even realized something was wrong until the "game" had gone too far.

"It's a sick world we live in, people," Colson said.

Chapter Ten

"Go on with life as usual. Right," Hannah muttered. Her voice seemed to echo in the half-empty rooms of the new office.

She glanced down the hallway, positive she had heard a footstep.

Impossible. Xander had walked her to the office and made her wait in the front while he checked out every room. Then he called Quarry Hall to tell Vincent they were taking him up on his offer to check security. Then he locked her inside. No one could get into the office unless they unlocked the front door or came in through a cellar door with a bar and heavy chain to reinforce it. Then they had to knock down the sturdy, dead-bolted door at the top of the stairs. All that would create enough noise to alert Hannah, even if she was foolish enough to wear headphones and play CDs at chop-and-liquefy volume. Right now, she preferred utter silence, thank you very much.

Hannah made a mental note to hang that old-fashioned bell over the front door, so no one could sneak in on her. Maybe she should hang bells by all the windows, and at her apartment, too.

"You're not crazy if you talk to yourself," she told the paint roller as she bent to slop it through the paint tray again. "Only if you start answering back."

They had all agreed that since she insisted on staying in Tabor and working on the office, they would go on as if nothing was wrong. Curt and Angela at the newspaper would know, but only because they were pursuing their own leads, trying to track down the identity of the White Rose Killer. Hannah didn't want her family to know until absolutely necessary. They hoped the lack of media coverage and no change in her routine or any reaction from the people around her would drive the White Rose crazy and make him act out of character.

If he really had targeted her.

If there was a copycat involved, they hoped Hannah's lack of reaction would prompt him to break the White Rose's pattern, so they could catch him. If the White Rose had chosen Tracy Brickman, alerting the media would reveal that she had dropped out of school. The longer he waited for her to come back from Christmas break, the longer the women of Tabor would be safe from his attentions. Then the White Rose would find another target, if he didn't try to track the poor girl down and punish her for running away. Either way, silence was the best course of action.

Hannah had chosen to stay in Tabor, rather than going to the Padua office to try to work. She wouldn't be able to concentrate or help anyone with their problems. Physical work, she had learned long ago, was the only release for the tension that threatened to turn her muscles into frayed knots.

That and lots of praying. Chief Cooper had told them he was going to call Pastor Glenn and send a discrete message around Tabor Christian's prayer chain that a member of the congregation was in danger. No mention of a stalker or gender, only the danger. Hannah had felt sick at the thought of Mr. Montgomery's reaction if he found out she was being stalked. He had made quite clear his opinion of women in their church who insisted on taking on a supposedly male-only occupation, and who refused to get married and raise children.

"Not that I don't want to get married, because I do," she told the echoing room that slowly filled with paint fumes. "I'd love to have kids and keep house, but why can't I help save my corner of the world at the same time? Why would God give me these talents if He didn't want me to use them?"

Such arguments meant icy, glaring silence from Mr. Montgomery and his clique at church. They were the kind of people who, once they made up their minds, couldn't be swayed by facts. Even when they were blatantly wrong.

Hannah wondered how poor Lisa survived being his daughter-in-law. It didn't escape her that if she had a husband right now, she wouldn't be a target of anyone.

At least, she hoped not.

She *could* imagine enemies of Xander taking pot shots at her, though, if they were married. After all, it had happened before, when that lunatic bailiff at the Justice Center poisoned her to put the blame on a rival lawyer who threatened Xander and the Arc Foundation.

That thought made her pause and then her thoughts went off on several new tangents. Several drops of paint hit the floor and she didn't notice right away. A few moments later, she put her roller down in the paint tray and scurried out to the front rooms, where she had left her coat with her cell phone in the pocket.

In that debacle at the Justice Center, Mendoza had made threats against the Arc Foundation because it supported Xander. Why not the same kind of thing now? Someone tried to distract or hurt the Arc Foundation or Xander through her?

"Distraction," Xander said slowly, after Hannah reached him at the office and spilled her theory. "Makes sense. I'll call the Chief. Maybe I should call Joan and ask if anyone has run into any really nasty trouble lately that would send someone out on a vengeance quest."

"Do they do that a lot?"

"When you fight the forces of evil in high places..." He sighed. "How are you doing? I assume it's been quiet enough to give you time to think of things like that."

"I'm calming down. Enough to think of all the work that didn't get done today because you were holding my hand."

"Hey, I like holding your hand. I don't like thinking of you facing all that alone. Or something happening because I was too busy somewhere else," he added with a slight growl in his voice. "Donovan called a little while ago to ask for your cell number. They're putting together a schedule for surveillance, and he's going to want to do a walk-through of your building, to look for weak spots, hidden places, that sort of thing. He'll be calling you to let you know when he's on his way over."

"Good. Otherwise I might see an intruder and attack him with a can of paint." To her surprise, jagged laughter spilled out of her. It sounded almost normal and brightened the atmosphere. Like a storm that cleared the electrical charge in the air.

"Remember, no going anywhere alone or without telling someone where you're going and when you'll be back. And no going out after dark without an escort or two."

"My life is going to be so boring."

"Better a boring—well, let's hope you're right, and it's just Montgomery having his second childhood and trying to scare us out of Tabor."

"How do we prove it? That's the problem." Hannah closed her eyes, fighting the dizzy sensation that came over her when her mind filled in Xander's unspoken words. *Better a boring life than no life at all.*

"Hey, you're the organizational genius who keeps my life from falling apart, and I'm Sherlock Holmes, remember? You just concentrate on having fun with the office and let me watch your back, okay?" he said, with a definite teasing growl in his voice.

"Okay." She had to smile.

Well, at least Xander was paying more attention to her, even if it was just her back.

"That's my Hannah. What time is dinner?"

"Dinner?"

"Hey, don't muzzle the ox that treads the grain, the workman is worthy of his hire, and the watchdog earns his chow. Or something like that."

"That's not in the Bible!" she sputtered, and another cleansing burst of laughter escaped her.

"Didn't say it was. Come on, Hannah, save me from stale bread and goose liver for dinner."

"Yuck, is that all you have at home?" Hannah caught a glimpse of movement from the corner of her eye and turned to see Maggie stomping up the steps to the front door. "Haven't you seen enough of me today?"

"Considering somebody threatened to keep anybody from ever seeing you again... I don't think I can see you enough." Xander's voice went scratchy. He cleared his throat.

Hannah had an instant image of him sitting at his desk, his feet up on the paper-covered surface, with his shoes off. Probably wearing those awful plaid socks. She imagined him rubbing at his eyes, hiding any hint of sentimentality.

Fear for her.

It was a step in the right direction, wasn't it?

Should she be grateful for this terror in her life, if it made Xander notice and value her more than usual? "Everything works together for good," she whispered.

"What was that?"

"Nothing. How does toasted cheese and salad and chili sound to you?"

"Heaven. Or the next best thing." Someone spoke close to Xander's desk. Hannah thought it might be Walter. "Look, I gotta go. I'll meet you at the office and walk you back to your place about five-ish?"

"Rene's meeting me, and it'll still be light enough out we can walk twenty steps down the sidewalk. The lights will be on at the theater and it'll be rush hour, so we'll have plenty of witnesses if somebody tries something," she hurried to add.

"Smart alec," he growled. "Don't let anybody in there without five forms of identification and a police escort, hear me?"

"*Seig heil, mein Fuhrer.*"

Xander's snort of laughter hit just before the connection broke. Hannah sighed, grinning wider than she thought she could ever grin again. What would she ever do without him?

"Thank You, Lord, for sending him into my life," she whispered as she switched her phone to standby and turned to go back to her painting.

"Yep, friends are great, aren't they?" Maggie said.

Hannah yelped and staggered back two steps from being nose-to-nose with Tabor's resident eccentric.

"How did you get in here?" She turned to glare at the front door. Hannah knew the door was locked. Every time she had to come out to the front, she had checked it just to be sure.

"Walked right through." Maggie shrugged, mischief sparkling in those mismatched eyes, one blue and one sea green, under her iron-gray, heavy brows.

She had on her winter outfit of two stocking caps, one green and one black, pulled down tight over her tangled silver and black curls, and five sweaters of graduated sizes buttoned up to her neck. A scarf long and colorful enough to rival Tom Baker's version of *Doctor Who* wrapped around her neck enough times to make her shoulders merge with her head. Maggie wore neon orange rubber boots that were about three sizes too large. Olive green camouflage patterned pants peered out from under the bottom sweater, which hung down to her knees, half-hidden by sagging leggings in faded pink with blue kittens all over them.

"Just wanted to tell you, Counselor, you're okay. Nobody's gonna hurt you." Maggie winked. "I'm keeping an eye on the place and on you and another eye on that silk suit with ice where his heart should be. Don't you worry none about no roses or —"

"Roses?" Hannah knees tried to fold. She reached out an unsteady hand for the desk to sit on the edge. She nearly missed and would have fallen if Maggie hadn't caught her with an amazingly strong grip.

"Angels rush in where fools fear to tread," the old woman whispered.

"How did you get in here? If you can pick that lock, anybody can."

"Did you ever read about Brother Andrew?" Maggie asked as she backed away toward the door. "God's making a lot of idiots blind lately, and that's good for you." She winked and twisted the doorknob. The door stuck for a few seconds. Long enough for Hannah to stand up and open her mouth to tell Maggie the door was locked. Then it opened. "Better get a bell or something up here, y'know? It's okay to trust God to take care of things, but we all gotta do our part, too. God wants you helping people. Can't do that if you're scared and hiding, y'know?"

Grinning as if she had just delivered the perfect present, Maggie turned and skipped outside, yanking the door closed behind her. Hannah hesitated a few seconds, then leaped for the door. She twisted the knob. It wouldn't open. She turned harder. It still wouldn't open. She pulled out her keys, and the stubborn lock resisted her.

By the time she stumbled down the steps to catch up with Maggie, the frustrating, quixotic woman had vanished.

Which, as Hannah knew, was par for the course with Maggie.

She came back to her senses and hurried up the steps and inside and locked the door behind herself again. Hannah found she could smile. Even laugh a little.

Truthfully, Maggie was one of the most beloved and trusted people in town. Newcomers looked askance at her, but parents who had known Maggie since they were children didn't think twice about her spending time with their children, or even walking them to the playground or the Mission. Maggie seemed to be everywhere in Tabor, in-the-know about everything and everybody.

Witness her reference to roses. Hannah didn't think it at all impossible for Maggie to have heard what happened to her. Though Chief Cooper was trying to keep this quiet, how could anyone keep Maggie from knowing something?

Hannah felt better, knowing Maggie knew she was in trouble and had vowed to keep watch. Nothing would happen without Maggie seeing. Stick-in-the-mud types like Judge Foggerty or Mr. Montgomery might want an excuse to get Maggie committed and off the street, but the entire town would rise up against them. Maggie belonged to them, their good luck charm and mascot.

"Thanks, Lord," Hannah whispered as she went back to work. She didn't doubt God had sent Maggie at just the right time to comfort and assure her.

~~~~~

"Uh, excuse me?" Walter hunched forward in his chair, resting his elbows on the knees of his baggy, hunter green dress pants. "If this White Rose guy is in Tabor, wouldn't it be safer for Hannah if she spent the day here, or maybe even left town for a while?"

"I wanted her to do that, but Hannah wants to keep working on the new office." Xander sighed and rubbed at his eyes, wishing he could close them for a few seconds, and when he opened them all his co-workers would be gone. Maybe start the day over again. Heck, why not start the entire month over again? "We're not sure if Hannah's the target of the White Rose Killer or a copycat. The only way to be sure is to gather evidence. If Hannah stays in one place, it's easier for the police to watch her. It's also harder for a stranger to get at her on Main Street in the middle of the day. Too many witnesses. " He met the eyes of all the staff sitting and standing around his desk and tried to summon up a cheerful smile to reassure them. "I let Arc know, and they're going to send someone to look over the security and make doubly sure she's safe."

Hannah had interviewed all the clerks and errand-runners and lawyers who worked part-time for Xander while trying to set up their own practices. She took care of their questions and problems. Hannah made sure all the disparate personalities complemented each other instead of clashing, and turned them into not just a team but a family.

Every person in the office liked her. Cared about her enough to be worried and angry over the news Xander had just given them.

He felt a little jealous. Could it be possible she was closer to some of the people here than she was to him? That wasn't fair. Hadn't he known Hannah years longer than the rest of them?

Why didn't you do something about it before now, moron? a sarcastic voice growled at the back of his mind.

"How about some of us go over there, take it in shifts to help out?" Nelson suggested. "We shouldn't leave her alone, right?"
~~~~~

"Hannah's not alone. Between her cell phone and the locked door and the police tripling their patrols down Main and the street behind the office, she'll be fine. Remember, the idea here is to trick the stalker into revealing himself, not drive him into hiding or get him so mad he does something stupid." Xander hadn't wanted to say "nasty" or "in revenge." Just thinking those words brought up images of Hannah lying pale and cold in that room she had been painting, with a mangled white rose in her hand.

After a few more questions and suggestions for things to do to help protect Hannah, Xander ended the meeting. He was glad to know they all cared about her and would work together on this. He had considered not telling anyone what was going on. After all, why worry them when they couldn't do anything? He was glad he had told them. Their office would pull together and get through this just fine, and they would be a tighter, more cohesive, harmonious unit when all was said and done.

Unless, of course, the intent of all this was to shut them down?

Xander thought back to Hannah's theory. What if someone attacked her to bring harm to Common Grounds or the Arc Foundation? He almost hoped so, because it took the personal element out of the picture. Hannah wasn't the target because she was beautiful, witty, intelligent and compassionate. She was simply convenient.

That option wasn't much better.

The phone rang, and Xander let it ring twice more before he decided the new receptionist, Brad, was on another line, and picked it up. The rules stated the only phone he picked up himself was his private line, and very few people had that number. All other calls were supposed to be picked up by Hannah or Brad.

"Common Grounds Legal Clinic," he said as he reached for his cold, half-empty cup of coffee.

"How the mighty have fallen, Mr. Finley," a chilly voice said with razor sharp enunciation. "The only redeeming feature of your alleged business is that efficient Miss Blake. She can't be at lunch already, can she?"

"What Miss Blake does when she's away from the office is her personal business." Xander bit his tongue to keep from adding, 'too bad you don't trust your people enough to let them live their own lives away from the office.' He recognized that voice. He wouldn't put it past his nemesis to record the phone call in the hopes of gathering ammunition to use against him. It wouldn't do for him to be snippy on the phone, no matter how provoked and justified. "What can I do to help you, Mr. Montgomery?"

"I don't need any help, Mr. Finley." Just a tiny pause, and Xander imagined the elder lawyer rearing back to gather his ire and prepare for the attack. "You, however, are biting off more than you can chew if you think you can trick Tabor Heights into keeping you on retainer. Even a city this small and peaceful has more legal action than you and your half-trained staff could ever manage. Finding it hard to deal with the dregs of society now, so you're moving up in the world?"

"Tabor doesn't have me on retainer," he forced himself to say slowly and calmly, but letting some inflection enter his voice. After all, sounding like a robot would give his enemy just as much satisfaction as screaming at him through gritted teeth. "If they're considering it—which I doubt—I haven't heard anything."

Then he wondered if Montgomery was referring to his discussion with the Chief and Mayor Amorrato about defending the city and Butler-Williams University if Tracy Brickman's family decided to sue. He had declined. What would day-to-day exposure to the case do to Hannah?

She mattered most in all of this. It might not be good business sense or legal wisdom, but everything pivoted off her.

When had he grown so protective of her?

"That's not very efficient, is it?" Montgomery said in a tone Xander could only think of as "oily smug." "How can you expect to get ahead if you don't stay on top of things?"

"All I know about the decision to put legal counsel on retainer is the *rumor*," Xander emphasized, his voice only a few degrees warmer, "that you've been pressing City Council for years to put you on retainer. Considering your friendship with Judge Foggerty, the Ethics Committee has always voted down the motion. Of course, that's also just a rumor, isn't it?"

Long silence. Xander grinned, until it occurred to him that he might have gone too far.

Chapter Eleven

"Rumors have a way of gaining a life of their own and turning into snakes that bite their handlers," Montgomery finally responded. "I only called to give you fair warning, Finley. If you weren't at the bottom of such a foolish proposal, I thought it only common courtesy to give you some good advice."

"I appreciate that. And when I see you acting foolishly, you can be sure I will return the favor." Xander held back his chuckle as Montgomery icily seethed through his farewell.

"Open your eyes, Finley," Montgomery added. "What appears to be an angel in white may just turn out to be a filthy whore."

The phone clicked and the connection died. Xander felt like something had scorched in his throat and lodged there, choking him.

What was that all about? Had someone started the rumor just to irritate Montgomery? Or was it truth? Maybe someone on City Council had suggested putting Common Grounds on retainer, once the move to set up the second office in Tabor Heights became official?

Montgomery was right. Going on retainer as legal counsel to the city of Tabor Heights would interfere with Common Grounds' caseload. Nearly half the cases Xander's people handled were *pro bono* or at a large discount. With all expenses and salaries funded by the Arc Foundation, Common Grounds had no need to generate income or make a profit. That was the whole purpose of Common Grounds. Xander's dream since entering law school had been to provide legal help for those who needed it, whether they could pay or not, given by people who cared and had the freedom to decide if the case was worthy and moral. Public defenders were a fine concept, but with people stuck defending the very obviously guilty, those lawyers burned out quickly, became cynical and bitter and hardened, until they either got out, or they just no longer cared, no longer tried. And the innocent people who needed help, who were looking for justice, still had no relief or support.

Common Grounds didn't need the income generated by working on retainer for Tabor Heights. The time taken up with research and all the complications of a municipal entity would take too much time, attention, and energy away from the cases Xander truly considered important.

Xander froze, reaching for the file that had been sitting ignored on his desk for too long. What had Montgomery said, just before he hung up?

An angel in white, and *a filthy whore.* Why did those words set up a reverberation in his memory?

Xander choked as the connection slammed into his consciousness with the impact of a brick wall toppling over on him.

Al Colson's message from the White Rose Killer had warned him what would happen if he tried to tempt his *angel in white* and lead her into sin, so she turned into a *filthy whore.*

Colson had promised not to tell anyone about the note or Hannah's involvement. He wouldn't have broken his promise and told Montgomery, would he?

Xander felt sick. It had to be a coincidence. Montgomery had a habit of turning his Bible into a weapon to batter people until they were so dizzy, tired, and mentally bruised, they gave in to his demands.

But what if it wasn't a coincidence?

What if Arthur Montgomery was the White Rose?

Stranger things had happened. And it made a kind of twisted sense. The man had been a widower for many years. He openly criticized the young women of the church for too much makeup or jewelry or short skirts, or a dozen other complaints. Especially the ones who chose a career over marriage and a family. What if he were lonely, trying to regain the wife who, according to the church stories, supposedly had been a saint? What if he found a girl, maybe one who looked like his dead wife, and tested her before approaching her?

Was Montgomery mentally sick enough to believe a girl deserved to die for not living up to his standards? In essence, betraying him.

Xander reached for the phone to call Donovan. His theorizing could come from his dislike for the man. He would tell Donovan what had just happened in the conversation with Montgomery, maybe find out if the rumor that got his rival so incensed were true, and let Donovan make the connections and formulate his own theories.

He wouldn't tell Hannah. At least, not right away. She had enough to worry about without giving her another problem to distract her. He would tell her tonight, after supper. Maybe after Donovan had worked on the clue for a while and gave them some feedback.

Still, what if it were Montgomery? Could the case be solved that quickly?

Hannah would be safe. That was the important thing.

~~~~~

Hannah heard the voices. She came up to the front of the office after rinsing out the paint pan in the bathroom and saw Vincent leaning against the thick post that supported the porch, talking to Maggie, who stood on the sidewalk. Just before Hannah picked up her keys to unlock the door and let him in, he tipped his head back and laughed, making his whole
~~~~~

body shake. Maggie flipped him a jaunty salute and sauntered down the sidewalk.

"How's it feel to be an object of desire?" Vincent said when she got the door open and stepped outside.

"No, thanks." Hannah moved to the front of the porch and looked down the street. Maggie had vanished, just in the two seconds she had looked away. How did the old woman do that? More important: Did she give lessons? "Thanks for coming," she said, when she could have threatened to punish his smart remark with a wet brush.

"Hey, Arc takes care of its own, and you're family." Vincent slung a lean, muscled arm around her shoulders and led her back into the office. "I did a quick look-see outside already. Your landlord takes good care of things. All the doors and windows are solid. Let me check it out from the inside, and we'll see what needs doing. I hope you're planning on feeding me before I head back home," he added with a grin.

"Why is everyone trying to turn me into a—a—a domestic goddess, all of a sudden?" she sputtered.

Vincent just grinned when she explained about feeding Xander tonight. Hannah watched him walk around the front rooms, testing the windows, tugging on the frames, examining the locks, the thickness of the glass, and the freshness of the seals.

"So, you seem to get along with Maggie just fine."

"Oh, so that's the famous Maggie. Yeah, Joan told me about her." Vincent looked like he was about to say something, then shook his head and turned back to what he was doing. "Well, I'll tell you, Maggie says you're safe and she's looking out for you. That's good enough for me."

"Uh huh." She didn't know whether to be amused or disgruntled.

"Hannah... just because you can't see the armies of Heaven surrounding you doesn't mean they aren't there. Anne led the charge, heading up to the War Room to start praying heavy duty for you as soon as Xander called. You're going to be fine." He winked. "Of course, being scared and ticked probably doesn't fit your definition of fine, but—"

He was interrupted by a knock at the door. Hannah bit her lip to keep from muttering about her supposedly empty office turning into Grand Central Station and went to the door. Mark Donovan stood outside, ready to do his safety inspection of the office and her apartment. Hannah decided to be amused at the way he and Vincent sized up each other, just for a moment, like two big dogs trying to decide if they would be enemies or work together to protect one very small, helpless dog.

Or was she nothing more than a bone to protect from another, nastier dog? Hannah pushed that thought aside to concentrate on what Vincent had told her. She was going to be fine. Between Maggie watching out for her, Vincent checking out the office and apartment, the Tabor Police

Department on the alert, and dozens of people praying for her at the Arc Foundation and at church, what did she have to worry about?

She reminded herself of that thought every time she got that hair-raising, chill sensation on the back of her neck that made her think someone watched her.

Sunday, December 22

"You really think he's going to come after me in the church parking lot?" Hannah said, uncertain whether to laugh or snarl.

She stood at the end of the driveway between her apartment house and the next house with her Bible clutched against the front of her pine-green wool coat and her purse hanging from her shoulder. Xander's car waited in the street, blocking access to the driveway. He stayed there with his hand on the open passenger door and just looked at her.

"Or on the way to church," he finally said. "Or in the bathroom. Remember Taylor's theory?"

"You really think a woman like that would even come through the front door? Pastor is very vocal about what the Bible says about—" Hannah sighed, giving up, and walked the last three steps to Xander's car. "It's nearly Christmas."

"That doesn't stop some lunatics. The fact that it's the holidays gives a lot of them justification for being especially nasty. If they're alone and miserable, why keep it to themselves?"

"You know, the White Rose is going to think you're trying to defile me." She slid into the passenger seat.

"I've given you and Rene plenty of rides to church on snowy days, it's habit. Speaking of Rene—"

"Her father got to town early. He picked her up for breakfast before church."

"And you were just going to walk all by yourself?" Xander let out a sigh that was part groan.

That set Hannah laughing. She tried to muffle it, so it came out a snort, which made her laugh harder. Xander glared at her for a few seconds after he got into the car, until a smile inched partially across his face. He shook his head, slammed the car into gear, and drove the few blocks down Main to the Triangle, turned left, then left again on Church and took the first driveway entrance to their church's parking lot.

"I was planning on walking with the Holwoods," Hannah finally said. "Who would try to stop me during a one block walk? It'd be smarter to try to ambush me further down the street. By those big bushes or from behind the sign."

She gestured down the street to the parking lot entrance, where the church sign hung mounted on a low brick wall, flanked on either end by thick pines. On the other side of the driveway were more pines and bushes that looked positively black in the early morning brilliance off the snow.

"Okay, so you weren't being unusually courageous." Xander turned off the engine.

"Or brainless?" She batted her eyelashes at him until he smiled.

"Optimistic. Just because Sunday is sacred to you doesn't mean..." He shook his head and unlocked the door.

Nothing in the world would persuade Hannah to tell Xander just how much she appreciated him stopping by and worrying about her. How warm it made her feel to know he was worried. It would embarrass him, and she might just make a fool of herself, presuming on a nonexistent depth to their friendship. When the crisis was over, the White Rose Killer or the copycat caught, they would go back to their friendly partnership. Just like after the last crisis.

Partners. That was all they would ever be to each other.

Once again, Hannah prayed for the serenity to accept what she could have and be grateful, so hunger for what she couldn't have would not poison it.

Xander caught hold of her arm after only a few steps across the parking lot.

"What will the White Rose think?" she asked under her breath.

"That I'm keeping his angel from falling on the ice and breaking her neck." He gestured at the blacktop before them, then stepped sideways to lead her around it. The change of angle revealed black ice, just dull enough with a dusting of snow to be nearly invisible.

They said nothing during the remainder of the walk to the back door. Xander didn't let go of her arm until they were inside and hanging up their coats in the first hallway outside the fellowship hall. He stayed by her side as they went in, searching for coffee.

They often sat together in church, so Hannah doubted anyone would remark on it today. Unless of course the White Rose attended for the first time today, just to keep an eye on her.

Hannah mentally slapped herself for giving in to those fears. Hadn't she prayed hard enough last night? What had happened to that peace she thought she had found, after what seemed like hours of praying and studying her Bible?

Was she wrong to enjoy Xander's attentiveness?

Reverend Ackley had arrived in town last night and insisted on taking both roommates out to dinner, despite Hannah's protests that he should spend some private time with his daughter. Rene had told her father before about the White Rose Killer. She waited until their appetizers came and the noise in the steakhouse around them grew loud enough to nearly require shouting, before telling him Hannah was the newest target. Hannah's gratitude outweighed her guilty feelings when the minister spent most of the evening giving them both encouragement and advice. Working in the rescue mission in Chicago, he had plenty of experience in counseling women who had been stalked, harassed and attacked. He had even offered to teach Hannah a few self-defense moves that all members of the mission's staff were required to learn.

Hannah had thanked him and agreed to take a few lessons while Reverend Ackley was in town. She had gone to bed last night with a renewed sense of peace, assured God was watching over her, no matter what happened. Even if the unthinkable happened, what mattered most was her soul, and her destination was assured. All she had to worry about was maintaining her testimony in the face of fear and evil.

She hadn't dreamed at all last night and woke up this morning feeling as if she had indeed slept the whole night through. Maybe it was that sense of renewed stability and peace that made her think she could walk to church. Fortunately, Xander seemed to have dedicated his life to worrying about her. It was almost amusing, in the midst of the uncertainties.

A bigger problem hit them at the start of the service, though, when Xander passed her the bulletin, turned over so she could see the announcements printed on the back. Hannah glanced down the list and didn't see anything that could dig those new lines of worry across his forehead, or those grooves of tension around his mouth. She frowned at him and shook her head. He reached over and underlined one announcement with his finger, then rolled his eyes for emphasis.

Hannah muffled a groan. Preparations for the Sunday School Christmas program and open house that evening necessitated some classes being combined during both services. Hannah and Xander went to different classes. He studied Romans with Dr. Holwood, and she had a class on church history taught by Pastor Wally. Their two classes were being combined. Hannah still couldn't understand his frown. Wouldn't sharing the same classroom be a relief? Xander wouldn't have to give up his class or ask her to leave hers, since he was so set on escorting her today. Then she read further down the list. One other adult class was combining with theirs: Foundations. Mr. Montgomery taught the Foundations class.

After what Xander told her of the phone call he received Thursday, and the odd coincidence of Mr. Montgomery's word choice, Hannah didn't want to be anywhere near the man. Leave it to Mr. Montgomery to see evil where there was none. If a girl had been attacked, her clothes torn to shreds, Montgomery would see evil intentions in the police officer who wrapped a blanket around her to cover her nudity.

What if that cold-hearted, self-righteous man had guessed her interest in Xander? Her boss. In Montgomery's book, that had to be as bad as prostitution. Maybe Xander's theory about Montgomery being the White Rose Killer wasn't so off base after all. Maybe he saw himself as an avenging angel, a protector of purity throughout the community. Maybe—

"Let's skip class today," Xander whispered, as the congregation stood to sing the hymn between the offertory and the sermon.

Hannah nodded. That sounded good to her. She had to fight to concentrate on Pastor Glenn's Christmas sermon, just to keep from gnawing on the idea that their greatest nemesis could be the villain the entire town had been hunting for months.

Such thinking was not proper for Sunday. Especially when it kept her from listening to Pastor Glenn. Hannah brought to bear all the skills she had learned during some particularly boring, required classes in college, to keep her mind on the sermon and off the topic that screamed for her attention. She succeeded and could even repeat the sermon points if someone asked. But she didn't enjoy it at all.

"Hard concentrating on anything lately?" Xander asked when they were back in his car. They had to wait for three cars to pass so they could pull out of the driveway onto Church Street.

"Hmm? Oh—yeah. And Pastor Glenn's Christmas sermons are the best." She tried to smile.

"I don't know what's worse. Sitting through class, getting glared at, with two-edged remarks thrown into the discussion, or confirming his belief that we're both heathens."

"How come legalistic slimes get all the press, and the ordinary, healthy, balanced people get ignored?" Hannah murmured as they drove down the street.

"What you said—balanced. And the world's not balanced, so..." Xander shrugged and gave her that crooked smile that said it all. *Life in general is unfair. End of story.*

Hannah felt very tired, suddenly, worn out with the wishes she thought she had abandoned and these new fears and worries crowding her mind. If only she and Xander could be this much in accord all the time, life would be perfect. Why couldn't she be like her brothers and parents, who found the people who fit them perfectly, like two pieces of a puzzle, made for each other? She had seen her parents complete each other's sentences for years, and it was scary and yet amusing to see it happening with her brothers and their wives. When would it happen—would it ever happen—for her?

Xander turned left down the next street, to take them out on Main so he could make a right turn into her driveway. Neither of them said anything during the few minutes of the drive. Hannah tried to turn her thoughts to what was in the refrigerator, what she could offer him for a very early lunch and what she had to hold back for the holiday menus she and Rene had put together.

"Hey!" Xander stomped on the gas, passed her apartment house, then half-turned into the driveway of the office, slammed on the brake, hit the gearshift and leaped out, leaving the engine running.

A dark shape darted across the front of the old house, almost lost among the bushes, but standing out in stark relief where snow had piled up nearly to the porch decking. Xander leaped across piles of snow and the figure suddenly darted around the side of the building, into the alley driveway between it and the funeral home on the other side.

Hannah turned off the ignition, yanked the keys out, and made sure the car was locked before she followed. Her hands shook as she reached for her cell phone.

"What do you think you're—" Xander growled from behind her. He stopped short when Hannah turned, revealing the cell phone pressed against the side of her head.

In another moment, Hannah had reached the police department. Taylor was on duty today. Hannah briefly explained what had happened, then passed the phone to Xander.

She shivered as he described the prowler: dark blue stocking cap, dark complexion, curly brown hair, football player build, patched jeans, muddy work boots, muddy green sweatshirt jacket, dark gloves. She turned to look at the office, wondering what the prowler had been doing there, as Xander described his chase on foot.

"Fire!" she squeaked. Without waiting for Xander, she ran up the driveway.

Chapter Twelve

A line of smoke trickled up from the side of the building, visible through a side window on the first floor. It was the storage room, where she had all her wallpaper and painting supplies, the rug samples, and the extra paper for the copy machine. Hannah shook her head to get rid of the list of office supplies that were surely feeding the fire by now. Judging from the way the smoke thickened and darkened in only a few seconds' time, the fire was new and growing fast.

"Fire!" she screamed, and fumbled for the keys that would let her in the side door. It led down into the basement, where all the tenants were allowed to store things, but it also led to the stairs for the two apartments on the second floor and the garret apartment on the third floor. If someone had decided to sleep in today... she refused to complete the thought.

"Stay out here," Xander ordered, just as Hannah got the door open. He shoved the phone into her hand, pushed past her before she could argue, and took the stairs four at a time.

"Xander?" Taylor's voice sounded tinny, before she thought to bring the phone up to her ear.

"He went upstairs to warn the others," Hannah reported, clutching the cell phone close to her face. Like a security blanket.

"I've called the fire department," Taylor assured her. "What do you see? Do you know where the flames are?"

Hannah surprised herself with how calmly she recited the details before her, and what she knew was inside the room now on fire. In the background, she heard the wail of the hook-and-ladder as it left the station, only three blocks west and two south. Above that, she heard Xander banging on doors and shouting the news.

Xander came down the stairs with a massive, bald, white-bearded Black man who clutched a Gold Tone Gym bag in one hand. He wore neon green sweats and Hannah hoped he had been preparing to head to Rene's gym when it opened at noon.

"Is that everyone?" she asked as she folded up her cell phone and slid it into her coat pocket.

"I'm the only one here. The attic apartment's been empty two months, and Evie moved to Florida just after Thanksgiving." He grinned, displaying two gold teeth in the bottom row. "Joe Hooper," he said, holding out his hand to shake Xander's and then Hannah's hands. "Don't know what I'd have done if you folks hadn't happened by. Got a head cold. Wouldn't have smelled the smoke until it was too late for me."

The fire truck screamed up to the end of the driveway. Two firefighters leaped off and ran up to the three of them before the truck had come to a complete stop. Before she knew it, Hannah, Xander, and Joe were herded down the sidewalk and out of the way.

"Don't know about the folks downstairs," Joe continued, when Xander stepped away to move his car at the request of one of the firefighters. "Somebody's getting ready to move in, but that's all I know."

"We're the folks downstairs," Hannah said with a shaky grin. "I live two doors down. Xander was bringing me home from church and we saw the smoke coming out of our office and..." She shrugged.

She felt very cold, though the Weather Channel had said they would experience an unusual warming trend up until Christmas Eve.

The clock tower on the Triangle just finished chiming for eleven-thirty when the firefighters started packing up their equipment. Chief Abernathy waved for Xander, Hannah and Joe to come back up to the house, while his men uncoupled the hose from the hydrant just past the funeral home.

"Not too bad. It was pretty much contained in that one room. We'll have to go upstairs and check the damage to the floorboards in the apartment directly above it. This one of the Gordons' houses?"

"Mandy's at church," Xander said, nodding. "I heard Fred stayed home today. Still fighting pneumonia."

"Well, when a guy insists his waders will keep him dry and warm and goes fishing after the ice forms, that's what he gets." The fire chief managed a one-sided grin. "Better send somebody to catch Mandy at church, instead of bothering Fred, then. Come on. Let's get the inventory done, and you can get on with your day."

Hannah peeled off her coat and left it with her purse in the front of the office. She could wash her dress, but her wool coat had to be dry-cleaned. That was what she got for wearing her Christmas present to herself before Christmas actually arrived.

At first glance, the fire didn't seem to have done that much damage. All the wallpaper, dry paste, and copy paper were a loss. Where they hadn't been charred, they were soaked. The strips of carpeting she had laid down to protect the floor while she worked were soaked. She hoped the hardwood floors weren't too badly damaged.

"That's not ours." Xander pointed to a gallon can of cleaning fluid lying on its side in the corner furthest from the fire.

"You sure?" Chief Abernathy glanced from him to Hannah. Joe Hooper hovered in the doorway, staying out of the way.

"The paint is all water soluble, and so is the wallpaper paste I'm using," Hannah said.

"And I brought over most of the office supplies on Friday," Xander added. "We don't buy that brand, and we buy pint cans because we don't use it that much."

"Then this does look like arson, doesn't it?" the chief murmured. "How did you know to stop? How bad was the smoke?"

"I didn't see anything," Xander said, and glanced at Hannah. "I was driving Hannah home, and I saw somebody come out between the office and the house. When he saw me stop, he ran back into hiding."

"Suspicious."

"With everything else going on lately, I jumped out to try to chase him, or at least get a good look. Hannah saw the smoke before I did."

"Well, sounds like the work of an amateur. Which might be worse than a pro."

"Why's that?" Joe asked from his post in the doorway. The other three startled and turned to look at him. He had been so quiet, they forgot he was there.

"Amateurs either do it for spite or revenge, or we have a firebug who likes to watch the pretty flames."

"Was somebody after us, or Mr. Hooper, or to get revenge on Mandy?" Hannah murmured, thinking out loud.

"Somebody doesn't want us moving in here." Xander met her gaze. Hannah felt sick, positive she knew what he was thinking.

Who would profit the most by keeping them from moving into Tabor? Who would take the most satisfaction from seeing them stymied, and consider the fire damage justified punishment for Mandy Gordon?

The biggest problem lay in proving Montgomery had something to do with this, without ending up on the wrong end of a lawsuit for defamation of character.

Monday, December 23

Hannah went to Gold Tone Gym that morning, for something to do and for company. Xander had told her to take the day off after the stressful Sunday they endured, filling out reports and talking with Mark Donovan about his progress in the White Rose case. Hannah would rather be busy. Staying home to finish the decorating just wasn't enough distraction. Reverend Ackley planned a leisurely morning, sleeping in at his hotel and then visiting some friends in the area, so Rene could still do her morning shift at the gym. Hannah went in with her roommate. After all, now was as good a time as any to get back into her much-neglected exercise routine.

Maybe physical pain would fog her brain enough to let her get through the day without gnawing on the clues, problems, and multiple layers of the whole situation that threatened to suffocate her.

It was only two days until Christmas—couldn't the bad guys of the world take a break?

~~~~~

Xander wasted ten minutes trying to reach Hannah after getting the call from the police. He closed his eyes, refusing to give in to the sensation of panic. Why wouldn't she pick up her cell phone? He took a deep breath, opened his eyes, and saw the blinking message light on his phone. Hope wiped away the panic as he pressed the code to play the messages. How long had that light been blinking, and he hadn't noticed?

"Xander? How come you aren't at work yet?" Hannah asked, with a breathy chuckle at the back of her voice.

He flinched, wondering if that was frightened, nervous laughter or she was in the middle of something strenuous when she called. Why didn't he know more about what Hannah would do when she wasn't at work? He felt like he had been going through life with blinders and earmuffs on, only guessing at the lives the people around him led when they left the office or the courtroom.

"I'm going to the gym with Rene. Might as well start working off all this holiday eating before it even starts, right? Then we're going shopping at Kingsbury Mall. Rene's father is meeting us for lunch. We should be fine, so don't start worrying. I'll check in with you before we do anything else. Have a nice day—and thanks for making me take a day off work." The breathless tone changed to something warm. "I really needed it. You're the best, Boss Man."

Xander slowly shook his head, a grin creeping across his face. If he had thought to check his messages when he came in, he wouldn't have gone halfway to a heart attack now, would he?

But that still didn't answer the question of why Hannah didn't answer her cell phone. She knew better than to leave it at home now, of all times.

"Hi."

For a moment, Xander thought the message was still running on the machine. Then he raised his eyes and saw Hannah standing in the door of his cubicle. She wore jeans and a black vest jacket with the snowflakes along the hem. Her cheeks were red with cold and she held out her cell phone.

"Were you trying to get hold of me?"

"Why didn't you answer?" He stayed seated, when he wanted to leap out of his chair and either hug her or shake her for scaring him.

"Because we were sitting in traffic, and I knew we'd be here in a few minutes anyway." She settled down in the chair facing his desk.
~~~~~

"We?"

"Rene and her dad and me. What's up?"

"They caught our firebug."

"But—"

"But what?" Xander tried to smile. Now that his worry for Hannah had evaporated, other problematic details grew more insistent in his thoughts.

"You don't sound as happy as I'd expect you to."

"Chucky Timkin." He sat back and waited for her to make the connection.

It only took a few seconds for Hannah's eyes to widen and a small sound of disappointment to escape her. It had taken him nearly twice as long to place the name and remember the case file it belonged to.

Chucky Timkin was a *pro bono* client of Common Grounds. The young man had no money and his only relative, an aunt, lived on Welfare and the weekly delivery from the Food Cupboard ministry at the Mission.

~~~~~

"What do you mean, he turned himself in?" Xander turned away from the one-way window that showed his erstwhile client sitting in the interrogation room at the Tabor Heights police station.

The young man had just turned eighteen and had a long history of shoplifting, truancy, running away from home, vagrancy, and underage drinking. He had come to live with his aunt in an attempt to straighten out his life before he ruined the record that had been wiped clean when he lost his minor status.

Chucky stayed in his seat, but he couldn't sit still. His legs jerked up and down like someone giving a toddler a horsy ride. His fingers pounded the table like a manic pianist. His head bobbed up and down and left to right as if he needed to see every side of the room at once. The boy was scared. Xander thought back to his last talk with Chucky, trying to get through to him so he wouldn't continue his streak of shoplifting and staying away from home for days on end. The young man had sat still, calm, almost smiling. He had even talked about attending church with Xander.

Hannah turned away from the window. "How and why?"

Xander remembered the time she spent on the young man, talking with him until he relaxed and started opening up. Chucky had dreams of being an artist and loved his loud, bouncy music. He had been delighted to talk to someone who actually listened. Hannah seemed to like the young man. Xander felt sure it hurt her even more than him, to know what their client had done.

"He heard the talk about the fire around town," Donovan said. He slouched in a chair set against the wall vertical to the interrogation room,
~~~~~

so he wouldn't see the frenetic movements of the prisoner. "He said it freaked him out, major league, when he heard the fire was in your new office. He said the guy who made him do it didn't tell him it was your place."

"*Made* him do it?" Xander echoed.

"Kid gave us a stack of twenties he said the guy paid him to set the fire. Either he stole the money, or he's legit."

"What's the story? I find it hard to believe Chucky would lower himself to arson."

"I know." Hannah stepped closer to the window, to press a hand against the glass. Almost as if she could reach through and touch the miserable, nervous young man. "Stealing, I believe. He justifies it in his head, because he needs it so badly. But he wouldn't willingly hurt someone or destroy someone else's property."

"According to him, he was being blackmailed. Not in those words, though," Donovan added with a chuckle. "He claims some guy cornered him and said he had proof the kid was involved in that mugging outside Progressive Field in November. The guy promised he'd hand over the proof, once the kid took care of this job."

"Could Chucky describe him?"

"We finished with the sketch artist just before I called you. The picture's out on the street as we speak."

Xander expected Donovan to smile or show some pride in that statement. After all, how much faster could anyone expect this case to be solved without using a time machine? But the officer looked grimmer.

"What's the rest of the story?" Xander asked. He settled in to make himself more comfortable. Gut instinct said this was going to be a long, rough afternoon.

"The guy gave him a wad of money to buy the cleaning fluid and gave him a box of roses he had to deliver."

"Roses?" Hannah's voice cracked. "Like—white roses?" She took a shaky step to the nearest chair when Donovan nodded.

Chucky was supposed to leave a white rose on Hannah's doorstep and on the steps of the new office every day, starting with the day of the fire. He didn't know Hannah lived there, which Xander could believe. They didn't make a habit of discussing their private lives with their clients. The man who hired him would be back at the end of the week with more roses.

They had a stroke of luck there. The man who bought the roses had left the hand-written receipt inside the box. Donovan planned to visit the florist that afternoon, along with a copy of the sketch of the suspect, and hopefully talk to the clerk who had sold the roses.

Chucky hadn't thought anything of it, other than to reason that the man who hired him had gotten in an argument with his girlfriend and was trying to make it up to her. How Chucky could factor the fire into an apology, Xander didn't know. He didn't want to know. The world was warped enough as it was without trying to twist his brain around it.

What mattered most to him was that when Chucky found out who was involved in the fire and who was to receive the roses, he had turned himself in. He was terrified, positive he would end up in jail, or the blackmailer would find him, or he would be punished for something he didn't do.

Yet despite that terror, he had chosen to do the right thing. Xander had high hopes for the young man.

"If he needs someone to defend him, tell him we're more than willing," he told Donovan as the three of them walked through the station to the side door. "In a way, Arc owes him for this one."

"He shouldn't be in too much trouble, since he's turning everything over to us," the officer said, nodding. "Besides, he already has an alibi for the day of the mugging." He grinned when Xander and Hannah gave him puzzled looks. "He was here. He had the flu and he tried to shoplift some medicine from Heinke's right in front of me." He snorted. "I was picking up something for Melissa in the same aisle. Poor kid spent most of his time in lockup in front of the toilet. Felt really sorry for him, let me tell you that."

"I think it paid off," Hannah said softly.

"Chief?" Donovan called, turning to look across the lobby of the department.

Chief Cooper was just coming in through a side doorway. His forehead immediately creased with concern as he saw Xander and Hannah standing there with Donovan. When the officer gestured toward the police chief's office, the man nodded. The three settled into chairs in front of Cooper's desk. Donovan filled him in on what had happened.

"Well, that answers some other questions," Cooper said slowly. He nodded as he spoke, and his eyes were fixed on some distant point.

"It might," Donovan said.

"Excuse me, but could you let us in on the secret?" Xander asked. He couldn't manage a smile to lighten the mood in the office. It took all his control not to grit his teeth.

"Either the man who paid the boy to set the fire and deliver the roses is the copycat, or you have another enemy out there, trying to make you very uncomfortable," the chief said slowly. His gaze shifted back and forth between Xander and Hannah as he spoke.

"I have a good idea who you want to blame for all this," he continued, and offered them a crooked smile. "The fact is, with something like this, the smart bet is to run away from what we *want* as the answer. If even a whiff of what we suspect gets out, we'll be hobbled with nuisance suits, and all the details of this case will get blown wide open. The closer we can hold the cards to our vest right now, the better I'll feel. Ever since Annalee died, it's been just Mark and me working the case. I haven't even put anything in the computer, just in case the White Rose can hack into our system."

"Hack into your system? Why?" Hannah asked.

"Like you speculated, he figured out that we were planning on getting Annalee out of his reach. That's why he killed her. In some of his notes, he even warned her not to leave town, not to hide from him." Cooper nodded. "The less information available to anyone not involved in this case, the safer the White Rose's next target will be."

"I'd just like to be sure once and for all that Hannah isn't a target of the real White Rose Killer, cold as that may sound," Xander added.

"We're pretty sure she's not." Donovan let out one bark of laughter when Xander turned sharply to face him, fast enough to make his neck ache. "She doesn't fit the physical profile. If there really is one, after only three victims."

"Four," Xander had to say. "The girl who ran away from college."

"Granted." The officer nodded. "The thing is, they're all dark-haired, dark-eyed, and still living at home, or at least dependent on their parents. Hannah is blonde. She's been on her own since her second year of college. And she dates — the other three girls didn't have much of a social life."

"Neither does Hannah." Xander couldn't quite believe himself. Was he arguing to keep Hannah on the victim list?

Chapter Thirteen

"She's more active in the community, and she spends a lot of time hanging around with the guys in her classes." Donovan cracked a smile. "We've been asking a lot of questions."

"It makes me sound kind of... I don't know. Loose?" Hannah tried to laugh. It sounded like she choked on it a little. Xander admired her for trying to smile in the face of everything she had endured and might still endure. She had to be afraid, but she refused to burden them with it.

The funny thing was, he *wanted* to be "burdened" with her fears. Because she wouldn't be a burden.

"I'd like to know how Montgomery knew the words from Colson's note. Some could argue he wrote the note," Xander said, thinking out loud to get his mind back onto track.

"Some could argue," Chief Cooper said, "that he got hold of Colson's note because he's that type of autocrat in his office. Everything is his property once you cross that threshold."

"Including the minds and souls of his employees," Xander grumbled. He nodded. The chief had made his point.

Still, who could say it *wasn't* Montgomery? The sketch of the man who paid Chucky wasn't anybody Xander recognized. Montgomery certainly wouldn't do his own dirty work. He'd hire someone. A smart man would hire someone nobody knew, an outsider who could never be traced back to him.

Face it, Xander told himself, *the man's defended enough slimy types. He has connections.*

"So my rose was from the copycat," Hannah mused. "Is that good or bad?"

"Remember, sometimes copycats can be nastier than the real thing," Donovan said. "They don't think the same way the original does. All they can do is follow in the footsteps that everyone knows about. Maybe they aren't as flexible. They don't know the agenda."

"Obviously not, if the copycat is going after me."

"The thing is, you could be in more trouble."

"It takes a pretty sick mind to do the things the White Rose is doing," Xander offered, when she frowned a little, not quite following Donovan's mental trail. "Just how much worse is a copycat, who is thrilled enough by the original to follow in his or her footsteps?"

"Zero creativity, and a thrill-seeker." She nodded. "So, let's hope that receipt for the roses is all the clue we need. If we catch this guy, what do we charge him with? Being un-original?"

"There's nothing new under the sun," Chief Cooper quoted softly.

~~~~~

With Chucky's help, and the cooperation of the *Picayune*, they hoped to set a trap. That night, after the newspaper had been put to bed and the Tuesday edition was already at the presses, Angela Coffelt and Curt Mehdlang were to meet with Chief Cooper and Donovan at the police station. Hannah didn't know the details, only that a slightly misleading story would be written for the Thursday edition, aimed at the man who hired Chucky. If it worked, he would panic badly enough to make several strategic mistakes.

Xander was still at the apartment when Angela Coffelt stopped by to talk to Hannah. He and Reverend Ackley had challenged Rene and Hannah to a game of dominoes, guys against girls. Hannah thought maybe it was one of the downstairs neighbors when the knock came on the door at nearly ten o'clock. They had grown a little too noisy, laughing and arguing over the rules. The old walls were thin, the heating system transmitted sound better than an intercom, and the apartment on the ground floor had small children.

"Hannah?" Angela looked like a Christmas card, her blue-black hair topped by a fuzzy red stocking cap, with a green and white striped scarf over her black coat, and the snow lightly falling, dusting her with diamond speckles. "I saw the light on as I was heading home and I thought..." She offered that wry little smile that could put rival politicians at ease during election interviews.

"Donovan thought he had a plan. I assume you've worked out something?" Hannah stepped back and gestured for the editor of the *Picayune* to come inside.

The next few minutes were taken up with introducing Angela to Reverend Ackley and offering her tea or eggnog. Angela accepted the eggnog but didn't take off her coat, only unbuttoning it before she perched on the edge of the green paisley loveseat.

"We're going to print a story about the college girl who left, and why she left," she began.

"But the White Rose will simply find another target," Xander said, almost at the same time Hannah thought it.

"Or he could hunt her down at home," Reverend Ackley offered. "I've had some experience with stalkers of one type or another. Some of them will hunt down their supposed sweetheart, no matter what it takes. They won't take no for an answer. Will he be able to find this girl?"

"Donovan is working with the administration over at the university
~~~~~

to seal her records and keep watch on anyone who might try to get access. We're trying to catch two jailbirds with one blow, so to speak," Angela said. "For you, Hannah, we're going to report there were witnesses to the fire at your office. We're also going to put a small piece right next to the story, saying new evidence has cleared several suspects in that mugging at Progressive Field."

"Making whoever hired Chucky panic. He'll lose his hold over him and get implicated at the same time," Xander said, nodding.

"Hopefully, he'll come looking for Chucky, and we'll have him."

"We?" Hannah couldn't help asking.

"A problem like this is doubly bad when it happens in a place like Tabor," Angela said with a quiet intensity that made Hannah shiver deep inside. "I don't want any more victims, let alone any more frightened girls. If the *Picayune* can help nail the creep who's stalking you, and slow down the White Rose, we'll be doing what a newspaper is supposed to: help the community. I take every tragedy personally because this is my town. My next door neighbor's daughter could be the next victim, and I don't want that to happen."

Angela, Hannah realized with an icy shiver, could be the next victim. She fit the target profile: dark hair, petite, living at home with her slightly eccentric father, and not much of a social life. Her name came uncomfortably close to the White Rose Killer's label for all his 'true loves'—Angel. Hannah felt a crazy urge to advise Angela to start dating as soon as possible. She swallowed the panic that tried to choke her and kept quiet.

Tuesday, December 24

"Merry Christmas, angel," he whispered as he stared at the city's brightly lit tree that towered over the Civil War monument and the gazebo. His breath puffed out in a white cloud that rose to the sky. He smiled, remembering how his aunt had told him that the clouds were angels carrying his Christmas prayers to God.

The strains of organ music filtered through the frosty air. On the other side of the Triangle, up the street by the Post Office, the Christmas Eve service was starting at the church. Hannah's church. He frowned, thinking of Hannah.

Something was wrong. Someone was trying to frighten Hannah. Ever since they found Annalee's body in Hannah's office, everybody had been so secretive. He couldn't find out anything. Nobody was talking to anyone.

He honestly regretted putting Annalee's body in Hannah's office. He wouldn't do that to her. She was nice to him. She didn't deserve to be scared, polluted by the body of a deceitful little whore anywhere near her. That was what Annalee became, when she wouldn't obey, when she wouldn't trust him and let him love her, and prove she was pure.

Annalee didn't matter anymore. His angel was safe at home with her parents, far away. In another week, the students would come back to the university. He would see her around campus. He could watch over her again, protect her, keep her safe and pure for him. He wished he could ask her if she liked the angel he gave her for Christmas.

"Merry Christmas, angel," he repeated, and started down the street. He had to watch over the whole town, to make sure it was worthy of his angel when she came back to him.

She had come back to him, just as she promised when they were children. Just like in the Greek myth when the singer Orpheus had gone down into Hades to bring his true love, Eurydice, back from the dead, his faithful waiting had brought his angel back from the dead. This time, she was the one.

~~~~~

Hannah wished Christmas Eve could linger twice as long as it did. Rene was singing with the choir and Xander had been running late and couldn't catch up with her before the service, but she hadn't been alone for a second. She shared a pew near the front with Reverend Ackley, Vic and Baxter, and let herself relax into the warm sense of security that always came from worshipping with her friends. All too quickly, the candle lighting part of the service came, and then they were heading out, going their separate ways to parties and get-togethers and late dinners. She nodded to Dr. Daniel Morgan, walking with the Randolph family. A few steps later she greeted Dr. Holwood, his wife, Doria, and their three current foster children, with Nikki bringing up the rear and laughing with the boys.

"Mind if I hitch a ride?" Baxter asked, appearing next to her at the side entrance as she shrugged into her coat.

There was something elfin about Baxter, despite his goatee, which he kept glistening and pointed with gel. Maybe it was the mischief that danced in his wide, chocolate eyes. Or his talent for bringing dead computers back to life, coaxing stubborn ones to work, and finding out anything anyone could ever want to learn through the Internet. He was an ebony-skinned magic-worker when it came to the computers, and a dear friend. Hannah had a list of things to do for the office before it could open for business, and one of them was to have Baxter set up the computer system. He ran a computer service from the back of Gold Tone Gym and divided his time between it and working the gym.

"Sure." Hannah bit her lip to keep from asking why he wasn't riding
~~~~~

with Vic. "Rene should—"

"Vic's driving Rene, and the Rev is heading down the road to his hotel for something he forgot. Personally, I hope Vic's finally letting her know how he feels, but—" He shrugged, a mischievous twist to his lips.

"Vic's interested in Rene?" She didn't know whether to laugh and accuse Baxter of teasing or feel rather oblivious.

"Yeah, but he's got this thing about not putting his problems on anybody. He's got issues in his past, and he's not going to add them to Rene's."

"She's the same way. They're made for each other." Hannah finished buttoning up her coat. She had to laugh when Baxter swept a deep bow and opened the door for her.

"Tell me about it." They strolled through the parking lot, both content to be quiet and listen to others calling Christmas greetings. "So... you know what Rene's problems are?"

"Nope. Somebody hurt her. Really bad. That's about all I can pick up." She cocked her head to one side and studied him for a few seconds. Baxter didn't meet her gaze. "Do you know?"

"Eh, what kind of problems could a sweet little preacher's kid like Rene have? Except maybe she can't see Vic's dying for her to throw herself into his arms."

"Let's do our best to convince her, shall we?"

"Miss Blake, I like how you think." Baxter held out his hand. "Partners?"

They shook hands. A few more steps took them to Hannah's car.

"So, why is Vic driving Rene back to our place?" she asked once the heater finally managed to generate slightly warm air.

"They're talking business, like usual. They don't want to ruin the evening discussing some glitch in the checkbook, so they thought they'd get it over with now. And I thought maybe now was a good time to show off my famous roundhouse kick," he added, with a noticeable softening of his voice.

Hannah shivered, but not from the chill air lingering in the car. For just a moment, half-hidden in the shadows, Baxter seemed all too capable of doing harm to anyone who got in his way. It clashed with what she knew of him. He was a computer wizard, her friend. He helped her plan her workout routine when she went to the gym. Yes, all his physical conditioning made him a natural for any kind of martial arts. Hannah grinned at her silliness in thinking a computer genius wouldn't know the first thing about self-defense and infighting.

"So, maybe what we should do is fix you up with a permanent, live-in bodyguard, know what I mean?" He winked, and the sparkle of mischief came back to his eyes.

"You're a nutcase, you know that?" She glanced in the rearview mirror in preparation for backing out of her parking spot. It was far easier to tease with Baxter than admit to the choking feeling that came over her. How could she feel teary and grateful and exasperated and very protected, all at the same time?

"Hey, it's an ugly job, but somebody's got to do it. Got any mistletoe at your place? I figure we should just ambush Vic and Rene and not let them out until they see the light."

Laughing, they made the short drive down the snowy street, coming up with a half dozen plans and discarding them just as quickly. Maybe Vic and Rene wouldn't see "the light" this Christmas, but Hannah told herself there was always next year.

Besides, just because logic said to give up on Xander ever seeing "the light" didn't mean she couldn't help others along to clearer vision.

The only problem was, how to help others when she couldn't seem to do much for herself.

~~~~

"So, what are you doing tomorrow?" Vic asked Xander when they met up outside the choir room. Xander glanced inside and saw Rene talking with Mandy Gordon, both of them still wearing their choir robes.

"Driving down to Columbus to visit some friends of my folks. It's a pretty nice little retirement community. They're doing a potluck. What about you?"

Xander tugged his scarf straight and glanced down the hall one more time. Where had Hannah disappeared to so quickly? It amused him a little that he couldn't decide if he wanted her to give him one last invitation to spend Christmas Eve at the apartment, or if he just didn't like seeing her going anywhere alone. At least with the White Rose Killer supposedly stalking her, they had a pattern to follow. Shifting the focus to a copycat made everything a murky fog to work in, and he didn't like it. Nothing was predictable anymore.

"Looking for Hannah?" Vic said.

"I know she was here. Sitting with you, right?"

"Baxter hitched a ride with her since I have to talk shop with Rene, and her father's running down the road to his hotel first."

"Oh. Good." Xander tried not to slump against the wall. The relief he felt was a little startling. "What're your plans? You and Baxter want to come with me? There's always room for more."

"Thanks, but I plan on a quiet day tomorrow. Sleep in, catch up on things, visit the Randolphs. Joel's an old friend from... from the old days." Vic offered a shrug and a half smile, reminding Xander of all the little details he had finally revealed during their appointment just a few weeks ago. His friend's past had been a surprise in more than a few ways.
~~~~

"Baxter's planning on harassing Brenda — she doesn't believe in Christmas, but she does believe in charity work, so he's spending the day helping Downtown at the City Mission. I'm leaving Rene and her father alone for some quiet time. They don't get to see each other all that much." Vic shrugged and glanced at the door to the choir room. "What?" he asked when Xander chuckled.

"Seems like you don't see Rene all that much, yourself."

"Stop right there. It's bad enough I have Baxter playing matchmaker on me without you joining in. You know why I can't let things go any further."

"Yeah." Xander nodded. "Or at least, why you *think* you can't. You've been here two years, and nothing has happened. Maybe this is where God wants you."

"Maybe. But I also know how the bad guys like to play games with your mind. They could be watching me right now, waiting for me to be completely relaxed. They're good at watching without anyone knowing. That used to be one of my jobs."

"Speaking of watching." Xander offered a crooked smile. "If you could help me keep an eye on Hannah? Maybe set up some surveillance where the police can't?" He let Vic fill in the gaps.

"You're a day or two behind schedule," Vic said with a grin. "Baxter and I were talking about something like that. We have a couple little gifts to leave behind tonight, if you know what I mean."

"I appreciate it. More than you can guess. Especially when I have to be Downtown or somewhere out of touch."

"Uh huh."

"What's that grin for?" He decided he didn't like it when Vic gave him that lazy, almost predatory smile. He had a very good image of what his friend looked like back when he had been an errand boy for one of the crime families in New York.

"Sounds to me like Hannah's more than just a co-worker."

"The office would fall apart without her. Besides, she's my friend."

"Sounds like your life would fall apart, too. Why not get a little closer yourself? Maybe twenty-four hours a day?"

Rene's exit from the choir room saved them both from an argument. Xander had the horrid feeling that for the first time since law school, he had no idea how to argue against Vic's assertion.

"Yeah, yeah, Merry Christmas," he muttered as the other two bade him farewell and hurried for the door.

Right now, he would love to have the responsibility of looking after Hannah around the clock. The idea of sharing his condominium with her, seeing her influence on every part of his life, not just the office, seemed like a taste of heaven. What he would do when Tyler showed up in

January, Xander had no idea. But this was just a daydream, right, so why worry?

The problem was, he thought he knew Hannah well enough to predict her reaction if he took steps to change their relationship. She would see it solely as a reaction to the danger she faced. She wouldn't take him seriously.

"Please, God, what I'd really like for Christmas is some clear insight on what's going on," he whispered as he headed for the door to the parking lot.

Xander glanced once at the church office, tempted for two seconds to ask to speak to Pastor Glenn. But that glance showed the senior pastor and his wife, Rita, chatting and putting on their coats and heading for the door with Jeanette Marshall and her little boy, BJ. They looked like a family. They had been surrogate parents to Jeannette ever since the young widow returned to Tabor Heights. Xander refused to intrude.

For the first time, he truly regretted turning down Mrs. Blake's invitation to spend Christmas day with Hannah's family.

Then again, maybe not. Xander grinned as he reached his car. Hannah had kept the problem with the White Rose Killer and the copycat a secret from her family. Chief Cooper had been angry when she admitted that. He considered family one of the key elements in keeping any stalking victim safe. Hannah had promised to tell her parents tomorrow. Xander didn't know if he wanted to be there for that. Something told him Hannah's parents might be angrier with him over the silence than they would be with Hannah.

On second thought, knowing that was kind of nice. Maybe it meant they saw a future for him and Hannah, together.

Chapter Fourteen

Wednesday, December 25

"You didn't." Hannah wondered where her father had put her coat. It wasn't too late to beat a strategic retreat and hide in her apartment all day. "Mother, please tell me you didn't."

"Sorry. Lying is a sin. Especially on Christmas day." Mrs. Blake shook her head, still the same vibrant strawberry blonde she had passed on to her only daughter. She chuckled, her double chin wobbling. "What is so wrong with inviting your boss to spend Christmas with our family? You two are friends, aren't you?"

"Remember what happened last time you invited a friend of mine—a guy friend—for a holiday with us?" Hannah decided to slide into the only chair remaining at the kitchen table. "The guys put him through the third degree, as if they expected us to elope that night!"

"Xander Finley is different." Her mother sniffed and turned back to basting the turkey.

"I'll say." She rested her chin in her hands and watched her work. It always amazed Hannah how her mother managed to keep three different pots going on the stove, mix and cut biscuits, set up yet another batch of bread in the bread machine and pull out dishes for the long dining room table, all without missing a beat, burning something, or forgetting a few ingredients.

"For one thing, you're not dating him."

"I didn't date Kyle, either. We were in a study group and he got stranded for Thanksgiving because of snow."

"You have to admit, if you brought men friends around more often, your brothers wouldn't get so excited to see one with you."

"So now it's *my* fault? Mom, I am twenty-nine years old. I am living on my own. I have a decent bank account, and in just two weeks, I start my law studies. I don't need my brothers protecting me from the playground bully anymore!"

Hannah shuddered. An image of Annalee flashed before her eyes. Unfortunately, her mother turned around at that moment. She could read her children to the finest detail. Hannah sometimes suspected she could read minds.

"What's happened?" She shoved the rack and roaster pan back into the oven, let the door slam shut, and came over to the table to rest her hands on Hannah's shoulders. "Something's bothering you, sweetheart. Scared about starting classes? You've wanted to complete your legal training for such a long time. Are you having second thoughts?"

"Haven't had time for second thoughts." Hannah managed a shaky grin. How had her mother known she had doubts whether she was doing the right thing? She had barely begun to second guess the providence that let her go to John Carroll, and then they found Annalee's body and the white rose arrived at her door.

"What's wrong?"

"Well, I was planning on waiting until the kids were all napping. I mean, I know better than to let you find out in the paper..." Hannah took a deep breath. "Maybe you'd better get Daddy, and then we can figure out how to tell the guys."

"Tell the guys what?" Mr. Blake asked, coming into the kitchen. He frowned at the closed oven and shook his head. "You're too fast for me, Cyn. I keep hoping to steal a drumstick and you just get faster, every year. Something wrong?" he asked, apparently seeing the somber looks on his wife's and daughter's faces.

The only room in the house not denuded of chairs for the dining room, or occupied with brothers, sisters-in-law and nephews playing games or watching TV, was the tiny den where Mr. Blake did the bookkeeping for their family moving business. Hannah perched on the hassock, waiting for her mother to settle into the easy chair with the threadbare upholstery, and her father to take the desk chair.

"Well... first of all, Xander and I found the third White Rose victim. He put her in the back room of our new office," Hannah hurried on, when her parents gasped in unison. "The paper's kept a lot of details from the public, to help the police. And then last week, we found out there's a copycat of the White Rose, and he's got something against either Xander or the Arc Foundation or... me." She shrugged and tried to smile. It made her face hurt.

"Copycat," Mr. Blake murmured. "So I assume you got a white rose, and you didn't tell us?"

"I didn't want to worry you. It was bad enough having Xander get all protective and panicky and angry for me, and we wanted to keep things quiet to help the police and... I guess I was ashamed." She nearly laughed as that admission slipped out. Where had that come from? The funny part was, she realized it was the truth.

"Ashamed?" Mrs. Blake leaned forward and caught hold of Hannah's hands. "Honey, what's to be ashamed of?"

"I guess... I'm a snob. Maybe subconsciously, I figured all those girls who get stalked did something wrong or stupid, to make themselves a target. I didn't want anybody to know. Talk about old-fashioned thinking! I ought to work for that slime, Montgomery! I'd fit right in. He actually said in court one time, if a girl got raped, it was her fault because she acted provocatively and — " She stopped, struggling against an urge to burst into tears.

For an awful moment, she thought she would lose that battle as both her parents wrapped their arms around her and held her. Then a tightness moved up through her body and vanished, like a heavy, foul-smelling bird had finally left its perch on her shoulder. But she hadn't even known it was there until it was gone.

"We should tell your brothers," Mrs. Blake whispered into Hannah's hair. "Did you say it was going to be in the paper?"

"Tomorrow. Curt's writing a couple stories to help the police flush out the White Rose and the copycat. I figure, you should know before our friends in Tabor start calling and the other papers pick up the story."

Amazingly, after unburdening herself to her parents, Hannah found she was more able to enjoy Christmas day with her nephews than she had anticipated. Her parents agreed with her, reluctantly, that keeping the story quiet had been a wise move. Her brothers would have overreacted, either starting a vigilante search of their own, or insisting she move in with one of them, or even leave the state until the White Rose Killer and his copycat were found. Her parents could get her brothers to act and react with a semblance of sanity.

Thursday, December 26

The newspaper fell to pieces at his feet, but he could still see the words — the lies — branded into the paper.

No, the words themselves weren't lies. He had to remember that. The *Tabor Picayune* wasn't like other newspapers, leaving out facts and twisting the truth to make stories exciting so they could sell papers and make a profit. The *Tabor Picayune* didn't lie. Curt Mehdlang always told the truth. Curt was his friend. But the reporters had to repeat the lies that other people told, so everyone would know they were liars.

Someone was pretending to be the White Rose.

That liar was frightening Hannah.

He had to stop the lies. He had to protect Hannah, because she was nice to him. Hannah was nice to everyone.

Who in Tabor didn't like Hannah? That was the person frightening her. That was the liar, who pretended to be the White Rose.

No one was allowed to pretend to be the White Rose — because he was the White Rose.

White, for purity. For the angel, his new angel, his sweet, young, pure angel.

He walked away, leaving the torn pieces of newspaper on the damp concrete floor, and concentrated on thoughts of his new angel.

She was the right one, this time. Despite what the paper said, she would come back to him. She belonged to him. She loved him. She would stay true. She had promised to come back from the dead, just like Eurydice. She would come back.

~~~~~

Rene and Vic came to the office to help Hannah clean up the mess from the fire. The police and fire departments had all the evidence they needed and she wanted to wipe away as many reminders of trouble as she could. Hannah and Xander agreed they would only communicate by cell phone, and Rene turned off the answering machine in the apartment. The phone was in Rene's name, but how long would it take before people learned the two were roommates and tried to contact Hannah at home? Hannah and the Padua office were sure to be inundated with calls once people started reading the *Picayune*.

The day was quiet. The daughter of the owners of Floor-to-Ceiling was a police dispatcher. When she told her parents about the fire, they had insisted on giving Hannah a discount on the supplies she had to replace. Maggie arrived with the delivery truck and wandered around the rooms of the office, her voice echoing softly as she told stories about the stores that had been in the space and the family who used to own the house. The house had been divided into apartments and a store since the thirties. Maggie had to be making it up. She couldn't be old enough to know the original owners, could she? Either way, Hannah was grateful for the distraction. Having Maggie around gave her a sense of being protected that she hadn't felt even while sitting in the police station.

Rene went out at noon to pick up pizza and get the paper. Hannah let her first slice grow cold while she read the promised stories.

According to Curt's story, the unnamed college student had gone home to Colorado as a direct result of the White Rose Killer's first contact. Her fiancé had proposed the night she graduated from high school, and he was pressing her to get married two years early.

"What are the chances the White Rose will get angry enough to follow her to Colorado and punish her?" Vic said, after Hannah read that part of the story aloud.

"For one thing, she's been engaged nearly two years," Hannah began. "She isn't betraying him, because she belongs to someone else."

"Common sense and logic aren't part of the serial killer's mindset. Besides, what if he knows it's a lie? Did you say she had a boyfriend she had been arguing with here at BWU?"
~~~~~

"For another—" She paused to stick her tongue out at him, earning a spurt of laughter from Rene. "There is no fiancé, and the poor girl's from Pennsylvania, not Colorado. That story is to throw the White Rose off her trail if he does try to track her down. And her college records are sealed. Even removed from the computer, and the papers locked away. Kind of like in Jack Benny's vault."

The rest of the story cautioned the young, single women of the community not to hesitate to contact the police if they thought they were being followed or if someone started acting possessive or in any way that struck them as odd. Curt quoted Chief Cooper as saying he would welcome one hundred false alarms, knowing the women of Tabor Heights were safe, rather than have someone hesitate to ask for help and end up injured, terrified, or dead.

He ended with quotes from several psychology professors at Butler-Williams, diagnosing the White Rose Killer from his actions. Reading between the lines, Hannah could see they challenged the man to approach his love interest face-to-face instead of hiding behind notes; to earn her love and trust instead of demanding it and terrifying her.

Curt ended by quoting the love chapter from Corinthians, listing the positive qualities of love.

"That's going to get a complaint from the ACLU," Vic said with a chuckle.

"The *Picayune* is privately owned," Hannah said. "Curt didn't give the reference or even say it was from the Bible. He's not forcing religion down someone's throat, just offering a standard for what real love should be."

How patient am I? Hannah couldn't help wonder. *How much can I endure? If I'm really in love with Xander, can I give up on him? Or is it just a silly infatuation? He's being so protective of me. He's always there when I really need him. How can a girl resist falling in love with a guy like that?*

One of these days, when everything was cleared up, she and Xander needed to have a long talk.

"What about you guys?" Rene asked, after Hannah had been quiet too long.

"Oh." Hannah's face warmed as she scanned the front page. The fire at the office and the theory of the false White Rose only took two columns, three inches high, and the story continued on page ten. That was good. She certainly didn't want front page coverage if she had to go through what Annalee, Tracy, and the first two victims of the White Rose Killer had endured.

It was something of an anti-climax, she realized, to read the story. It repeated the facts from Tuesday's story, and then added that there were several suspects, including people who had been vocal in opposition to Common Grounds moving into Tabor.

"That'll get Montgomery in a snit," Vic said with a chuckle.

"Probably not," Rene said, shaking her head. "People like him never recognize themselves. It's always someone else who's disagreeable."

Hannah agreed. She read that one suspect had been taken into custody but was scheduled for release on Thursday, until other suspects had been examined. Chucky had stayed in a hotel in Toledo, to keep him out of sight and out of reach. Taylor Dunlop was driving up to Toledo that morning to bring him back to town, and several officers were to shadow him in shifts. The minute the man who hired Chucky to set the fire contacted him, the police would be on him.

She prayed the man panicked and hunted down Chucky in broad daylight, instead of abandoning him and hiring someone else. The sooner this was brought out into the open, the better for everyone.

Friday, December 27

"Something strange is going on at the office," Colson said, almost before he crossed the threshold into Chief Cooper's office that morning.

"He finally noticed?" Donovan muttered, just loudly enough for Xander to hear. The two men exchanged strained grins, then schooled their faces into calm concern.

Dr. Holwood had joined them for this conference, as a representative of Butler-Williams University, and because he had been student advisor to White Rose target number four, aka Tracy Brickman.

They certainly couldn't call the poor girl *victim* number four, because she hadn't been kidnapped or killed. Had she? Xander had a sudden urge to demand Donovan call the girl and make sure she was all right and had enjoyed a peaceful Christmas with her family.

"What do you mean by strange?" Chief Cooper asked as the other lawyer settled down in the last of the five chairs spaced around his desk.

"I didn't think Mr. Montgomery even knew I met Hannah after class last week, but he made a remark yesterday about my date with the enemy." Colson flashed a thin smile of apology at Hannah. "Then, he started talking about what a hard worker she is. He actually said he admired her dedication to helping the innocent, even if her venue was badly chosen." He rolled his eyes and shrugged when he met Xander's gaze. "Then he said he hoped she wouldn't get hurt by the White Rose."

"Like he believes she's not being stalked by a copycat?" Donovan said. "Or he merely wants you to think that's what he believes?"

"Please don't go into that," Hannah said with a breathy attempt at a chuckle. "It's too early in the morning to turn our brains into knots."

"Al, did Montgomery see the note you got from the alleged White

Rose?" Xander asked.

"Not that I know of, why?"

Xander repeated what he could recall of his phone conversation with Montgomery, and the words that echoed what had been in Colson's note. The others batted around theories, speculating on Montgomery's normal speech patterns and the odds of him choosing those words out of thin air. He refused to let himself hope this early in the game, but Xander still felt a thrill of hope. If they could prove Montgomery was behind the fake notes, the white rose, even the fire, they could put him out of business just like he tried to put Common Grounds out of business.

I'm acting like him, Xander realized with a jolt. *I'm starting to think like him and justify my actions like he does.* He felt the blood leave his face in shock. When had he gained such a vindictive streak? If he gave in to it, he would be just as bad as Montgomery, justifying every nasty thing he said or did in the name of justice and truth.

That was what made Montgomery such an unpleasant soul. Did Xander really want to follow in his footsteps?

"Where exactly did you find the note?" Chief Cooper asked.

"Taped to my office door." Colson rolled his eyes as he replied. "Haven't done that since college. There's a rack sitting on the receptionist's desk where all our messages are supposed to go."

"So the White Rose copycat could be a stranger to the office, and doesn't know the routine," Donovan said, nodding. "Hate to admit it, but I'm disappointed. I want it to be an inside job."

"We've all run afoul of Mr. Montgomery's verbal missiles and traps," Dr. Holwood said with his slow, deliberate eloquence that always made Xander think of James Earl Jones. "We're only being human when we hope for him to humiliate himself beyond redemption. But, we should also remember we have been bought and cleansed by the Blood, and we are *supposed* to be new creatures." He glanced around the circle, meeting the other four sets of eyes, and a moment later a brilliant smile lit his square, dark face. "That's just in case anybody missed their devotions this morning."

His words earned a few chuckles from the others. Most of the people in the office attended the same church.

"If it was taped to your door," Hannah said, "then anybody coming into the office before you could have read it. Meaning he could have been quoting what he read, instead of repeating what he wrote."

"But how would he have known the note was referring to *you* before the story came out?" Xander blurted, almost the moment the thought occurred to him.

Silence vibrated through the room for four heartbeats.

Xander had read the note. It said nothing about Hannah. Colson had promised he wouldn't tell anyone what was going on.

"He knew, somehow, that Hannah and I had plans the night before," Colson said after a few moments. "Maybe he saw us going inside Stay-A-While, or walked past the window and saw us and we didn't see him. There are a thousand explanations."

"And no proof," Xander muttered.

The remainder of the meeting didn't improve the mental and emotional atmosphere much. For the sake of the university, they went over everything that had been done to track down the White Rose and what had been discovered so far about the man.

Sunday, December 29

"Xander? Hannah?" Curt Mehdlang caught up with them at the back of the sanctuary after the service was dismissed.

The woman following close behind Curt caught Hannah's attention. Her big, dark eyes and pixie-cut dark hair made her look young and innocent, barely offset by the business-like, boxy, dark gray jacket and calf-length skirt. Hannah mentally chided herself for looking for potential White Rose victims every time she turned around.

"This is Toni Napolitano," he continued, gesturing at the young woman. "She just joined us over at the paper."

"Welcome to Tabor." Xander held out his hand to shake. The four of them moved over to the side to get out of the flow of traffic coming down all the aisles to the back of the sanctuary. "New in town?"

"Not really." Toni smiled crookedly. "I used to live here when I was a kid. Curt barely remembers me."

"Yeah, she keeps rubbing it in every time I give her pointers about getting around town, or the history of some people," Curt said with a shrug. "Look, could we buy you two lunch? There's something we need to talk about."

"Reporter to source?" Xander asked.

"More like a personal matter," Toni said.

"Ah... sure, why not?" Hannah said. A shiver went up her back, and she knew, as if she had read it in the paper, it had to do with the White Rose. Toni had lived in Tabor when she was a child. Hadn't Curt said the White Rose case was similar to something that happened when he was a boy?

Chapter Fifteen

The four picked up salads and sandwiches from Stay-A-While and went to Hannah's apartment. Rene and her father had gone to Playhouse Square to see *A Christmas Carol* with Vic, so the apartment would be empty, granting them privacy for their discussion. Hannah kept studying Toni, wondering how a murder twenty years ago might be personal to her now. Or was she a relative of one of the first two victims, and she was using her training as a reporter to try to piece clues together?

"Nice," Toni said, when they had settled in the living room, their food set up on tray tables.

They naturally divided into Xander and Hannah on one love seat and Curt and Toni on the other. Hannah found it amusing. Especially since Xander chose his seat after she sat down. Protectiveness, or something more?

"I remember walking by these houses on my way to school, thinking how cool it would be to live in one of them, above a store." Toni's smile grew strained. She glanced at Curt and nodded.

"Oh, no you don't, Lois Lane. You asked for this meeting. It's your show." Curt picked up his tuna deluxe and took a big bite.

"Coward." She looked down at her clasped hands for a moment, then picked up her salad fork and fumbled it, nearly dropping it on the floor.

"Curt said he had a theory about the White Rose, tied into a murder a long time ago," Xander said, leading the conversation.

"Yeah." Toni let out a long, gusting sigh. "If he's right—heck, I know he's right. The clues, everything that happened is so similar it gives me chills. Makes me want to string up the guy and use him for target practice with very dull table knives." She offered a grimace, took another deep breath. "You probably think I'm not quite all there."

"Nah," Curt said. "They're used to me taking off at a completely different angle from everything else. These leaps of intuition are an occupational hazard."

Toni groaned and elbowed Curt. He pretended to be deeply wounded. Hannah slowly put down her turkey club, which she hadn't bit into yet. Was what she thought was happening, happening? Had Curt, the Lone Wolf, the Untouchable, Mr. I'll-Never-Fall-For-A-Girl... fallen for the new kid in town? He rarely ever clowned, yet he definitely acted foolish to help Toni relax. Would wonders never cease?

"Tell me what you know, your impressions of the White Rose," Toni said. "I've read the police reports that are public, and what Curt put in the paper, and his notes for things that he's agreed not to put in the paper yet. But I'd like to get it from you, too."

Later, looking back on it, Hannah was amused at how little time it took to recount what they knew, separating the incidents surrounding her from what they knew or believed about the four 'real' victims of the White Rose.

"Okay." Toni toyed with her salad as she talked. "If Curt is right, my big sister was the first victim of the White Rose, almost twenty years ago." Her gaze flicked back and forth between Xander and Hannah. "Angel was twelve when we moved to Tabor. I was nine."

"Angel?" Hannah thought she was choking, but she hadn't eaten anything since Toni started talking.

"Angelique, actually. My full name is Antoinette." She shrugged. "Mom was really into fancy names. Anyway... Angel was gorgeous, and shy. She wanted a boyfriend, but the boys in school scared her. It seemed by the time we'd been here a month, every boy in her class, in the neighborhood, even two grades ahead of her, wanted to be her boyfriend. She said no. She wasn't stuck up, like so many of the girls thought. She was just shy. She didn't know what to do or say. And all these boys kept coming by and sneaking presents or notes into her desk at school or into her locker. They really scared her."

"And the White Rose was one of those boyfriends she refused?" Hannah guessed.

"The White Rose was her boyfriend, for real," Curt said.

"I missed something." Xander leaned back in the loveseat, put down his sandwich, and crossed his arms, visibly giving this his full concentration.

"Angel changed before she died. She was happy, she had some great secret that she wouldn't tell me, and she didn't want me to walk home from school with her. When she told me she had a boyfriend, and they were keeping the whole thing secret, I was so jealous I didn't want to know anything about it," Toni said. The old pain gleaming in her eyes made Hannah want to get up and cross the room to put her arms around her. Curt rested a hand on her shoulder and squeezed.

Yes, Hannah decided, there was something starting up between him and Toni.

"Rumors started going around that Angel was meeting boys behind the bathhouse down in the park. Some girls were jealous and spread the tales just to be nasty. But we found out one boy in particular was telling everybody that Angel let him kiss her, to get revenge because she wouldn't have anything to do with him. He suspected Angel had a boyfriend, but the boy wasn't bragging. Later, we figured he told the lies just to get the boyfriend to confront him. Probably so they could fight. How could he beat up Angel's boyfriend and make him give her up, if he didn't know who the guy was?"

"I bet that ticked off all the boys who couldn't get anywhere with her," Xander muttered.

Hannah wrapped her arms around herself, suddenly chilled with a premonition of where this story was heading.

"One Saturday, Angel went for a walk. She was going to meet her boyfriend, as far as we could tell." Toni swallowed hard and her eyes glistened with a threat of tears. "She didn't come back."

"Strangled with a wire?" Xander asked softly.

"Down in the park," Curt said. "There was an old access road blocked with some old fencing. They found her body there, tangled up and strangled with the wire from the fence. Everybody hoped it was an accident."

"Curt found her," Toni whispered. "He came to our house to talk with Angel about something at school. Our parents were starting to get worried because she was late coming home. So he went to look for her and..." She knuckled more tears from her eyes before they could fall, swallowed hard, and sat up straight. She took a deep breath, let it out, and regained her composure.

"My parents found letters from her boyfriend in her room. He begged her to stay faithful to him. He promised he'd take care of her forever and they'd be together and he'd make her happy. He didn't sign his name, and Angel never wrote his name anywhere, even though almost everything she wrote in her diary was about him. She was going through a Greek mythology phase, and she kept referring to the two of them with names from all those stories. The really horrid ones, where someone gets killed by jealous gods and—" Toni shook her head and raked her hair back from her face. For a moment, anger and grief darkened her eyes. She took a deep breath and swallowed hard and continued with a nod for emphasis.

"In her diary, Angel said he was quiet and smart and they were in love and they swore they'd be together forever. And they weren't telling anyone how they felt about each other because—" Toni's voice broke with a rusty, wry chuckle. "Because everybody in school was so infantile and just wouldn't understand. They swore they'd be together forever, and when they died, they'd come back from the dead to be together, just like Orpheus and Eurydice."

"I'm not up on that one," Xander said.

"Orpheus was a poet, he played a harp. He was in love with Eurydice, and she was so beautiful that one of the gods chased her, trying to capture her," Hannah said slowly, watching Toni for the first sign that she shouldn't finish the story. The young woman met her gaze, dry-eyed. "She died—from a snake bite, I think—and Orpheus was so upset at losing her that he went down into Hades and got permission from the king and queen of the Underworld to bring her back to the world of the living with him. But of course, there were conditions, and he messed up and Eurydice went back to Hades."

"Let me guess—Orpheus went around trying to force other women to be his true love, come back to life?" he said.

"No. He hacked off some Amazons, who... hacked him," Curt said with a shrug and a crooked grin. "I could never get into the mythology stuff in school. It always seemed so depressing." He shifted his hand from Toni's shoulder to hold her hand and rub it comfortingly.

"Angel was really big into mythology. I used to tease her she'd marry a librarian," Toni whispered. "She wrote in her diary, just before she... her boyfriend was upset about the nasty stories, and she was angry that he wouldn't believe her when she said she never did any of those things."

"He thought she was unfaithful to him," Hannah murmured. "So he killed her for it."

"And for a whole week after the funeral, someone kept dropping white roses on her grave," Curt said. "Every time they took the rose away, a new one appeared. Nobody ever saw who dropped it there. Which at the time was just as freaky as Angel being murdered. At the end of that week, the boy who started the nasty stories about Angel got ambushed, knocked out, and hung by his ankles from a tree in the park. He was beat up pretty bad."

"The same tree that Sam Conrad ended up in, when he pretended to be Katrina's boyfriend?" Xander asked.

"We're still trying to determine that. But do you see where we're going?"

"Something set him off." Hannah fought a shudder. "Maybe he thinks Angel has come back from the dead and he's trying to find her. Or maybe he's just tired of waiting for her, and he's looking for her."

"Any girl who looks anything like Angel is a possible target," Curt said.

"Have you started checking out anybody who was in school with her?" Xander said.

"It's taking a while," Toni said, her voice raspy with repressed emotion. "First, we have to get names of everybody who lived in Tabor and went to the same school, then we have to figure out if they're living here, or just living, period."

"Have you contacted the police, to use their connections?"

"That's the biggest problem slowing us down," Curt said, shaking his head. "Chief Cooper is pretty sure the White Rose has hacked into the

a half day today? She decided this at four-thirty yesterday afternoon. When all the workers came to me to complain, because they knew she wouldn't listen to any of them, she blamed *me* for the 'lack of harmony in the company', as she calls it. I'm not the one who made the decision to change the schedule. All the years Dad and Mr. Carpenter ran the business, they always gave people the whole day off, New Year's Eve and Christmas Eve." Bailey shook her head and lightly slapped her own mouth. "Sorry. I swore I wouldn't bring my problems with me. The last thing you need is to hear my petty little gripes."

"Hey, what are friends for?" Hannah bit her lip to keep from spilling her latest concerns to Bailey.

"As a friend, let me warn you to tighten things up with Xander before Jayne makes him her next target. Charlene has decided to set her hooks into Vic, and if those two aren't competing for the same man, they're giving each other advice. After Vic, Xander is probably the most eligible bachelor in the church."

"Thanks for the warning," Xander called from the front room. Hannah had given him the job of hooking up the new DVD player Reverend Ackley had given Rene for Christmas.

"Oops." Bailey grinned and didn't look at all repentant.

"Should we warn Vic?" he asked, appearing in the doorway leading from the kitchen to the front room.

"I say we let him suffer," Hannah said. "If he can't see Rene is the one for him, and he won't do anything about it, he's fair game for any husband-hunting woman in the church."

"Uh oh. That sounds like a universal judgment on all single men. Does that mean I need to hook up with someone to keep from being lassoed and hog-tied?"

Hannah's face felt scorching hot. She turned to the sink where she had been defrosting shrimp in cool water, putting her back to the other two to keep from betraying her feelings with her expression.

"Leave me out of this," Bailey said with a chuckle. "Are we waiting for Vic and Baxter before we head to church?"

"They have to head right back to the gym after the service to open it up for the youth group," Xander said. "They'll join us once the riot clears out. If you ladies are ready?" He reached for his coat, hung over the back of the kitchen chair, and bowed toward the door.

Hannah refused to look at Xander during the short walk to his car and the ride to the church. She didn't know whether to be grateful for Bailey's comments or mortified. Did she really want Xander to pay her more attention, maybe even get serious, just to ward off the husband-hunters at church?

Part of her leaped at any chance at all for Xander to consider her as more than a co-worker and someone to protect. Another part of her wanted to shove him away as hard as she could if he did turn to her for protection from Jayne and her ilk. What good was a relationship based on desperation? Just like she knew this new closeness would die once the crisis over the White Rose and the copycat died out, Hannah knew she should avoid taking advantage of Xander in a panic.

The bottom line, she fiercely told herself once again, was that Xander wasn't interested in a lifetime relationship with anyone, period. If he was, certainly he would choose someone whose life course paralleled his, wouldn't he? They were partners in so many things already, it seemed so natural and right to extend it to the rest of their lives. At least, it seemed natural and right to her. Xander was blind.

~~~~~

"This place is packed solid," Xander whispered after they had stood for several minutes at the back of the sanctuary, trying to find a place they could sit.

"That's because nobody is allowed to attend any of the parties connected with the church if they don't go to the service first," Bailey whispered back. "There were some kids who crashed the party last year. They were already drunk from two other parties they weren't invited to. The deacons made all the youth activities a lock-in this year. Nobody gets in or out, once the attendance list is filled in."

"Including the youth leaders?" Hannah muffled a snort of laughter. She was doubly glad she had avoided being drafted to help out this year.

Although, now that she thought of it, where else would she be safest from the copycat White Rose, than in a huge, amorphous crowd of rowdy church teens?
~~~~~

Chapter Sixteen

"Hi, Hannah."

She turned, then she realized she didn't recognize the voice. The man smiling down at her yanked his snow-dusted cap off and gestured at the crowded rows of pews in the sanctuary.

"I see two spots. Join me?"

"Uh—thanks, but I'm with..." She half-turned back to Xander and Bailey, indicating them. "Sorry, but do I know you?"

"Now that's a low blow to my ego." He chuckled. Laughter sparkled in his gray eyes, and his square-cut face was red from the chill outdoors. "I've sat behind you for the last four months in Singles class."

"Sorry. We have a big class."

"If you're really sorry, how about you let me take you out to dinner?" He stepped closer. Hannah estimated he stood maybe six-foot in his stocking feet, but he towered over her like Jack's giant.

"We have plans." Xander stepped up next to Hannah. "Funny, but I don't remember you from class, either."

"Makes sense." The stranger winked at Xander and tipped his head toward Hannah. "When you're watching this pretty lady all the time, why pay attention to string beans like me?" He shrugged. "Guess I'll sit by myself, then. Some other time, Hannah? Next week, maybe?"

"I'll think about it." She managed a thin smile and waited, watching him move down the aisle to a seat three rows from the back. "I've thought about it," she muttered, "and the answer is no."

"Good answer." Xander stared after the stranger.

Hannah could almost hear the gears turning in his head. A shiver ran up her back despite the heat of the crowded building.

"What was that all about?" Bailey asked. "I've never seen that guy before, and I always end up sitting in the last row of class."

"So we all know he's lying through his teeth. I don't even go to the Singles class," Xander muttered. "Hannah switched to a different class two months ago, so who has he been watching? Let's try the balcony, ladies, shall we?" He hooked his arms through theirs, turned them around, and headed through the crowd to the stairs to the balcony.

The short pew next to the stairwell was empty. Xander gestured for Bailey to slide in first, to sit next to the wall, then Hannah, and he sat on the aisle. Hannah caught him staring down into the stairwell several times. The prelude music stopped and Pastor Wally stepped up to lead the opening prayer. Xander nodded and turned his attention to the front of the sanctuary.

"What's going on?" Hannah whispered.

"Your boyfriend just walked out of the service."

Hannah bit her lip to stop a sharp retort. "He doesn't look like that sketch Chucky gave us. Should we go to the station and —"

"I know who he is now." The muscles in Xander's jaw clenched visibly. He closed his eyes as Pastor Wally started praying. Hannah followed suit, but she didn't think he prayed any more than she did.

That's been part of the problem, hasn't it, Lord? We haven't been taking all of this to You nearly enough. Please, God, it's a new year. Help me to trust You more and go to You first with problems, instead of saving You for the last resort.

~~~~~

Xander hurried Hannah and Bailey out of the church as soon as the New Year's Eve service was over. Any other time, he would have lingered and greeted and chatted, but gut instinct said to stay hidden among the crowd. With the rush of traffic as the Singles and youth groups hurried off to their first events of the evening, he knew Hannah's admirer wouldn't spot them, no matter where he might be waiting outside the church. Xander doubted he would try anything with the potential for witnesses around, but why take chances?

"Do I want to know who that guy was?" Hannah muttered, as Xander hurried her and Bailey to the parking lot.

"Oh, just a young up-and-coming law student who clerks at a certain law firm." He refused to look at her. Xander didn't need to look at Hannah to know her reaction, because her arm went rigid in his clasp.

"That could be the clue we need."

"Clue for what?" Bailey asked.

"Office business," Xander hurried to say. "And here we are. I don't know about you two, but I'm freezing."

He hurried to unlock the passenger door and shuffled around the front of his car to get in on his side. Fortunately, there was no new snow or ice to scrape or brush off the car. Xander wished he dared to camp out in Hannah's living room. He told himself it was enough that Bailey planned on spending the night after he, Vic and Baxter left. Hannah wouldn't be alone. He had to trust that Bailey's presence and all his prayers, building up over the last few weeks, would be enough to keep away the copycat.

What if the enemy was Montgomery's clerk? Would he stop harassing Hannah now that they had seen his face? But if he was the copycat, why had he made contact with her in a public, crowded place? Had he done it to throw them off the trail?
~~~~~

More important, was the clerk harassing Hannah on his own initiative, or on Montgomery's orders?

"Okay, ladies," he said as he slid into the driver's seat and slammed the door. "Any last-minute stops we need to make before we settle in for the night?"

By the time Vic and Baxter closed up the Gold Tone Gym and hiked the two blocks to join them, Bailey had a from-scratch pizza in the oven. Hannah turned her seven-bean soup down to simmer, and the five settled down with the veggies and dip, and two huge bowls of popcorn, to watch a movie and wait for midnight to ring in.

Xander told Vic about the latest development with Montgomery's clerk during the break between movies, when Hannah and Bailey went into the kitchen to retrieve the soup and pizza. Baxter shook his head, his lips pressed flat together like he tasted something foul. Vic sighed and gave Xander that chilling smile he saved for belligerent jocks who tried to commandeer the gym without buying a membership.

"I think we can help you," was all Vic said before Hannah hurried back into the room with a tray full of steaming bowls.

After that, Xander tried to relax and enjoy the evening. Hannah was safe, they were together, and no one was nasty enough to brave twenty-below wind chill for a chance to attack on New Year's Eve.

He indulged in an extra-long hug with Hannah when the ball dropped in Times Square. He relaxed into the warmth and companionship of the little living room and let his drowsy imagination take over. What if this were his and Hannah's living room? Would they have guests over on New Year's Eve, or would they be out celebrating in high style? Would they be with the Young Married class, or some other class at church? It was a nice dream. Maybe once this crisis had passed and half the town wasn't watching them any longer, he could pursue it.

At two a.m., they called it a night. Xander offered to drive Vic and Baxter to the gym. Vic had an apartment at the back of the gym and Baxter had left his car there. All three men took their time walking down the fire escape stairs and down the driveway to where Xander had parked on the street. Xander caught the other two visually searching the neighborhood. Main Street was the main drag through Tabor and there were plenty of lights on the street. Who knew what shadows lurked in the narrow backyards and alleys behind and between the houses? If Vic and Baxter, with their shadowed backgrounds, felt some need to be extra cautious tonight, Xander wondered if he had reason to worry.

"We have a friend in the FBI," Vic said, as soon as all three were in Xander's car.

"You'll have him check out Montgomery's clerk?" Xander asked.

"Heck, I can do that just as fast, and with fewer questions asked,"

Baxter said with a chuckle. "Nope, not that. We asked him about the legalities of any evidence we gather. If we set up some surveillance equipment around the office, we only need your permission."

"For Hannah's place, we take it from the angle of protecting our partner, since Rene happens to live there, too. We're all concerned that the copycat could go off on a tangent and hurt either one. So, whatever happens, we're covered," Vic added.

"What did you do?" Xander grinned as he pulled out of his parking spot, onto the eerily quiet, snowy street.

"Motion sensors attached to video cameras at Hannah's door, and at strategic spots around your office here. Nobody can get within ten feet of either place without a camera coming on and catching him. We have a feed to Baxter's office at the gym and a bank of digital recorders. If someone approaches during our off hours, we have an alarm rigged to go off in my apartment. I can check the monitors and call the police if it looks suspicious."

"For phone taps, we'd need Hannah's permission," Baxter added. "That doesn't seem to be the White Rose's pattern, though. Just watch the poor kid, leave notes, and scare her half to death."

"What do you think the chances are of him following Hannah to the Padua office?" Vic asked.

"We know it's the copycat, and now we suspect Montgomery's clerk." Xander shook his head. Amazingly, he did feel a little better. "There are too many people around at all hours for him to chance anything at the office. The guys there have already agreed never to leave Hannah alone for a minute, until she's in her car and pulling out onto the street. And she has her cell phone ready with 911 in the speed dial."

"And we found out the hard way, you guys have some very scary friends lurking in the shadows." Baxter grinned. Vic just shook his head.

"What?" Xander wanted to know. "What happened?"

"We were setting up the equipment Christmas Eve, after we left Hannah and Rene," Vic said. "This guy came out of nowhere and wanted to know, very politely, what we thought we were doing with the equipment we were setting up. I don't know how long he was sitting in the dark, just watching us, before he decided to talk." He shook his head. "I used to hang around with guys like him, back in the bad old days. I didn't like them even then."

"Ah." Xander knew who he was talking about. "Tall, Black, shaved head, something really elegant about him?"

"The kind of guy who uses a silk handkerchief to wipe up the blood after he slits your throat," Baxter muttered.

"Vincent. Head of security for Arc. He said he'd stop over a few times to check on Hannah, just in case."

"If he's watching out for her —" Vic shook his head and offered a wry grin. "She's safer than if you locked her up in a bank vault. How good is he against guns if our copycat decides to break the pattern?"

"If he's sticking to the White Rose as a pattern, he won't use a gun." Xander grinned, suddenly feeling much better. "Vincent is the best. He can handle just about anything. Let's pray you wasted your time with all that equipment."

"Amen," Vic whispered.

~~~~~

Despite the news from Vic and Baxter, and knowing intellectually that Hannah would soon be safe, Xander couldn't sleep when he finally reached his Medina condo. He paced the floors, imagining how the echoing, half-furnished rooms would look if Hannah were moving in with him, instead of Tyler.

"Lord, if this was a wake-up call, did You have to go this far?"

As a last resort, he made a mug of warm milk with a generous dollop of vanilla coffee-flavoring syrup and settled down on the couch with his Bible. Xander knew if he retreated to his bed, he would never fall asleep. The only sure way to relax enough to sleep was to use some reverse psychology on himself and pray the sleepless hours away.

Thursday, January 2

Donovan, Hannah and Xander met Chucky for breakfast in Stoughton. She didn't know what to think when Donovan showed a picture of Toby Halm, Montgomery's clerk, to Chucky, and the hapless boy didn't recognize him. Halm was a law student at John Carroll University, and Donovan had Taylor run a check on him. They found nothing unusual to indicate criminal connections. He was on a scholarship, covered most of his living expenses working at Montgomery & Associates, maintained a B-minus average, and had the usual assortment of college ruckuses and traffic tickets on his record.

"He doesn't go to our church," Donovan said, as he drove her and Xander back to Tabor. "So, we have Halm in an outright lie, in front of witnesses, claiming to know you from church when that's probably the first time he stepped through the doors."

"He had enough information about me." Hannah shivered as the implications raced through her head. "Who would have given him that information?"

"Colson, from dating you or just talking to you after class. Halm could have mentioned seeing you with him, and asked about you," Xander said. "Working from that information, he could have asked around town
~~~~~

and learned enough."

"You're such a coward, Xander." She turned around enough in the front seat to give him a teasing grin. "We both want so much to prove Montgomery is behind all this, we're afraid to even speculate that he gave Halm the information so he could fake knowing me."

"All this is off the record," Donovan said. "Speculate away. Nobody will get anything out of me in court."

"Let's hope it doesn't go to court," Xander muttered.

~~~~~

Hannah finished painting all the ceilings in the new office by that afternoon. She turned off the thermostat, unsure it would do any good with the old-fashioned heating system, and opened all the windows, no more than six inches at the top, to let the office ventilate. Then she cleaned up drop cloths and washed up the roller pan and brushes. More than the chill seeping into the office suite made her shiver. She knew no one could pry open one of those stubborn, cold-jammed windows without making enough noise to rouse her from a sodden sleep. She was perfectly safe, with extra patrols down Main Street, the workday traffic all around her, and her cell phone hooked to her belt. She still had visions of a masked man sneaking up behind her with a rag full of chloroform. The seeming proof that Montgomery *might* be behind a scheme to harass Common Grounds into retreating from Tabor didn't comfort her. Harassment was very different from a real threat to her life.

"Okay, Lord, where's my faith?" she whispered after she dropped the roller pan in the bathtub for the fourth time while she rinsed it clean.

Hannah froze, thinking she heard a footstep. She turned up the water pressure, to create more noise, and took her cell phone from her belt as she stood. She had closed the door three-quarters of the way when she went into the bathroom. Now, she crept up behind it and peered around the edge.

No movement in the hallway. She kept her finger a good inch from the speed dial button, so she wouldn't contact 911 accidentally.

I don't know if I want this to be my imagination or not. Lord, protect me from my imagination? She pulled the door open.

A quick tour of the office suite showed nothing disturbed beyond a twenty-degree drop in the temperature. The air seemed clear enough, but Hannah knew paint fumes would collect quickly enough once the heat built up again in the rooms. She checked the locked door, played with the bells hanging over the doorway to make sure they weren't suddenly sticking, and went back to cleaning the paint pan.

See, Lord, the thing about Xander is ... Hannah sighed and turned the pan over to dry. *I'm starting to think I wanted to get my law degree as some warped means of catching him. Xander is the kind of guy who can't be hog-tied*
~~~~~

and dragged to the altar. I don't want a guy I have to badger into loving me. I want him to chase me. I know that isn't politically correct, but the world is a mess because of political correctness.

A snort of laughter escaped her. If she confessed her thoughts to anyone right now, they'd think she'd lost her mind.

But when she really thought about it, Hannah wondered if she weren't actually *finding* it again. Most of her prayers lately had been rote, prayed along with others at church, while her mind ran in twenty different directions. Or else her prayers had been desperation prayers with not much beyond "Lord, help," or what she and Rene called "gimme" prayers. Asking God but not thanking Him for much, and certainly not including Him in her day-to-day life and concerns.

"What really got me thinking," she said to the empty hallway and to Heaven, "is that when I learned Halm is attending JCU, I immediately thought about canceling my classes. My whole program. If he turns out to be innocent, I could never stand running into him in classes. Not after all the things I've been thinking about him. I want him to be Montgomery's henchman. I want this whole thing solved—and Lord, I'm sorry, but I really want something to knock Montgomery down to size and run him out of town. I'm really a rotten Christian, Lord. I'm a vindictive, man-hunting schemer."

Hannah settled down in the future conference room and rolled a few unopened rolls of wallpaper up and down the long table she would use for papering. She really didn't want to do anything right then. Part of her wanted to pack up, flee the office and Xander and even Tabor. Starting over new in some place where no one knew her sounded heavenly.

And lonely.

God, I really wonder if I should be going after my degree at all. If it sounds so good to drop my classes, just because I might run into a guy, maybe I shouldn't be there in the first place. I'm jumping on any flimsy excuse that comes along. She rested her elbows on the table, her chin in her palms.

What do I really want? I'm happy with what I'm doing right now. What I really want is a life partnership, not a law partnership. Wrong motives to do the right thing don't add up to anything working out right, do they? Maybe Montgomery is right, and I'm chasing Xander. I should just quit.

A horn honked on the street and the sound echoed in the half-empty rooms. Hannah shivered and decided she didn't care about paint fumes. She only had another half hour until she could close up, walk—or run—up the sidewalk to her apartment, and lock herself in for the night.

Strange, but she did feel better already, as if she needed to confess the doubts and misgivings churning inside her heart and mind for the last few weeks. Maybe they had been there for months.

"Should I quit?" she whispered after she had closed half the windows.

"Where am I going to find a job like this one? Sure, the pay isn't the greatest, with all my experience and training, but I'm not strapped. I'm even able to save something every month. I love my apartment and Rene is the best roommate in the world.

"I love this town, I even love most of my life the way it is right now. I know what I'm doing in my job and I know I'm making a difference. Sure, it isn't being a missionary out among the savages, but I've sure had enough evidence lately that not all savages carry spears and go barefoot and... Lord, I really love it here. Should I give up on Xander forever and be happy with things just the way they are?"

She slammed and locked the last window and lowered the few shades that had been installed. She turned up the thermostat and turned on a few more lights, just to drive away the abandoned feeling.

No matter what, Hannah knew she had to stay until the Tabor office had been set up and the desks and rooms were filled with competent people. No matter how scrambled her heart and mind felt right now, she knew she wouldn't be happy anywhere else if she left this job half-finished.

The question was, could she just walk away once all the decorating and arranging and hiring were finished? Xander depended on her to run this office and train someone to take her place in the Padua office.

"Am I just making excuses?" Hannah unrolled the first roll of wallpaper and spread it out on the table. She wouldn't open the bucket of paste, but she could measure the first length and set up things, to make a good start tomorrow.

No. Tomorrow she planned to spend at the Padua office, to close out the week and clear up anything that nobody else there had been able to handle or find or think of while she was out. Hannah felt some measure of pride that she really was needed. Or rather, she was needed until she trained someone to take her place.

Maybe Arc has someone ready to step in. Maybe call Arc and see if they can use me somewhere else? But I love Tabor. This is home. Should I just stick it out?

Chapter Seventeen

A hard thud on the front door startled a yelp out of Hannah. The wallpaper roll went flying across the table. She kicked the folding chair back behind herself. It hit the wall and folded with a deafening clatter. Heart racing, hands shaking so drastically she could barely pick up her cell phone, Hannah stepped out into the main room.

Taylor Dunlop stood at the front door, one hand raised to knock again. She saw Hannah and waved, her face breaking into a grin. A desire to shriek choked Hannah for a moment, then she laughed. Taylor certainly couldn't know she had been working herself into a tangle, examining all her doubts and motives and fears. And Taylor certainly wouldn't grin like that if there were bad news.

"We need you to look at some photos that are coming in right now," Taylor explained, the moment Hannah opened the door to let her in.

"Xander's Downtown at the Justice Center," Hannah murmured.

"We don't need him for this. Where's your coat?"

Taylor drove a dented baby blue Fiero that sounded like it was on its last wheels but handled like a dream on the snowy streets. She slid into police officer mode and gave Hannah a thumbnail sketch of the situation before they reached the police station.

The officer assigned to shadow Chucky had called for someone to come get a memory card full of photos he had taken. Chucky had gone to his usual haunt at the edge of town by all the international shipping companies, the railroad tracks and auto dealerships. A message had been waiting for him, to go to Lake Abram for ice-skating. Chucky couldn't show the message to the officer following him, but he complained at the top of his lungs to his buddies and crumpled up the note, tossing it far beyond the garbage can. The officer retrieved the note before Chucky left the area.

"We're getting a lot of useful information on the underground element here in Tabor and the surrounding communities," Taylor added with a wry chuckle. "That's off the record, of course. The Chief isn't sure if we should take advantage of this and clean up what's basically a minor nuisance right now, or wait and keep an eye on things, and use it to track down bigger targets in the future."

"Hard choice," Hannah muttered, when what she wanted to do was grab Taylor by her uniform collar and shake her until she gave the rest of the report.

Taylor gave Hannah a grin and continued. Chucky had barely arrived at Lake Abram when a man met him and led him into the woods that surrounded the frozen Metroparks lake.

"The kid's smart. The other guy didn't get two words out before Chucky started yelling that he wasn't doing any more errands until he got paid five times as much. Then he listed everything the guy told him to do—and this idiot confirmed each one. McGuire got everything on tape, and he filled all the memory in his camera. We just have to wait for the techs to download and print." Taylor pulled into a parking spot against the building and hopped out of the car.

Hannah barely noticed the ice spotting the parking lot as she hurried to catch up with Taylor. It felt odd going through the back entrance into the police station. Only employees and captured offenders came through that particular door.

"What do you need me here for?" she asked, when she caught up with Taylor inside the empty conference room.

"McGuire doesn't recognize the guy. That's the main reason. The other..." Taylor shed her coat and dropped into the first convenient seat. "The guy's basically a bum. You know Tabor pretty well, and you've invested a lot of time working with street people and anybody who needs help. Maybe this guy came to Common Grounds for help and you either didn't give him what he wanted, or he was trying to scam someone and you caught him. Something to justify what he's doing." She shrugged.

"And he's behind all our trouble, out for a little petty revenge." Hannah silently laughed at herself for the dropping sensation in her gut. That was disappointment if she ever felt it.

"We figure, if that's the case, you'll recognize this guy before Xander would, since everyone who uses Common Grounds goes past you."

"Until recently, at least."

Hannah barely remembered to call the gym and let Rene know where she was, so her roommate wouldn't panic when she came to the office to walk home with her and she was gone. She called Common Grounds and left a message for Xander, giving him the news of this latest development. She didn't know whether to ask him to come to the police station or just promise to call when she had more news. How long would this take?

"I'm no photographer," Taylor said with a shrug. "I have no idea how long it'll take to download everything and print. Thank goodness we don't have to work with film and chemicals and all that anymore. Just go to the computer. Hungry? I can order something delivered."

"No. Thanks." Hannah managed a shaky laugh. Could the whole mystery be solved so quickly?

Then it struck her that she might soon be safe, but the mystery of the

White Rose Killer hadn't been solved. Somewhere in Tabor Heights, another innocent young woman had become, or soon would become, the target of a murderer who demanded loyalty and innocence, who grew angry when she reacted in fear, and who had already killed three times.

Donovan joined them only minutes before the photos came from processing. "McGuire is following the new man," he told them, "and we sent up another escort for Chucky. We're guarding him until we have things sewn up, just in case it gets nasty."

Though he managed a pleasant expression, Hannah caught a grim light in his eyes. Could this stranger be someone with lethal connections? When they trapped him, did he have the clout to punish Chucky for betraying him, maybe even switch to more harmful tactics against her and Xander? But if he had those resources to begin with, he wouldn't have hired Chucky, would he?

The photos were glossy and dry, fresh from the printer when the lab technician spread them out on the table. Hannah wrinkled up her nose, remembering when two of her brothers had been shutterbugs for three years in high school, and the stink that hung around them in a cloud from all the chemicals they used developing film. She grinned, thankful for the improvements in technology, and leaned in just as close as Taylor and Donovan to get her first glimpse of her unidentified enemy.

After studying only three photos, Hannah could almost smell his unwashed odor; a combination of desperation, anger, hunger, dirty sweat, clothes that hadn't been washed in weeks, bad nutrition and sleeping in filthy conditions. Dirty, salty, metallic, sometimes as strong as the stench of a grocery store dumpster on a hot summer day.

The man's multiple layers of clothes were dull tones of sepia and gray, all running together. She had a clear picture of him. A stocking cap under a ball cap with holes in it. Matted, tiger stripe earmuffs that might once have belonged to a little girl. A discarded Tabor Heights High School varsity-style jacket with holes on the sleeve where the year numbers were missing, stretched tight over a ragged raincoat that hung past the man's knees. He wore an oddly new-looking, matching pair of rubber boots. Stolen? Or had someone taken pity on him in all this snowy weather and simply gave him the boots.

His square-cut face had heavy jowls and dark smears under his eyes, but that could have been his natural coloring. Hannah frowned, knowing something was wrong with that face. Then it struck her.

"He's clean-shaven. How does a guy like him get a shave?"

"Maybe he lifted a disposable razor from somebody's garbage," Donovan said. "Or that's a disguise, and he slept in his own bed last night."

"Maybe."

She studied the man again. In two photos, the officer had caught him with his hats off. His hair looked dark, cut short. Recent barbering, or was his hair simply greasy dirty and clung to his scalp? His eyes were dark, too. Impossible to tell if his eyes were brown or dark blue or black. A receding hairline topped his fleshy face.

Strangely, she did think she had seen him before, but not at the Padua office. Where? Hannah knew better than to pursue the niggling sense of recognition. Too much pressure would drive the subtle clues completely out of her mind.

Finally, she reached the end of the photos. She sat down and Donovan gathered them up into a neat stack. He settled down next to Taylor, across the table from Hannah. For several seconds, silence dominated the room. Hannah swallowed down a nervous giggle.

"I know I've seen him before, but I don't remember where."

"Does he always look like this, or is this a disguise?" Taylor offered.

"I think... this is him. All he has in the world, on his back." Hannah shook her head. "But where would he get the money to hire Chucky, and how would he get the roses if he's a street person?" She flinched. "The roses—anything yet from the store?"

"The girl who worked the counter that day is a student at Cleveland State, and she went home for break. She'll be back to work in another day or two," Donovan said with a sigh. "The problem is, that was an extra busy day, and the guy who bought the roses paid cash."

"What are our chances she'll remember one man out of dozens?" Taylor said.

"Where would this guy go, if he really is what he seems to be?" he continued. "No cars anywhere in sight up at the lake, and no tracks in the slush to indicate someone dropped him off, so he walked there. From where? McGuire won't be reporting in until his replacement meets up with him. I'd sure love to find out this guy is working for someone big and nasty and we can nail them all."

He offered Hannah a wry grin. They both knew better. Such easy solutions and convictions only happened on television, in deference to the audience expectations, time constraints, and ratings.

"Okay, so where would a bum go in Tabor?" Taylor said, taking up the thought. "The Mission?"

"We're not up to that kind of ministry yet," Hannah said, shaking her head. "We have the Senior Center and the Daycare and the Food Pantry, and a soup kitchen in really bad weather. We won't have housing for the homeless set up for..." She felt breathless for a moment, as an idea struck her. "But he wouldn't know that, would he? If *you* think the Mission would offer shelter, wouldn't other people?" She slapped her hand down hard on the table, making Donovan's empty coffee cup jump. "That's it! I saw—at least, I *think* I saw him talking with Claire."

"Donnelly?" Donovan snapped. "The Mission's assistant director?"

~~~~~

"Henry Ford," Claire said, after only looking at three of the stack of thirty photos. She nodded, then finished raking her wheat-colored hair back into a ponytail. "That's what he calls himself," she added, as she bound her hair with a twisty.

"Is he for real?" Donovan glanced from Claire to Pastor Wally, the Mission's director, aiming the question at them both.

He and Hannah had come directly from the police station to the Mission, just managing to catch Claire before she left for the night. The four of them stood around Claire's always-full desk in the front office of the former elementary school.

"Very real, unfortunately," the elderly, barrel-chested minister said, nodding. "He's highly educated, just from his manner of talking. I think something tragic pushed him out of a comfortable job and way of life, and his mind snapped. He comes in every day to use the bathroom to brush his teeth and shave for job interviews. He's been in a good mood lately, saying he has something 'in the works', as he puts it. But he hasn't been very forthcoming about the details." He frowned deeper, rubbing his chin as he thought. Then he sighed and shook his head. "I'm not sure if it means anything. Half the time, Henry lives in a fantasy world. I've seen too many people who just closed the door on their lost lives and failures and started all over again."

"Why come to Tabor?" Hannah whispered, not really intending to speak the thought aloud.

"The Metroparks," Donovan answered her with a snort and a shrug. "Lots of places for the homeless to find shelter, even in the winter. Heck, we've caught folks who managed to trap the ducks and geese for food. All those ice fishing holes you see in the old quarries aren't just from sportsmen."

"There are also a good dozen deaths from starvation and exposure in our section of the Metroparks every winter," Claire added. "That's why we're so desperate to get the funds to set up the shelter here in the Mission. To get them indoors and fed and clothed in bad weather."

Hannah thought of the Arc Foundation. Wouldn't this be something they would want to get involved in? The foundation had ties to Tabor through Nikki, Joan's friendship with Xander, and now Common Grounds moving in. She searched her purse for a notepad to write down the idea before she forgot it.

"What about this Henry Ford guy?" Donovan asked. "How does he get along? Has he come into any money lately? Is he the kind of guy who would kill somebody on a grudge?"

"Henry?" Claire exchanged a glance with Pastor Wally.
~~~~~

"I meant it when I said he snapped," Pastor Wally said in that somber, mournful tone of voice Hannah had heard him use on the rebels and delinquents in their church's youth group. "Henry's a sweet soul, normally. If he decides you're his friend, he'll protect you, and do anything for you. But if he's angry, he can be a nasty, vindictive...child, I suppose you could say. He yells and punches and kicks. He even spits and bites, on occasion. But let a few days pass, and you can be his best friend again. Just buy him a hamburger and talk to him about Shakespeare."

"He has no real sense of right and wrong anymore," Claire added. "The world revolves around him, so everything is judged by how it affects him. He loves us, because we feed him and let him read the books people have donated for the children's library."

"Would he pay someone to set a fire, if he was angry with someone?" Donovan asked.

"Henry?" Pastor Wally thought for a moment. "Where would he get the money? He does odd jobs for anyone who asks him, for just a few dollars or a meal. He's reliable and smart, but if he isn't interested, he just doesn't stick to it. He doesn't have the mental power for long-term projects or attention to even the simplest details. We tried to fix him up with a few jobs, but he never came back after the weekend."

"Odd jobs?" Hannah shivered. "What kind of odd jobs?"

"Oh... anything that's fast and pays under the table," Claire said after thinking a moment.

Hannah and Donovan locked gazes. She knew he was thinking the same thing: could someone be using poor, broken Henry Ford as a go-between?

"If Henry's involved in some kind of trouble, maybe we could help," Pastor Wally said. "Can you tell us what's going on?"

"Hannah, do you mind?" Donovan sank down into the chair next to her.

"The more people who know, the better they can pray," Hannah said. "I have the feeling we're going to need some heavy-duty praying, soon."

Friday, January 3

"Hannah?" The male voice on the phone was unfamiliar.

After a long, busy, tiring day cleaning up a week's worth of work at Common Grounds, all she wanted was to go home, curl up on the couch and watch a totally brainless movie while she indulged in a super-deluxe pizza and a chocolate peanut butter malt. Would anyone be upset with her if she spent the entire weekend in a deliberate coma?

"Speaking." She closed her eyes and hoped whoever it was would identify himself before she had to reveal she was clueless.

"How about that dinner date now?"

Hannah stopped herself just before asking "what dinner date?" She remembered Toby Halm from the New Year's Eve service and everything learned about him later. But if she revealed she knew who he was, what would he do? After all, he didn't go to their church, so she wouldn't know who he was. Or would he expect Xander to recognize him and identify him to her? If she pretended not to remember him, would he know she was on her guard against him? All this trying to think circles around him was tying her brain into knots.

"I'm sorry, but I'm busy."

Two could play this game. He hadn't specified a day or time and she hadn't said when she was busy.

She almost laughed when the silence stretched out on the other end of the phone. Xander stepped around the corner of the dividers. She signaled him to come to her desk when he would have gone to the coffee machine.

"When are you busy?" Halm finally asked.

"Constantly." Mentally crossing her fingers, Hannah decided to put the ball into her court. "Why don't you call me when I get home, and I can check my calendar for when I'm free, okay?"

"Uh — sure."

"Oh, hello officer." Hannah crossed her eyes at Xander. "I'll be with you in a minute. Um, let's talk about this tonight, all right?" She barely waited for Halm to stammer agreement before she hung up.

"Officer?" Xander propped himself against her desk with both arms stretched out straight. "What was that about?"

"Halm just called to ask me out again. Without identifying himself," she continued, ignoring it when Xander's left arm buckled. "He has no idea if I recognized his voice or if I mistook him for someone else."

"Your new number is unlisted, so how can he call you at home?"

"How fast can Donovan set up a wiretap for me, or something to at least prove Halm called me if he does call me?" Hannah took a quick, deep breath and plunged on. "If he calls me when I have an unlisted number, he has connections in the wrong places, which might give us legitimate reason to dig further into his activities. At the very least, we can establish a record that he's harassing me."

"Wow. That's pretty fast thinking for a rough Friday afternoon." Xander's grin, lopsided as it was, warmed her.

~~~~~

Donovan made arrangements to install a trace on Hannah and Rene's phone within the hour. Xander fought the temptation to order Hannah to let him drive her home. Her car would be exposed all weekend in the
~~~~~

parking lot behind the Padua office, so what good would that do her? Thanks to Vic and Baxter's surveillance equipment and Vincent adding a helping hand with security around Hannah's apartment, her car was safer sitting on Main Street than anywhere else. If Halm had the connections to get her unlisted number, he had the connections and wherewithal to do something nasty to her car. It would be that much easier doing it in the shadowy lot behind the building in Padua, where most passersby wouldn't see, much less notice and ask questions. As Hannah had already proved, it was better to pretend they didn't suspect him, or even think anything was going on. If they seemed to relax, so would he, and they could catch him before he could cause any harm.

Any more harm than he had already done to Hannah, frightening her as he had.

Xander followed Hannah home down Pearl Road to Sackley and thought hard. Half the office staff would be at the Tabor Heights office all day Saturday, for the last big push to put the office together, moving furniture and papering the walls, hanging light fixtures, all the fussy last-minute details. Hannah wouldn't be alone, even when Xander couldn't be with her. He wished he had the right and the responsibility to be with her day and night.

Chapter Eighteen

Xander knew what he faced in the mirror, even on his best days. Hannah wasn't the shallow type of woman who would only look at his face and bank account. Still, he found it hard to believe she would wait for him so long, when he had been oblivious to her, distracted with so many other concerns in his life. He knew Hannah dated. There had to be an even dozen men who were just waiting for the chance to go out with her, if her schedule permitted.

What if Toby Halm truly was just interested in her as a woman, and had deliberately come to their church to look for her? He could have asked around town about her and then came to their church, hoping to see her. Maybe he even thought Hannah knew who he was, and when he saw she was busy with other people, he left.

"Then why did he pretend to be in her class?" Xander asked the radio announcer who extolled the virtues of a local used car lot.

None of that mattered, he told himself. Nothing mattered but Hannah's safety. He concentrated on the taillights of her car, following her through the end-of-the-day congestion on Main. He pounded one fist against the dashboard and vowed that when this whole mess was straightened out, he would figure out how he felt and then work on finding out how Hannah felt. And if she didn't feel like he did, then he would just have to work on changing her heart and her mind.

Saturday, January 4

"Anything?" Xander asked the next morning, as he walked Hannah from her house to the office to start their marathon day of decorating and arranging.

"Not a peep. I would have called you if something happened." She cocked her head to one side and studied him as they walked up the sidewalk to the office door. Did he look like he hadn't rested well? A stab of guilt made her wince. Hannah knew she had no right to even think about bailing out on Xander and leaving Common Grounds, just to run away from her own tangled feelings. Certainly not while all these problems pounded on him. "Do you think maybe Donovan turned off my phone service instead of setting up the tap?"

Xander grinned and let out three sharp barks of laughter. He held onto that grin even after he unlocked the door and ushered her inside. He paused just a little too long on the porch to be casual, looking up and down Main Street. It was too early for any traffic to speak of, but Hannah knew that meant little to a demented stalker. Even when he was a copycat.

"So, did Halm run into a roadblock getting your number, or did he think you were in the book, and when he looked you up later he couldn't find you? Or does he realize we're on to him?" He punctuated his words by locking the door with a hard click.

"Or was it someone I should have recognized and didn't?" Hannah added.

"How many guys have asked you out in the last few weeks?"

Xander didn't look at her when he asked that question. Something tight in his voice, a forced brightness, made the hairs rise on Hannah's neck. It was just her imagination. Xander wasn't the sort to get jealous.

"I can't honestly remember. My social calendar is just so full, I turn down dozens every day." She flashed him a grin when he turned sharply to look at her.

Walter and Nelson banged on the front door then. If Xander had been about to say anything, the opportunity was lost.

With so many hands helping with the work, what might have taken Hannah a week to do on her own got finished in less than six hours. The office felt crowded and rang with the clatter of two radios set to two competing stations, nineteen pairs of feet running back and forth and as many pairs of hands helping to measure and cut, carry and clean. By the time dinner arrived — wings, ribs, salads and pizza from Mancuso's — the office was nearly ready for inhabitants.

"Guess you won't have to spend any more time alone here," Xander said, as he unwrapped the packages of paper plates and plastic utensils.

"You just arranged this work party so I'd have to come back to the office and straighten out your files," Hannah retorted. She finished prying back the lip of the aluminum pan holding the ribs and lifted the cardboard lid. A gush of spicy, tomato-scented steam bathed her face and she moaned, almost loud enough to drown out the rumbling of her suddenly aching stomach.

"Guilty!"

Donovan showed up when the work crew was only halfway through the dinner line. Hannah had retreated to her section of the office, to stay out of the crush and enjoy the organized, nearly pristine look. She knew it wouldn't last very long, once the staff was hired and she was busy juggling dozens of records every day. Xander had followed her and braced his arms on her desk, visibly ready to say something important. Donovan rapped on the locked door before she could think of something to say. Xander sighed, grinned, and stepped into the entryway to open the door.

"Just wanted to let you folks know, McGuire followed our man to a meeting tonight. Recorded a lot of the conversation." Donovan didn't step inside, just braced himself against the doorframe. His smile was grim, and the weariness in his eyes sent a bolt of sadness through Hannah.

"Incriminating?" Xander asked.

"Henry Ford might have been a very intelligent man at one time, but he needs a lot of coaching and gentle handling to get him to do anything. Seems Toby Halm isn't very patient anymore." Donovan's smile grew sharp.

Hannah gasped. Whether from relief, surprise, or anger, she couldn't decide, even when she thought about it later.

"They said enough to prove Halm hired Ford to do his dirty work?" Xander slid a hard, strong arm around Hannah.

"That's what McGuire said when he called for backup. They're bringing them both in, probably in the next ten minutes. I'm heading down to the station to do the initial questioning. With Montgomery for his boss, I expect Halm to get out with no bail and no questioning, and charges of entrapment slamming down on our heads before we have time to think."

"But it could be over, right?" Hannah had to ask.

"Hope so, folks. I'll keep you updated." Donovan backed off the porch. "I'd keep the doors locked and be careful in dark places for a while, just in case." He nodded to them and stepped down onto the sidewalk.

Hannah shivered, but it wasn't from the cold air that came in while Donovan held the door open to talk to them. Xander shut the door and locked it. He turned her around to face him and wrapped his arms around her. She let herself enjoy the warmth, the caring she felt in his arms for five too-brief heartbeats.

"The blinds are up. The whole town can see us," she muttered as she pushed free of his arms. What she wanted was to stay there forever.

This was probably the last time Xander would ever hold her tight and close. The danger was past, or nearly past. He could stop worrying, stop blaming himself for the threat to her, and things would slowly slide back to normal. Was that a good thing? Had she finally convinced herself to let the dream of a romance with Xander fade away, and just hold onto him as a good friend?

"Hey, you've been under a lot of pressure." Xander let her step back, but he gripped her shoulders so she couldn't get away. "It's natural to feel kind of shaky, now that it's almost over."

"You heard Donovan. Montgomery will probably be waiting on the steps of City Hall to bail out Halm. The way he twists everything around, we'll be up on charges of conspiracy and I'll be accused of stalking Halm."

"Maybe. Maybe not. Donovan's smart, and Chief Cooper doesn't intimidate. Montgomery's a smart man, too. He won't go after us until he's actually seen the reports and can publicly trace it all back to us."

"To me," she had to correct him.

"He's a self-righteous shark who'll cut his losses and sacrifice his own people to keep his hands lily white." Xander shook her a little. "It's almost over, Hannah. We've got a party going on in the other room. Maybe we should celebrate."

"Yeah, celebrate." Hannah remembered how hungry she had been just moments ago.

Xander was right. She should be celebrating, not bracing for a house to drop on them. They were the victims here and she had to remember that. They had the right to make sure the people harassing them were brought to justice.

They would have answers soon, one way or another. There would be some kind of closure to the questions that had haunted her for the last few weeks. Hannah looked around the room and recalled her half-formed plans to leave once her obligations to Xander ended. Now there was even less to hold her to Common Grounds and Tabor... and Xander. Was that her problem? Did she want the questions and dangers and darkness to remain, so she had an excuse to stay?

You're pathetic.

"Mind if I tell the rest of the gang?" Xander asked.

"Should we? I mean, what if it all falls apart?"

"They're family. Maybe this is the time to bring in the reinforcements, prayer-wise, instead of relaxing and expecting everything to go our way. Ever think about that?"

"No." Hannah let Xander hook his arm through hers and lead her back to the conference room.

A few of their co-workers called out teasing remarks about skipping out on the party or the bill, or threats that there wasn't enough food left to feed Hannah, much less satisfy Xander's legendary appetite. Hannah smiled at some of them and laughed at a few others. Judging by the amount of food left after everyone had taken their first serving, there would be seconds for all, and thirds for some. That was one of the nice, dependable things about Xander. He always overestimated the needs of any party or work project.

Xander raised his hands for quiet and proceeded to bring everyone up to date on the harassment situation. His words effectively stopped Hannah from thinking of the many other things about Xander that she liked. Things she would miss if she left Common Grounds.

"Thank God." Carolyn, Walter's wife broke the slightly stunned silence that reigned after Xander finished. She turned to Hannah and enfolded her in a hard, tight hug. "I don't know how I would have handled all that, if that sicko had targeted me."

Others echoed her sentiments as talk suddenly flooded the room. Others hugged Hannah. Speculations rang out, and the after-work festivities turned into a celebration. Hannah listened to her co-workers and their families talk, expressing the concerns they had carried for her the last few weeks, and warmth moved through her. It drove away some of the chill, prickly misery that had filled her since she started thinking about leaving. All these people were her friends, as dedicated to helping the helpless as she was. In the last few days, most of those men and women had expressed how valuable Hannah was to the office. She made a valuable contribution to the work of Common Grounds, didn't she? They were her family as well as her friends. How could she consider leaving them?

To her disgust and amusement, Hannah found her appetite had returned in full force. When Xander and Nelson helped her carry the leftovers to the apartment, she was worn out, full to the point of discomfort, her tension had seeped away, and she had come to at least one decision. She wouldn't leave Common Grounds. Not until a specific sign came from God, as in a job offer from a much larger, more powerful firm that would let her serve just as effectively.

What she would do about her churning, tangled feelings for Xander, Hannah didn't know. She was too tired and relieved to let that bother her right now. God had taken care of other, bigger questions and problems. She felt sure she could trust Him to handle this, too.

Sunday, January 5

"Would you mind going to second service today?" Hannah met Xander inside the door from the church's main parking lot. She hooked her arm through his and headed back out the door before he could answer.

The excited flush in her cheeks and her breathless voice finally registered. Xander slid his arm free to wrap it around her waist and led the way down the steps, around the remaining patches of ice that the morning's dose of salt hadn't tackled yet. It was early enough that the main rush of church goers still hadn't arrived.

"News?" he asked.

"Mark called. He needs us down at the station. He also said Halm didn't ask for his boss or for a lawyer until this morning. Something weird is going on."

"Should we wear flack jackets to the station, in case Montgomery is waiting for us?"

"Probably. But Mark would warn us, wouldn't he?"

"Hope so." Xander opened the passenger door of his car for Hannah and hurried around to his side. His hands shook a little as he inserted the key. "Might take less time if we walked," he joked.

"I'm not going anywhere on foot with those storm clouds rolling in from Canada, thanks very much." She grinned at him as she buckled her seat belt.

Donovan waited for them when they walked into the main lobby of the police station.

"We have Halm dead to rights with the fire, the notes, and the roses. He's already signed a confession, with one of his lawyer buddies from Montgomery's office present. Seems he wants to be sure he's not accused of being the White Rose." Donovan snorted his disgust and beckoned for them to follow him, across the lobby and down the hall to Chief Cooper's office.

Arthur Montgomery waited for them, impeccably dressed for a church service. He sat in front of the chief's desk, a briefcase sitting next to him, his hat on his lap and his overcoat neatly folded on the table behind him. His somber expression didn't change as Xander and Hannah walked into the room. No anger, no shame. Hannah gripped Xander's hand. She had taken off her gloves when they entered the station, and her hand felt damp and cold and trembled a little in his grip. Despite that, she looked just as composed as Montgomery when Xander pulled out a chair for her.

What would I ever do without her? Xander asked himself for what seemed the thousandth time in just the last ten days.

"Thanks for coming in," Chief Cooper said. "I hope we can get this over with quickly, so we can all attend second service." He nodded to them before bending his head to study the papers spread across his desk. Then he looked up at them again. "Hannah, Xander, I'm sure Officer Donovan has kept you informed of the progress of the investigation. The homeless man who calls himself Henry Ford led us to a Mr. Toby Halm, who hired him to find people to deliver the roses and notes to Hannah, and to set fire to your office. Chucky Timkin, of course, has identified Henry Ford as the man who, in turn, hired him to set the fire and deliver the roses. We have a full confession, signed in front of Halm's lawyer and notarized." He held up a sheaf of papers.

"Did he say why he did all this?" Hannah's voice was calm, full of the poise Xander had come to admire in her.

He recalled, for a split second, how Hannah had stayed calm when a pregnant teen in a drug-induced craze came into their office, demanding help, and then went into early labor right there on the dusty linoleum. Hannah had held the girl's hand and talked to her until she calmed down, then persuaded her to accept medical help. Xander knew that Hannah would have been able to face down the real White Rose murderer with the same calm strength and poise. He prayed she would never have to do such a thing.

"According to the confession, he wanted to frighten you away because you're so valuable to Common Grounds, and he wanted to discourage you and Xander from setting up the branch office."

Xander bit his lip against sighing his relief or giving away his feelings with a wide grin. This was all small-time and aimed at Common Grounds, not some major vendetta against the Arc Foundation or a personal grudge against him or Hannah. He could handle this without crippling guilt or the need to call in the "big guns" from the foundation.

"Why?" he asked, when it became apparent Chief Cooper wasn't going to add anything else to the explanation.

"Because of hero worship, I suppose," Montgomery surprised them all by saying. His voice stayed dry and cool, and no emotions showed in his eyes as he looked at Hannah. Xander wondered if the man did that to avoid looking him in the eye. "I'm ashamed to admit Mr. Halm overheard me in a fit of pique, expressing a wish for you to be driven away, at any cost, because I knew Finley couldn't move his office into Tabor without you. I recognized early how valuable you are to the overall operations of Common Grounds, Miss Blake, and I quite honestly envied your unswerving loyalty to your employer. If only I had more employees like you, so reliable, intelligent, and full of the proper sort of initiative." A tiny, frosty smile flickered across his face.

"He took my angry words as... well, as an indirect order. Hoping to prove himself to me, he took it on himself to make those shameful arrangements. I find I must apologize, most ashamedly, for the actions prompted by my unwise words. I would never seriously want either you or Mr. Finley to be harmed. Though I must admit, I do still want you to keep your business out of Tabor."

"There's enough crime in this town for ten times as many lawyers. Unfortunately," Xander added.

For a moment, Montgomery did meet his gaze. Nothing changed in his expression.

"Yes, unfortunately." He turned back to Hannah and held out his hand. "Miss Blake, please accept my apologies. And please do take it as the compliment I intend, when I say that if you should ever leave your current employer, I hope you will seek a position at my firm."

Xander thought—hoped—Hannah would refuse to shake their nemesis' hand. She smiled coolly, inclined her head, and held out her hand. Xander wished she had put her gloves back on. She let Montgomery break contact first.

"If you're finished with me, Chief Cooper, I do have some obligations at church." Montgomery stood and reached over to pick up his coat. He nodded to them all, made frosty eye contact with Xander once more, and left.

"So Halm was just buttering up the boss?" Xander asked, once the door thudded softly closed behind Montgomery.

"Looks like it. I wish Halm had slipped up just once and said his boss told him to do it, but..." Donovan sighed as he sank into Montgomery's vacated chair.

"I can believe it. For the most part," Hannah said. She gave Xander a shaky, too-bright smile. "It's nice to know someone else appreciates my contributions."

"Hey, I gave you a raise last month, didn't I? And a Christmas bonus." Xander grinned back, delighted with her ability to break the tension with humor. If they had been alone at that moment, he knew he would have wrapped his arms tight around her, maybe spun her around the room in celebration.

He suspected he might even have kissed her in the exuberance of the moment. That didn't shock him at all. On the contrary, he rather enjoyed the momentary fantasy.

Chapter Nineteen

"What surprises me," Hannah said, after Chief Cooper let them read a copy of Halm's confession, "is how Mr. Montgomery reacted to all this. He's too calm. You'd expect him to be livid, just to be casually implicated. And I've never known him to apologize for anything."

"Technically, he didn't do anything wrong," Chief Cooper pointed out. "Expressing your opinion still isn't a crime. And it's easy to apologize for someone else's crimes when you're innocent."

That thought stayed with Xander after they cleared up a last few details and left. They still had time to catch the second service at church. He considered stopping at Stay-A-While to get some cappuccino or maybe hot chai to celebrate. Maybe his favorite blueberry scones would be available. He wondered if Hannah liked blueberry scones. There was so much he still didn't know about her, all the little, day-to-day, ordinary details that made her the unique person she was.

"I really expected him to blast us," Hannah said, when Xander was about to suggest they go to Stay-A-While.

Distracted, he turned right on Span, instead of left. Sighing, he smiled and continued up to Church Street.

"Not with the Chief and Mark there as witnesses. And a lot of the proof in those signed documents was pretty embarrassing to him, even if it didn't convict him," he added with a slight grudging feeling.

"He usually manages to twist things around. I really expected him to rant and rave that it was *our* fault Halm decided to break the law and embarrass him."

"Don't you know it *is* against the law to make Arthur Montgomery look bad?" Xander chuckled when Hannah just sighed at his words.

Maybe, he speculated, Halm had done all his dirt on Montgomery's orders. Maybe he had been paid off. Maybe it had been understood from the start that if he got caught, he would take the blame. Clerks didn't make that much money, and not even scholarships could cover everything for law school. Xander knew that fact all too well. Maybe he had been paid enough to guarantee his loyalty and silence. If Halm got a suspended or reduced sentence, he might be able to attend this semester's classes at John Carroll University. How much would a successful, entrenched lawyer like Montgomery be willing to pay to keep his name clean?

"I can hardly believe it's really over," Hannah murmured.

"Yeah. Over." Xander felt like he had awakened from a sound sleep.

He looked around and realized that he had driven the short distance to church and parked the car without noticing what he did. Moving on autopilot was fine in some situations, and certainly safe enough with the sparse Sunday morning traffic in Tabor. He mentally shook himself and swore not to do that again. Not in his driving, and most definitely not in other parts of his life. He had to keep his thoughts focused and centered, or he might get into trouble the next time. Well, he knew a way to get a few things off his mind and out in the open. That would help. No more autopilot, as far as Hannah was concerned.

"What are you smiling like that for?" Hannah paused with her hand on the latch to open the door.

"A guy can't smile when he's feeling good?" Xander wondered if she would stay in that position while the engine was still running. He didn't want her to leave just yet. They still had a good fifteen minutes until they had to go inside for the service. He was quite willing to spend fifteen minutes' worth of gas to keep Hannah in the car with him.

"We've spent a lot of time together, the last couple weeks." Xander wondered if he should reach over and take hold of her hand.

He hadn't felt this awkward and unsure about such a simple thing since he first started dating. He had been so busy getting Common Grounds up and running, he hadn't even thought about dating in years. He knew he was out of practice. Come to think of it, he really hadn't dated that much in high school and college, so what practice he had once wasn't worth mentioning.

Back on track, idiot!

"Sorry." Hannah's hand slid along the door latch. "I've been taking up a lot of your time." She looked away. Xander had no idea what she might be feeling. Now he really felt lost, out of his depth.

"If I didn't want to spend time with you, I would have hired a bodyguard. In the final analysis, all your problems are my fault. Maybe even starting with Simons poisoning you."

"Funny. I've been thinking about that weird time too." She made a funny little coughing noise. Laughter or nausea, Xander couldn't be sure, because she insisted on looking out the side window instead of at him.

Did Hannah want to get away from him? Her life had been in danger, whether real or bluff, because she worked for him.

"I don't want you to — to run away, Hannah." The moment the words left his lips, Xander knew that was the wrong thing to say.

Hannah slowly turned to look at him now. She frowned, but he dared to hope it was confusion that wrinkled her forehead and not anger or fear.

"What makes you think I'd run away?"

"I'm glad we've spent a lot of time together," he hurried to say, running over her words. "We've really gotten to know each other a lot better. A lot closer. I like that."

He mentally kicked himself. What had happened to his eloquence? Facing an unfriendly jury, he could talk the moon down out of the sky and save an innocent, framed man's life. Facing the lady he wanted to keep in his life, his tongue turned into knots and his IQ dropped fifty points.

"Xander?"

"Maybe we should take advantage of how close we are and ... I don't know, keep it going?"

"Don't let the momentum die?" Hannah made that coughing sound again. It was definitely closer to a laugh than nausea or choking.

"Well, that's not how I would put it." He honestly wasn't sure anymore how he *would* put it, but Xander knew a lame line when he heard it. If he could avoid saying those lines, he knew he would be ten steps ahead.

"You're feeling guilty right now." Hannah smiled and tugged on the door latch.

"Yeah. Guilty. I didn't realize before how important you are to me." He couldn't let her run away from him now. "I mean, you've always been important to me, and I know I don't tell you often enough or show you, but the thing is, I've been so busy and — okay, scared — and I should have done something about it a long time ago." What was he going to do if she got out and walked away? Chase her down in the snowy parking lot and drag her back to the car?

"Xander, don't ruin things. Don't push things. I think we should let everything calm down. Wait until the crisis is over and we go back to normal."

"I ignored you when things were normal."

"Well, yes, you did." Her smile widened a little.

Hannah's lips trembled. Gut instinct yanked Xander's gaze up four inches, and he saw glistening in her eyes. Was she about to cry? Why?

"I don't want things to go back to normal. We're good together, Hannah. I don't know what I'd do without you."

"And what happens if we try to prolong this closeness and it gets really awkward in a few months when things calm down?" The door clicked and inched open next to her. "I'd have to leave, wouldn't I? Can't ask the boss to leave when things get uncomfortable, can I?"

"I think we'd be great together. More than just defending the innocent and fighting off the creeps."

"You don't date much, do you, Xander?" Daylight slipped in between the door and the car frame.

"What does that have to do with it?"

"Much as I would have loved this moment a few months ago... I'm convenient. I'm there, I'm useful. You don't date because you're too busy saving the little guy from being trampled. With me, you don't have to make any effort. Man, when you pray for something, watch out what you pray for," she said with a chuckle.

The door creaked like a dungeon door. Hannah blinked back more glistening wet from her eyes and turned to climb out of the car.

"Hannah, I'm serious!"

"Right now you are. Just like a guy in a foxhole who vows to become a priest if God will save his life. I don't want a foxhole romance any more than God wants foxhole religion."

Hannah slammed the car door before Xander could protest. She ran the distance of four parking spaces before he could unbuckle, open the door, and climb out of the car. He slipped on a patch of ice and grappled at the open door to stay upright. By the time he got his feet underneath himself again, she had climbed into her car and started the engine. Xander leaned against the hood of his car and watched her drive out of the parking lot.

Somehow, without being quite sure how he got there, he ended up in the service. He spotted Montgomery sitting two pews ahead of him. Xander wondered if the other lawyer was watching for him or Hannah to show up. Knowing how much Montgomery hated being humiliated or proven wrong in any degree or form, Xander felt he had done at least one thing right by coming into the service instead of skipping it. Both he and Hannah missing the service would give Montgomery some fuel against them.

Remembering Montgomery's innuendos about improper behavior between him and Hannah, Xander knew how it would look if they both missed the service. Especially after Montgomery was forced to apologize to them.

Maybe those innuendos had prompted Hannah to turn him away? Xander caught his breath as his mind latched onto that explanation. Yes, he had been spending an unusual amount of time with Hannah lately. All those hours could be explained away as his concern for her safety, stemming from his responsibilities as her employer. If they continued to spend time together and displayed an interest in each other, people would find a new interpretation for those hours together. People, Xander had learned long ago, were more prone to see filth in any situation than to accept innocent explanations.

Somehow, he couldn't make himself care if people thought he and Hannah had acted improperly. Not if he lost this closeness between them and could never regain it.

~~~~~

Where was she? His angel should have returned to school by now.
~~~~~

Why wasn't she at school, where she belonged, where he could watch her and protect her and teach her to be faithful to him?

He walked past her dormitory three times in the darkness, ignoring the cold, wet lash of the storm. He circled the parking spot in the sheltered corner behind the dormitory building, close to the trash collection bin, where no one else wanted to park. That was her parking spot. Why wasn't her car here? He returned to the front of the dormitory and watched her room.

A light came on, and it felt as if his heart had just remembered to start beating. Tears warmed his frozen cheeks and he laughed into the storm. They lied, when they said his angel wouldn't come back. They lied when they said she had given her heart to someone else long before he saw her. His angel loved him. She had come back to him, just like she promised.

He waited, watching the movement between the light and the blinds covering the window. He wanted his angel to open the blinds and look out, to feed his starving heart with the sight of her pure, sweet, beautiful face. When the blinds didn't move, he told himself to be glad she protected herself from cruel, evil eyes.

A door opened, behind him across the street. He ducked into the shadows of the lightning-struck pine tree and watched the people coming out of the side door of the Mission. He relaxed, smiling, as he saw Claire Donnelly and her brother, Tommy, come out of the building. Tommy was a good boy, watching out for his sister. He admired Tommy, able to laugh and make others laugh, even though he was tied to a wheelchair for the rest of his life. He knew he could love Claire, if he hadn't found his angel. Claire was good and kind and fierce when someone threatened the children under her care. He had seen Claire tackle and sit on a bully who climbed the fence of the Mission's playground to threaten the children. Claire was a good person, and she was nice to him. He was glad Claire and Tommy and the Mission were there to watch over his angel.

He waited until Claire and Tommy worked the wheelchair lift and got him into their van. He stayed in hiding until the taillights vanished into the snowy darkness. Then he stepped out to watch his angel's dormitory window. He smiled, smothering happy laughter when the light finally went out. Good, she was asleep. She needed her sleep. School started this week, and she had to take care of herself, stay healthy, stay beautiful, and wait for him.

Would it be so bad if he went up to her room, just to look at her sleeping, just to wish her happy dreams? She wouldn't know he was there, but he would sleep better, finally able to see her again after weeks without a glimpse of her face or the sound of her voice.

He had the keys for the back door of the dormitory out of his pocket before he finished thinking about it. He snorted disgust for the idiots who thought they could keep him away from his angel, just by changing the locks on the dormitory. He knew how to get all the new keys, and even make new keys for new locks if he had to. He was here to guard the whole town, so nothing could stay locked away from him for long.

Angel lived on the second floor. He crept up the back stairs, wincing every time his wet boots squeaked on the linoleum. Her door was second from the end, next to the empty lounge. He wished his angel would wake up and come into the lounge, so they could talk. She would be glad to see him. He knew she would be glad. But the time wasn't right for them to be together. Not yet. She had to be tested a little longer.

He tried the doorknob of the dorm room and it turned easily. Unlocked. That pleased him, so a funny, happy, choking sensation filled his chest with warmth. Angel knew he was coming to visit, and she left her door open for him.

The streak of light from the hallway illuminated the empty bed on the right side of the room. Cold tore the happy warmth away, making him hollow inside. All his angel's books and posters, her computer and Teddy bears and her fluffy unicorn slippers — gone.

"Where is she?" he growled and yanked the sleeping girl out of the other bed by her hair. She let out one squeak as he flung her across the room, so she slammed against the cinderblock wall under the window. "Where is my angel?"

The girl wiped blood out of her eyes and stared up at him. He knew she couldn't see his face, with the light coming from behind him. He would have to kill her, if she had seen him. She wasn't pure. She wasn't allowed to see him. She wasn't his angel.

"Where is she?" He reached down to shake her until she talked.

"Tracy went home," she squeaked, and scrambled back away from his hands.

"Liar," he whispered, choking on something that wanted to come out as a scream.

For just a moment, his angel was there in front of him once more, trapped inside his hands, her flesh soft and fragile, bruising under his grip as she struggled and begged, crying, fighting to breathe. Pleading, swearing that the nasty stories were all lies, and he was the only boy she had ever kissed.

He swung, backhanding the roommate, so her head slammed against the cinderblock wall. She slumped, unconscious, without making a sound. Trembling, wanting to howl his pain and the old terror and guilt, he fled the dorm room, left the door hanging open, and slipped and skidded down the stairs. He almost forgot to lock the back door behind himself, to cover his trail. He dropped the stolen keys and almost didn't go back for them. He almost ran right past his car, hidden on the other side of the trash bin, where he had been waiting for his angel all afternoon.

She left him. She ran away. Why did she run away?

Monday, January 6

Monday morning, Hannah rolled over and opened one eye to glance at her bedside clock. Five twenty-eight. For some reason, she felt sure she had to get up at five-thirty. She lay for a moment, wondering why she had to get up so early.

Her thoughts and decisions from the past week and yesterday's argument with Xander flooded her conscious thoughts. Groaning, she tugged the blankets up over her head. Today, she should be starting classes at John Carroll University, working toward her law degree.

But she had decided not to go for her degree.

She still had to cancel her registration and return those books she had bought so eagerly a month ago. That meant going Downtown. Maybe she should just go and take care of it today? She hadn't told anyone but Rene of her decision not to pursue her degree. Xander wouldn't expect her to show up at the Padua office until after lunch. There was nothing more to do at the Tabor Heights office until the Arc Foundation started sending candidates for the lawyer and paralegal positions, and the ads running on the Internet started bringing in respondents for the support positions. She could take care of those responses from her notebook computer, in bed.

If she didn't go Downtown this morning, she would have to go to the Padua office. That was the last thing Hannah wanted to do, after that weird non-argument she had with Xander.

Rene had laughed and cried with her yesterday, when she related the twisted, unbelievable conversation they had had. Hannah could hardly believe herself. Finally, Xander wanted a relationship that went beyond the office. So, what did she do, after years of hopeless yearning and praying and counseling herself to be patient? She told him to take a hike. She told him what he felt for her wasn't real and wouldn't last.

Why had she listened when she told herself to give up on Xander?

"I don't know what You're trying to teach me, Lord," she mumbled into her pillow, "but could You spell it out a little clearer for me?"

"If you're wrong, and what Xander feels is real, solid, not rooted in this crisis," Rene had said yesterday, "this will prove it."

Hannah had stared at her roommate, her head aching and her stomach knotted, and wondered if Rene had flipped. Maybe the whole crazy encounter, starting in the police station with Montgomery and ending outside Xander's car, had been a warped dream. Would she wake up soon?

"If his feelings are real," Rene continued, with that concerned smile that made Hannah want to burst out crying all over again, "he won't give up. He'll keep trying."

"If he has any common sense, he'll send me packing and find someone new to run the office. I have definitely lost my mind." Hannah had slumped on the couch and rubbed the last traces of tears off her cheeks with the heel of her hand. "This is so weird. I mean, I finally convinced myself to be happy with what I've got. What does Xander do? He offers me exactly what I've wanted. And I couldn't believe it was real. He has to think I'm crazy."

Rene had disagreed. She dragged Hannah with her to Gold Tone Gym that afternoon and talked her into making her sporadic exercise routine more constant. Working up a sweat had helped, and what that didn't soothe, a trip to Rick's Bakery and the leftovers from Saturday's feast healed the ache quite nicely. Or at least the combination of agony and ecstasy fooled her into believing it was healing.

But now, early Monday morning, Hannah still had problems looming ahead of her. She watched the blue numerals on her clock switch to five forty-three. She had to make some kind of decision and do something, or she might still be lying in bed at noon.

Maybe she should go to her first class and check it out. She certainly didn't have to worry about running into Toby Halm at the university.

Her stomach twisted when that thought flicked through her mind. Hannah shook her head and resolved not to let that situation bother her. Halm had been caught, and even if she didn't believe Montgomery was innocent of everything but nasty words, there was nothing she could do to prove otherwise. She had to go on with her life. It was up to her how she reacted to the things people said and did to her. She didn't have to let anybody ruin her life.

Chapter Twenty

A hot shower helped. Rene had already left to open up the gym, so Hannah didn't have to explain anything to anyone if she ran behind schedule. A pot of tea waited for her, and fresh cinnamon rolls. She nearly burst into tears, grateful for her thoughtful roommate who thought today was a day for celebration. Hannah filled an insulated cup with more tea, packed up all her books, snagged a new notebook and a blister pack of pens off the shelves by the door and headed out to her car.

It felt odd not to watch over her shoulder as she walked down the driveway to her car parked on the street. Hannah glanced across the yards to the office, half-expecting to see footprints in the melting snow, maybe a broken window. No signs remained that anything odd had happened in the building.

By the time she got off the highway near the university, Hannah had made up her mind about a few things. She would check out her first class, which had sounded interesting enough she would have taken it even if it wasn't required. After that, she would decide whether to continue the class, but she would definitely cancel the other two and return all the books while she still could get the full price refunded. The Arc Foundation would appreciate that much. Why lose more of their money on late withdrawal fees and penalties?

"Okay, Lord," she whispered as she got out of her car in the student parking lot. "Please show me what You really want me to do, and make the sign easy to understand, please? I'm kind of dense today."

Hannah double-checked that she had locked her car and that the parking permit decal was clear in the corner of the window. She made a mental note to remove it if she decided to drop this one class along with the others. The fewer reminders of her abandoned dream, the better.

She prayed she wouldn't need to rid her life of all reminders of Common Grounds and Xander, too.

~~~~~

Xander had meetings Downtown all day. Hannah didn't know whether to laugh, cry, or simply wilt into her chair with relief when she got to the office and found his scribbled notes about his meetings and appointments on her desk calendar. She had dreaded her first encounter with Xander after that awkward scene yesterday, but it looked like she had worked herself into nervous knots over nothing.
~~~~~

Maybe God was teaching her, through her own blindness, to relax and trust Him?

She had decided to keep her Monday-Wednesday class to leave her options open. Her decision came partly from an honest interest in the class, and partly grasping for any excuse to be out of the office a little more.

When, she wondered, was she going to get her head on straight and her mind made up?

The chime over the door startled her and she half-stood up from the desk before she recognized the windblown figure stomping snow off her boots on the reception mat. Hannah started to smile, putting on her professional face and voice to welcome Toni. Then something twanged deep in her chest, warning her. They had caught the copycat, so why would Toni be here? Not to do a story, Hannah hoped.

"Hi, Toni. How are you doing?" She gestured for the reporter to take a seat in the reception area, which was mercifully empty right now. "Coffee? Hot chocolate? It looks pretty vicious out there. I'm glad I got in before the heavy stuff hit us."

"The White Rose attacked Tracy Brickman's roommate," Toni said. She finished pulling her gloves off and raked her fingers through her snowy hair, shedding the last few flakes before she stepped off the rug.

"Is she—" Hannah sank down into her chair again.

"Concussion, stitches, scared out of her skull and ready to quit school." She managed a flat smile. "But very alive."

"He didn't believe Curt's story, that Tracy went home to stay," Hannah guessed. "He thought he was going to find her in her room, and when he didn't—"

"He went ballistic. Well, at least we know it's a man now. No." Toni shook her head. "There wasn't enough light for her to get a description. She just got a general outline and the sound of his voice. Tall, baritone voice, really angry and raspy, big shoulders, dressed all in dark clothes. No mask, though. She was pretty sure there was no mask. Which doesn't make sense. Isn't he scared of anyone identifying him?"

"Maybe he was planning on snatching Tracy and didn't care if she recognized him later or not." Hannah swallowed hard. "Because there wouldn't be a later." She rested her head in her hands and didn't care that they were visibly shaking. "When is this going to be over?" Then she realized who she was talking with. "Oh, Toni, I'm so sorry. This has to be twenty times worse for you. Living it all over again."

"It'll be over when we catch the psychotic who killed my sister." Cold calm washed over Toni's face, as if she pulled a coat on over her pain. Her eyes lost their teary gleam. Only two spots of color remained in her cheeks to betray her inner turmoil. She nodded and stood up to go. "I thought you should know."

"Does—I don't even know her name. Does the roommate need any help? Someone to stay with her until she's feeling better? Has the university called her parents?"

"Taylor from the department is with her, and her name is Samantha. She's made friends with some of the folk across the street at the Mission, especially that guy in the wheelchair." A snort of something that came close to laughter escaped Toni. "He got across the street despite all that snow and barged his way into the RA's apartment and practically dragged her back across the street with him. Taylor says she's doing better, just surrounded by the kids. She wants to be a kindergarten teacher, so she loves kids. Claire—you know Claire over at the Mission?" Toni waited for Hannah to nod. "She says she'll take Samantha home with her tonight, and she's staying with them until her parents can get in from Vancouver."

"Good."

"I'll tell her you offered. All of us collateral damage folks have to stick together, y'know?" Toni reached for the door. She stopped when a man appeared out of the heavy, blowing snow and yanked the door out of her grip.

"Do you need someone to talk to? Somebody to stay with?" Hannah winced when an icy gust of wind wrapped around the divider set up to deflect some of the weather, and slapped her face and yanked her hair.

"You are in so much trouble," Curt growled, grabbing hold of Toni's arm at the elbow.

"Thanks, but I don't think I need that." Toni smiled a little more warmly at Hannah. "My bodyguard just caught up with me."

"What did you think you were doing, just taking off like that? Hi, Hannah. Bye, Hannah. Say good-bye, Toni." Curt turned and pushed the door open.

"Curt thinks I'll be the next target, since I look so much like Angel. At least he cares that much!" She gasped a little as Curt dragged her out into the snow.

Hannah stared after the two of them until they walked out of the window frame. She sank down in her seat again and took a few deep breaths. In a situation like this, she could either cry or scream or laugh. She chose to laugh. Especially when Nelson and two of the part-timers came from their cubicles in the back at that exact moment, wanting to know what just happened.

~~~~~

"Something wrong?" Vic asked, as Xander finished his fourth set on the butterfly station. He rested a foot on the end of the bar, effectively stopping Xander from doing any more reps.

"What makes you say that?" Xander wiped stinging sweat out of his eyes and looked around the gym.
~~~~~

He looked again. There hadn't been much of a crowd when he arrived at eight, after a long, stressful day of one meeting after another at the Justice Center and then an hour-long traffic jam thanks to three accidents in a row on I-71. Now, the gym looked like a ghost town.

"You're going to wish you had stopped half an hour ago when you get up in the morning. If you can get up," Vic added with a chuckle. "Something must be pretty heavy on your mind, to keep you pumping iron for so long without feeling it."

"Yeah. Heavy on my mind."

Or my heart, he added silently.

Xander had been grateful for his heavy load of work, which had kept his mind occupied and away from the tender subject of Hannah most of the day. At least yesterday afternoon and evening, he had been able to escape by concentrating on preparing for today's heavy schedule of meetings. Now, though, those priorities had vanished, and he couldn't find any other excuse to keep from hashing through his confusion.

Okay, his approach had been wrong. Just the approach? Would she have been more receptive if he had taken her out to dinner? He should have rehearsed his words. That much was for certain. Xander knew he could be ten times more eloquent. The timing had to be part of the problem. Why had he rushed things?

He knew Hannah was right, though. A little bit. He had certainly brought it up too soon after the mystery of the copycat had been solved. He couldn't really imagine how it looked to her, how she had to feel, hearing him stumble through his explanation yesterday. Sitting in the parking lot of the church, no less!

"Hey, Earth to Xander." Vic snapped his fingers in front of Xander's eyes. "You really need to talk this over with somebody before you zone out in traffic."

"Yeah, talk to somebody." Xander shook his head, sending sweat droplets flying. "Have you got time?"

"Go get a shower and I'll get a fresh pot of coffee going in the office." Vic put his foot down and stepped back. "Does this have anything to do with Hannah?"

"Does it ever." Xander slid his arms out position and groaned. He had stiffened up just in those few seconds he sat still.

"Make it a long, hot shower."

"How did you know — about Hannah, I mean."

"Rene mentioned something this morning. I heard they got the guy who was after Hannah, so what are you worried about now?"

"What did Rene say?" Xander levered himself off the bench, hissing to keep from groaning like a wimp.

"Hannah's upset about something and scared she made the wrong choice and you're all wrapped up in it." Vic shook his head and hooked a thumb toward the front of the gym. "Decaf or regular?"

"I'm tense enough as it is." He managed a grin, caught the towel Vic tossed him, and stumbled toward the locker rooms at the back of the gym complex.

Xander stood under the steamy spray of the shower as long as he could endure it, letting the near-scalding stream soak into the iron ropes of his muscles. How had he functioned like this all day? How could he let one rejection tie him into knots? He slapped the shower control bar, using more force than necessary. His hand stung and the dial spun over to off with a click and a thud in the pipes.

He had been a coward. He had been lazy. He had been content to keep Hannah in the office, keep her busy, watch over her at church, satisfied there was no one in her life to steal her away from him. Had he been so afraid of upsetting the equilibrium that he hadn't dared take the risk and deepen their relationship?

He remembered Joan's words those few weeks ago. Both she and Anne thought Hannah was interested in him, but Xander hadn't been able to believe it. Was his self-esteem that low, his self-image so gruesome and pitiful he couldn't believe an intelligent, beautiful, caring woman like Hannah would want him? Was he so frightened of rejection he couldn't take the risk of asking for a simple date?

It had taken the fear of losing her to propel Xander past those self-pitying fears. Then, still in a panic, he had moved too soon and made the largest fumble of his life.

The downside of being analytical and dedicated to justice was that he couldn't lie to himself, and he couldn't avoid figuring out problems and flaws for very long. Even in himself.

"Good going, ace," he muttered into his towel as he dried off. Xander was grateful no one else was left in the gym this late at night. He didn't need word spreading through Tabor that Common Grounds was run by a lunatic who talked to himself.

Vic had the coffee waiting, doctored with a good dollop of almond-flavored syrup and real cream so Xander couldn't tell it was decaffeinated. The jumbo-size cup of liquid heat helped soothe those bands that persisted in tightening around his chest as he spilled all the events of Sunday morning.

"I'm all in favor of maintaining the status quo," Vic said, breaking the comfortable silence. He offered up a lopsided grin. "The problem is that you can't go back to the way it was. The genie is out of the bottle."

"I don't want—well, maybe I do. Want to go back to the way things were. It was a lot easier."

"Easier isn't always good." He took a long sip from his own mug of black decaf. "Safe is just existing. Not living."

"So would you and Rene—you know, get closer, if you could?"

"This isn't about me and Rene. She's better off not knowing about my past. She deserves better than an ex-hood who could get her killed if someone finds out where I'm hiding."

"Maybe she hasn't shown any interest, and you're afraid to take the risk?" Xander held up a hand to stop Vic before he could retort. "That's out of line. I'm sorry. We're talking about the mess I made with Hannah. Your problems are a whole lot bigger than mine."

"Oh, thanks for that bit of comfort." Vic grinned and raised his cup for another long gulp of coffee.

"Somebody else has been talking with my mouth today, because I seem to have forgotten how." Xander stared into the creamy brown depths of his scarlet mug and watched the slow swirling of the coffee. "So, what are my options?"

"Win her or lose her. Convince her you're serious or let her leave you—and everything you've built together—behind."

"She can't leave. What would I do without her?"

"Is that the lawyer talking, or the man?"

That stopped him short. For so long, Xander had convinced himself his concern and need for Hannah had been based solely on her contribution to Common Grounds. It was truth, just not the entire truth. How many times had he daydreamed about her presence brightening up his condo? He looked forward to Mondays because he could share his weekend with Hannah and hear about the things she had done.

He remembered how he had ached, sitting in the hospital room after Hannah had been poisoned. Watching her sleep, afraid to trust the doctors when they said she would be fine. Wanting to watch out for her for the rest of his life. So scared he hadn't known what to pray. Blaming himself because she had been attacked in an attempt to affect him and his actions and choices.

"I am so stupid," Xander said with a ragged chuckle, after relating the incident to Vic. "I knew then she meant more to me than just a good right hand, but I let things slide back to the way they always were. She should have left me then."

"Maybe she's stupid, too."

"What?"

"Why should she hang on, waiting for a big, half-blind dope like you to wake up and really see her? She's just been wasting her time." Vic set down his mug and leaned back in his chair. "Unless..." He cocked his head to one side, eyebrows raised in question, and waited for Xander to respond.

"She's waiting for me to wake up." He choked on laughter that didn't want to escape. "But she told me what I feel is just foxhole romance."

"So? Prove she's wrong."

"How? I don't want to lose her, now that I've made a mess of things. You just said, either I win her or she leaves."

"She's waited this long. I think she'll wait a little longer. Convince her you're thinking about what she said and you're letting things cool down between you. Then when she relaxes, start turning up the heat."

"Turn up the heat?"

"Let her know how important she is to you. She wants you to chase her. Hannah just doesn't want you chasing her for the wrong reasons, that's all. Smart girl."

"How do you know so much about women?" Xander tried to laugh. It sounded rusty and ached in his chest. "Is this how you sweet-talked the ladies in the old days?"

"There were no *ladies* to sweet-talk, in the old days." The humor died from Vic's eyes, replaced by that aching Xander had seen when the other man revealed his shadowed past. "No good, smart ladies like Hannah and Rene. If I hadn't walked away from that life... Rene wouldn't have anything to do with me, and I know you'd never take me on as a client." He reached for his cup, tipped it back and drained the last mouthful.

Xander shivered deep inside, sensing the regrets and shame that still haunted Vic. He didn't want to live his life with regrets, growing bitter over might-have-beens. He certainly didn't want to spend the rest of his life alone, wishing for someone like Hannah to complete him.

Step back and wait, convince Hannah he agreed with her, and then turn up the heat. He thought he could do that. He had learned patience when it came to delicate, life-and-death court cases. Xander knew how to manipulate witnesses and juries and even opposing lawyers, to bring the truth to light and win sympathy for his clients. He had to apply that same patience and skill to Hannah.

Tuesday, January 7

The phones weren't working when Hannah settled into the Tabor office that morning. A few urgent calls on her cell phone finally got her a promise of installation within the hour and an apology, because the phones should have been turned on Monday. Her ads were to run that morning in the *Fish Wrapper*, the local Christian weekly broadsheet, and Hannah didn't want to lose prospective workers because the phone company couldn't get things done on time.

Baxter would be coming after lunch to set up all the new computers, install the software, and link everything into the office network with the

Padua office. Hannah wanted to get everything in place before he came. That meant moving desks into their final positions, portioning out the chairs to each room, locating all the boxes of files, and getting them into the new filing cabinets and off the floors so she and Baxter wouldn't trip over them.

Hannah was grateful for the hard work, the concentration needed to make sure everything had been shipped from the office supply stores or from the Padua office. It freed her from having to think about Xander and her recent decisions, and how she was going to tell him she wasn't going after her law degree after all. It felt strange not to talk to him every day, but she would have to get used to it. What use would she be as an office manager, coordinating the two offices, if she couldn't handle the everyday tasks and decisions on her own?

She had refused to center her life around catching a man; refused to become a man-chaser, a female who had no identity unless she was a Mrs. So-And-So. She had been right to reject Xander's affection and interest under strained, false pretenses, right?

So why did she feel like she had made the worst mistake of her life?

"Please, Lord," she prayed, eyes open, down on her knees in front of a filling cabinet and her hands full of folders. "This is where I belong. I'm depending on You to fix things. Am I supposed to break the wall down with Xander, or should he?"

The jangle of the bells on the door startled a yelp out of her. Hannah dusted off her hands, finding two more paper cuts in the process, and stood. Her knees ached and her ankles felt stiff from kneeling so long. She laughed at herself and made a mental note to get back to the gym tonight after work as she hurried down the hall to the front room.

Chapter Twenty-One

Bekka Sanderson, from the Singles group at church, stood in the entryway. She looked around, slowly tugging off her neon green stocking cap. A grin lit her cold-reddened, long face as she turned and saw Hannah.

"This place looks fantastic. Is it true that Ice Man Montgomery tried to swipe it from underneath you?"

"Partially." Hannah gestured for Bekka to go into her office area and have a seat. Much as it would have felt good to spill all the sordid details of the rival lawyer's activities, she chose to keep her mouth shut. The truth had a tendency to be warped by too many re-tellings and might turn into a weapon Montgomery could use against her or Xander in the future.

Bekka settled into a chair facing Hannah's desk and let her threadbare Army surplus backpack slide to the floor. Hannah recalled that Bekka's grandparents, who raised her, had been part of Montgomery's clique at church until they moved to Florida the previous September. It must have been misery for Bekka until then, constantly encountering the man. The perpetual college student was a free spirit and quietly, calmly defied the restrictions her grandparents tried to put on her life. She lived in blue jeans, loathed skirts, and pursued a theater degree and a career writing fiction. The elder Sandersons wanted her to get married, and subscribed to the belief that good Christian girls never wore slacks.

"We can always tell when he comes to our building to visit Todd and Lisa," Bekka continued. "The lights dim and the temperature goes down about ten degrees." She grinned. "Enough about the Grinch. I came to ask you about this." She unzipped her navy blue down vest and pulled out a much-folded copy of the latest *Fish Wrapper*.

"If you're asking about the office sitter position, you're hired." Hannah laughed when Bekka stopped short and her big brown eyes widened. "You do understand it's only part-time, and only until we get the office fully-staffed. Maybe three months at the most."

"Answer phones, direct people to the main office, and sort the mail." She nodded and mimed sagging with relief. "Perfect for me. It'll let me get some schoolwork done and keep me off the streets during the worst of the winter. I love my courier job, but I'm having a hard time finding chains for my bike tires!"

Hannah laughed with her, delighted to have that one position taken care of so quickly. The part-time college student was perfect for the job.

She would be discrete, because as far as Hannah knew, Bekka never talked about anything that happened on her many and varied jobs, and younger singles at church seemed to flock to her for advice.

They chatted for a few minutes about the job requirements and Bekka's schedule. Hannah was relieved to learn Bekka was Internet-savvy and could access the different Web sites where the want ads were posted, to download resumes and applications.

"How about I put you on the payroll starting today, and you can help Baxter get the system put together this afternoon?" she offered.

"That sounds great... but I have a class during the lunch hour. A stupid time to schedule a class, when everybody wants to eat, but hey, that's what the administration does best." Bekka grinned. "You heard about the fiasco last spring, when they tried to schedule a series of lectures, complete with audio-visual, in the theater right in the *middle* of the two-week run of *Much Ado About Nothing*? And some bozo thought it would be easy to disassemble an entire Shakespearean theater set and put it up again in time for the performances that he assumed would be easy to re-schedule, after all the tickets had already been sold. Considering they make the General schedule his plays a year in advance, they had no excuse."

"Bureaucrats are the same everywhere." Hannah knew then it would be a delight having Bekka working in the office. She only wished she could offer her a full-time job.

"How long will Baxter be working here? I could come after class."

"Sounds great. I might just abandon you and get some errands taken care of."

Hannah took Bekka on a tour of the rooms, giving her a general idea of where everything was stored. She showed Bekka the circuit breaker box, the thermostat, the supplies, and nearly forgot to give her a set of keys and the code for the security system.

"Not a good idea to forget that one." Bekka nodded, the laughter dying from her eyes as she and Hannah settled down in her office again. "Um... I heard Annalee was found here. Is it true that he goes after brunettes only?"

"Seems like it. We can only guess the pattern, but he targets girls who don't seem to date."

"Uh oh. What an excuse to get a boyfriend. Think I can hire one?" She fiddled with the frayed cuff of her heavy, cherry red sweater.

"If it's any comfort, he picks on girls who live at home, not on their own. That girl from the college is a break from the pattern."

"Not really much of a pattern, is there, with only four? When do you think he'll pick number five?"

"I hope he never does." Hannah shivered. She wouldn't wish on her worst enemy the feelings that had gone through her, when she thought she was the next "true love" of the White Rose.

"There are so many sickos in this world. Sometimes I wish I could run around with a... I don't know, a handful of grenades and just blow them off the map." Bekka shrugged and offered up a lopsided smile. "Could I ask you something? Semi-legal advice, really. Employee discount, maybe?"

"On the house." Hannah reached across the desk and rested one hand over Bekka's. "What's the problem?"

"Not me—a friend. Her stepfather is a real creep. Was a real creep, actually, since he's divorcing her mother." She went on to describe the sexual harassment her friend had endured growing up, doing a stumbling but still admirable job of protecting her friend's identity.

Hannah's mind raced, trying to decide who in the Singles group at church could have been going through that torment without anyone knowing. It definitely wasn't Bekka, changing the details to hide her identity. Bekka had learned how to walk the straight and narrow while getting what she wanted from life. She wasn't afraid to fight for something that mattered. Hannah couldn't imagine anyone harassing Bekka and getting away with it. So who was it?

The girl, naturally, didn't want anyone to know what had happened to her. Hannah completely understood. Society claimed to be enlightened, but victims were still blamed for the damage they suffered. However, the stepfather owned a business that employed college students. If his stepdaughter had escaped him, maybe he would target the girls who worked for him. They had the right to be warned. Bekka thought they could drop hints and let the rumor mill do its job, without outright confessing what had happened to her friend.

"I need to know, is it illegal? I mean, we're sliming his reputation. It could affect his business. He never really *did* anything that we can prove in court, other than drool a lot. He always made Amy real uncomfortable, like he was mentally undressing her. I don't want her mom to lose what's coming to her."

Hannah felt a man like that deserved far worse than to lose his employees and business.

"As a Christian, I wouldn't set out to destroy his reputation, but I'd feel an obligation to warn those girls who could become his next targets. If the rumors stay just *rumors*, he might never realize anything is wrong, but no one will walk into danger, either. Forewarned is forearmed."

"Balancing act, huh?"

"I could take it to my boss." Hannah felt some wonder that she didn't flinch at the thought of going to Xander. Then again, this was business, not personal.

"No, that's not necessary. Just advice. We haven't really done anything, told anyone major. At least, I haven't. Amy isn't too good at holding back when she's ticked." She groaned. "Yeah, and I'm really good at being discrete, huh?"

"Nobody will ever hear any names from me. If it gets serious and Chef Creepo comes after you or your friends, Common Grounds will represent you."

"Employee discount?" Bekka grinned, relief coloring her cheeks.

"Employee discount."

~~~~~

Why was everyone against him? Why couldn't he find the information he needed? He couldn't get into the college computers to find out where his angel lived. He couldn't ask any questions about her because no one would talk. The girls he approached around the university, especially around the dormitory, gave him frightened looks, even when he told them he was trying to help protect Tracy. The boys on campus got defensive, thinking he accused them of threatening or even attacking her.

What was wrong with the people at the university, that no one would help him find his angel?

The police department infuriated him. What was wrong with Chief Cooper, that he wouldn't put the information in the police computer, wouldn't let the files leave his office? Did the Chief suspect how easily he had found information on the other girls, the false angels? Was that why he wouldn't give information to anyone but Donovan?

He hated Donovan, his enemy since elementary school. Donovan the sports hero, the Eagle Scout, the lifeguard. He always did everything right. Who did he think he was, sitting in the front row in church every Sunday, as if God needed him there?

Snarling, he turned and slammed his fists against the solid panes of the wall beside him. The heavy plastic shuddered in its frame and the echo reverberated through the abandoned greenhouse.

His angel was gone. Stolen from him. Did he have to kill the ones who stole her?

"Angel." He cradled his bruised hands against his chest and stumbled across the damp concrete floor to the room that had been the office, back when his uncle ran the greenhouse. He needed to see his angel again. He needed to see her smile at him.

The school yearbook was worn out from handling, the binding cracked, pages threatening to fall out. He handled it with care as he took it out of the plastic tub that protected his treasures, his memories of his angel. The perfume of hundreds of white roses filled the humid air and soothed him.
~~~~~

She smiled at him, serene and quiet, standing in the back row of the choir picture. His hands clenched as her laughter filtered through the greenhouse, echoing against the dirty panes. Laughing at him? Why would his angel laugh at him?

"You promised you would come back," he whimpered. "Where are you hiding? Why are you hiding from me? You said you'd love me forever."

He stared at the picture of the choir and he trembled as an idea came to him. He was wrong, looking for his angel all grown up, waiting for him to find her and love her again. She didn't need to come back because she had never gone away. His angel was right where he had left her.

~~~~~

Xander debated with himself whether to include flowers when he picked up lunch for himself and Hannah and took it to the Tabor office. Roses were definitely out. He was desperate, but not stupid enough to take the heavy-handed approach. Maybe carnations, some daisies, maybe one of those plastic-sheathed bouquets he could buy at the grocery store?

He ordered Chinese, then got caught up in some last-minute work and left the office ten minutes later than he wanted. Despite that, the food wasn't ready when he got to the restaurant. Xander forgot to stop for the flowers, forgot he even intended to get flowers until he had parked in front of the office and started opening his door.

Hannah met him at the door with a smile that made him forget all about the flowers. Xander felt like an idiot, blathering about what he had brought for lunch, rather than asking her to forgive him for the mess he made of things on Sunday. Then again, considering that mess, maybe talking about food was the best track to follow. She thanked him, claimed she was starving and pretended to snatch the cardboard cartons from his hands. Just like old times. He felt half his nerves settle down.

Before he could think of what to say next, Hannah spilled out her report on that morning's progress while she set up their lunch in the conference room. She had taken four calls from the *Fish Wrapper* advertisement for support staff and had hired Bekka Sanderson to watch the office. Xander knew and liked Bekka, and approved immediately.

Then Hannah told him about Bekka's question and her response.

"You said exactly the right things. Definitely, Arc will fund the entire defense if this ever gets to court. I doubt it will, though. Taking a slander case to court will expose both sides of the story to the public. He has to prove he never acted improperly toward his stepdaughter, in word *or* deed. The fact that her mother left him so abruptly will work against him. I get the feeling you know who the stepfather is?"

"Bekka tried not to, but she dropped enough hints." Hannah sighed and rubbed her temples before diving into her hot and sour soup.
~~~~~

Xander watched her, curiously glad he had been able to give her the answer she needed. He wondered if he should be grateful for Bekka's problem, which helped to bridge the rough spots between them.

This proved once again that he needed Hannah in his life, if only in her capacity as his office manager and people-person. Hannah touched their spirits and saw their emotional needs while he saw to their legal defense. They were the perfect team. He prayed he had a chance to take that perfect unity into their personal lives.

Xander used the quiet time to catch Hannah up on what was happening in the office and to ask about her first class. He waited until they were nearly done eating to try to apologize and smooth things over. As Vic had pointed out, Hannah had shown patience with him so far. He owed it to her to be patient with her doubts and fears in return. He couldn't build the foundation of their new relationship until the old one had been repaired.

"You were right, the other day," he began, watching Hannah squeeze the last drops of duck sauce onto her egg roll.

"About what?" She didn't look at him, and her hand jerked just slightly, so she had to turn the egg roll to keep from losing the last blob of sauce.

That was one sign she knew what he was talking about, and that it still bothered her. If this conversation took place last week, she would have made a snappy remark. Something along the lines of "I'm right so often, which time were you talking about?"

"I was reacting in relief, when I talked about us getting closer." Xander muffled a sigh when Hannah still wouldn't look at him. "I want you to know that I never want to lose you. If all we can have is our working relationship, I'll be happy with that. I don't want my stupidity on Sunday to drive you away. Promise me you won't leave, Hannah."

"Scared you, huh?" She looked at him now, just for a moment. Her smile was a little stiff. Xander dared to think he knew her well enough to guess that she *had* contemplated leaving. Did he dare hope that the idea hurt her, just a little?

"I'll admit that something in the male chromosomes gives us tunnel vision. I've been a typical male and oblivious when it comes to you, how valuable you are to Common Grounds and to me, personally."

He waited, but Hannah concentrated on nibbling on her egg roll. The crunchy wrapper barely made a sound, despite the utter stillness in the office.

"This is where you're supposed to jump in and say 'Oh, no, Xander, you're much more observant and sensitive than the average male,' or something equally soothing to my ego." He grinned when a chuckle escaped her as a snort. "When you really think about it, Hannah, you're just about my best friend."

"That's why I don't want to ruin things." Again, she met his gaze only for a moment before looking away.

"I agree. So I'll step back and wait until things calm down with Halm and Montgomery, Chucky is taken care of, and the office is set up. Okay? But if, after a suitable cooling off period, I still want more than just Boss Man and Gal Friday, you'll give me a chance?"

"Anybody home?" Baxter called, accompanied by the jangling of the bells over the door. Hannah leaped up, popped the last of her egg roll into her mouth and hurried out of the conference room.

"Hey—"

"I'll think about it," she said with a teasing grin, and hurried to meet Baxter.

Xander stayed for another half hour, helping Baxter cart all the computer components and boxes of cables into the office. Then he had to leave, called away by appointments that couldn't be postponed. Hannah and Baxter were hip-deep in boxes and cables, monitors and disks of software, and barely looked up to wave when he said good-bye.

Xander decided his lunch hour campaign had been quite successful and most satisfactory.

Wednesday, January 8

"Hi, Boss," Bekka greeted Xander when he stopped into the Tabor office that afternoon after a brief appearance in Tabor Municipal Court. She picked up an envelope from a surprisingly large stack on the secondary desk in Hannah's office and slit it open.

"Hi, yourself." He stomped his shoes on the mat in front of the door and started unbuttoning his coat. "I hope you're not walking home tonight. That snow is getting pretty fierce."

"There's a meeting of the terminally backstage crew at the theater tonight, and I'm hitching a ride with someone after." She slit another envelope, pulled out the paper inside, then glanced at the front of the envelope. Bekka paused just long enough for Xander to notice as he peeled off his snowy coat.

"That's good. Something wrong with that letter?"

"Nope. I shouldn't have opened it—for Hannah." She slid the still-folded paper back into the envelope and tossed it onto Hannah's desk.

"Speaking of whom, where is she?" Xander tried to remember if Hannah had an afternoon class scheduled for Wednesdays. How was he going to convince her that all of her life mattered to him, not just her office skills, if he didn't pay attention to little details like that?

"She had to run down the street to the printers. The zip code was wrong on half the business cards."

"You're kidding." Xander tugged a chair away from the wall in the reception area and angled it so he could face Bekka. "Their business is in Tabor Heights. Our business is in Tabor Heights, two blocks up the street. And they couldn't get the zip code right?" They laughed together. "That's a lot of mail, after only three days being in business."

"From what the mailman said, it's been coming ever since you took the lease, they just haven't delivered it until office hours started. Most of it is from businesses wanting to sell you something. Copiers, office supplies, phone service, that kind of stuff."

"The phone calls will be starting soon."

"Tell me about it. I already fielded a call from some guy who claims he called this office and talked to our purchasing manager last week, but he can't remember his name, and wanted to verify his name and our address so he could send him a confirmation of our order." Bekka rolled her eyes in disgust, prompting more chuckles from Xander. "He got pretty snippy when I told him that he was mistaken. He got really quiet when I told him the phone had only been turned on since yesterday. I love it when you catch these pirates in their lies."

"Don't you know it's our job to catch the pirates and stop the lies?" Xander slouched in the stiff reception chair and raised his arms to the ceiling, stretching until he swore he heard his vertebrae pop. The doorway bells jangled, prompting him to sit up so quickly he nearly slid out of the chair.

Chapter Twenty-Two

"You look like you had a rough day," Hannah said as she entered.

"Thank God it's almost over. What's with the new zip code?" Xander got up and followed her over to her desk.

"They didn't even try to explain it. I could understand a simple typo if it was the entire batch, but it was half the run." Hannah peeled off her coat, tossed it over the filing cabinet sitting in front of the window, and flopped down into her chair. "Please don't tell me more office supply pirates called while I was away."

"Okay, I won't tell you." Bekka grinned cheekily at them and picked up the last envelope.

Xander shared a grin with Hannah. Then his gaze dropped to her desk and landed on the envelope Bekka had opened by mistake. At first, the return address made no sense. He thought he recognized it. The fancy silver embossing on the bottom left corner of the envelope confirmed it.

"What's Montgomery doing writing to you?"

"Montgomery?" Hannah followed his gaze down to her desk. She stared at the envelope several seconds, then picked it up.

"I opened it, but I didn't read it," Bekka said.

"Well, at least we know it wasn't rigged to explode." She stared at the envelope several seconds before pulling out the letter.

Xander stepped back while Hannah read it. He watched her eyes. Her frown deepened when she reached the end. She went back to the top of the letter and read it a second time. He fought the urge to fidget when she read it a third time.

"What does he want?" he finally asked.

"He's offering me a job."

"It's got to be a joke." He reached for it, then stopped himself. Something about Hannah's withdrawn expression made him uneasy.

"Bekka—"

"Hey, anything said inside these rooms is forgotten the moment I step out the door." Bekka stood up, hands raised in a gesture of innocence. "Except for those jerk phone calls. I'm taking notes on those and putting them in a book someday. Maybe I can sell a couple of the really dumb ones to *Reader's Digest.* But maybe I should take off? With the snow falling and all, I need extra time getting over to the theater building."

"Thanks." Xander waited until Bekka exchanged her sneakers for boots, wrapped up in her coat and scarf, grabbed her backpack and left. When the jangling of the doorway bells had fallen silent again, he moved over to sit on the edge of her vacated desk. "What did he say, besides offering you a job?"

"Not much." Hannah spread the letter out on the desk in front of her with deliberate motions. "Dear Ms. Blake," she read slowly, "I must apologize yet again for my indiscrete words which prompted an ethically deprived young man to take such drastic action against you."

"He must be desperate, to actually put an apology in writing." Xander cringed when his attempt at humor didn't even get Hannah to raise her head.

"Let me state for the record that your exceptional reputation as a paralegal and office manager is the foundation for my words. I continue to be dismayed at the threat to your safety and sense of security. As a consequence, I must here confess that I wish to permanently deprive Common Grounds Legal Clinic of your valuable talents. I would like to offer you a position as paralegal at Montgomery & Associates. As part of your terms of employment, you will have full access to the law library, time off with pay to pursue your studies toward your law degree, and tuition assistance."

"Assistance? Arc pays everything. You can't get a better deal than that."

"That's true." Hannah finally raised her gaze from the letter and studied his face in silence until Xander grew fidgety again.

"You could pretend you never got the letter. Or wait until next week to send your reply."

"I can't."

"Hannah, you know he'll go into his suffering martyr role and then lambaste you for refusing to bow to his greater wisdom and experience. I've seen him do it at a dozen board meetings and congregational votes."

"I can't ignore him or delay responding because he's going to call the office on Friday for my decision." She folded up the letter and slid it back into its envelope.

"Your decision?" His hackles rose. "What about an interview, discussing salary and benefits, your schedule, your duties, things like that? Does he think his firm is such a plum opportunity he can just snap his fingers and you'll come running?"

"Obviously, he does." She shivered a little and wrapped her arms around herself. That distant look touched her eyes.

"The only reason I can think for you to take up his offer—no, two reasons. First, a bigger salary—"

"What makes you think I care about money?"

"And second, if you work for him, we can date."

"What?" She sat back hard, shoving her rolling chair against the filing cabinet. "What makes you think King Arthur Montgomery would put up with me dating the enemy while I work for him?"

"So, I guess you can't take the job." Xander grinned, relieved that he had broken through her daze.

"Was that the problem? You ignored me all this time because you wouldn't date an employee?"

"Co-worker. Practically a partner," Xander hurried to say. What got her so angry? She was practically shooting sparks from her eyes. "And I never ignored you."

"While I was in the office, no." Hannah stood and snatched up her coat. "The moment I step out the door in the evening, I don't exist."

"Hannah—"

"I can't decide if you're a snob or a coward. You won't date an employee, or you're afraid what self-righteous idiots like Montgomery would think or say if you showed some interest in me as a woman." She pulled on her coat with angry stabs of her arms into the sleeves.

"I couldn't care less what he thinks. Especially when it comes to you." He cringed, positive that didn't sound right. He wished he stood in front of a hostile jury. He would know what to say to get them on his side. Hannah, he couldn't figure out if he had twenty guesses and unlimited time.

"It's nearly six, Xander. I'm going home. It's been a very long day."

"Let me take you out to dinner?"

"I'm not hungry." She gestured at the door. "Do you want to turn everything off and lock up, or should I?"

"I'll do it."

"Fine." She picked up her purse and slid the letter into it as she walked toward the door.

"Hannah!" For two agonizing heartbeats, Xander feared she wouldn't stop or look at him. She stopped and looked over her shoulder. "Don't leave me."

"You mean, don't go work for Montgomery?"

"I mean, don't leave *me*. I can't seem to do anything right lately when it comes to you. All I know is that I can't manage anything without you."

"Xander," she sighed. A tiny smile caught the corners of her mouth, and despite the darkening skies full of snow, it seemed like summer noontime filled the office. "You are such an idiot sometimes."

"Only sometimes. The rest of the time, I'm tolerable. Right?"

"Tolerable." She closed her eyes, and for a moment he thought she swayed. Her smile faded. "Good night, Xander." She turned her head away and walked to the door, opened it, and stepped outside.

Thursday, January 9

Hannah was on the phone when Tyler Sloane walked into the Padua office that afternoon. She had seen pictures of Tyler with Xander from their college years together. The reality of him was different.

He was tall, for one thing. She estimated he was maybe five or six inches taller than Xander. Chocolate brown hair and eyes. A lean, fit body fairly vibrated under that long, thick, black wool coat, as he turned around in the doorway to give the office the once-over inspection. Or maybe that was tension. Xander said his friend was driving in from Iowa, where he had been a drama teacher at a Christian college for the last nine years. Hannah couldn't imagine what it must have been like to drive two days, all alone.

In those few seconds before their gazes met, Hannah couldn't decide if he was naturally honey-brown all year round, or he used a tanning bed. His face kept drawing her attention as she waited for the person on the other end of the phone to take her off hold and answer her question. Tyler's face struck her as a little too long; but she liked it. He had wide cheekbones, nice angles that just escaped being chiseled, which always reminded her of cartoon heroes with no brains.

She waved to him when he turned around and looked straight at her. She pointed at the phone held against her ear and then gestured at the coffee machine, hoping he would take the hint to help himself. Tyler's face widened in a smile that wiped away several hours' worth of rough day. He nodded thanks and made a show of tiptoeing past her to reach the coffee machine.

"That's all we needed. Thanks," Hannah said, and fought to stifle a sigh of mixed frustration and exhaustion. All that waiting to get the answer she had been sure of all along, but still needed confirmation before she could do anything. She made her farewells to the obsequious little clerk who always made her think of naked, pink mice running mazes.

"You saved my life," Tyler said with a groan, the moment her phone clicked down into the cradle.

Hannah caught her breath. His voice was as chocolate brown as his eyes. No wonder Xander said his friend had been a successful romantic lead in summer stock, despite his unusual, not-quite-handsome face. She turned to see Tyler slouched in one of the reception area chairs, his coat spread to reveal faded jeans and a bright yellow Southeastern Christian College sweatshirt. He grinned at her and raised his cup in salute before taking a long drink.

"Xander's on the phone, Mr. Sloane, but I'll buzz him as soon as he's free."

"Tyler, please. And you must be miracle-worker Hannah. Xander told me a lot about you."

Hannah bit her tongue to keep from asking how much Xander had told his friend about her. Her face warmed at "miracle-worker." Well, at least Xander talked about her to other people. That was more than she would have expected only a few months ago, when she was convinced he forgot she existed after working hours.

"Has he been pacing the floor?" Tyler continued, when they exchanged smiles that seemed to solidify an instant friendship between them. "I know he was expecting me two hours ago."

"Well, a little. It's a good thing he's busy today or he'd probably be camped out up here."

"Or calling the State Troopers?" He got up and sauntered over to the coffee machine. "Do you mind? I've been running on fumes for the last four hours. I just can't eat when I'm on the road." He shrugged.

"Go ahead. Xander's the only one still in the office. Everybody else is out either doing research, interviewing people, or in court."

"Thanks." He filled his mug but didn't return to the chair. He leaned against the half-wall next to her desk after taking his first gulp of the fresh cup. "I went to check out my new theater, first."

"Royal Community. Xander said you're taking over as the manager and director."

"And whatever else needs doing. I love teaching, but after a while you want a change of pace. My aunt and uncle retired to the area a few years ago, and they're the only family I have left, besides my sister and her kids. And that dirt-ball ex-husband of hers." For a moment, Tyler's face tightened and something hot and hard flashed into his eyes. He shook his head. "Anyway, Xander told me about the theater. I contacted them, to see if they needed someone to fill in during the summer. We got talking, and the next thing I knew, they were offering me the full-time job." He took another gulp of coffee and leaned back to the table to set down the empty mug. "I decided to take a detour and check out the building before coming here. Xander's always giving me a hard time about being an irresponsible, artsy type, so why not live down to the image?"

"You two are going to be at each other's throats in about two weeks," Hannah said, fighting giggles.

"Yeah, just like old times." Tyler winked.

The one red light on Hannah's switchboard blinked off. She started to reach for the intercom button, to buzz Xander, then thought better of it.

"If you go down this center aisle, all the way to the back, and hook a right, you can surprise him."

"Ambush, you mean." Tyler peeled out of his coat and slung it over the chair where he had been sitting. "Remind me to give you front row seats for my first production." He winked at her again, then sauntered down the aisle between the cubicles.

Hannah held her breath, waiting for a ruckus to burst out. From what Xander had told her about his old college buddy, she didn't know what to expect. Would they yell, or indulge in one of those stupid he-man punching matches?

Silence. She couldn't even hear Tyler's footsteps. How long did it take a man with such long legs to walk to the back of the office?

"You!" Xander roared.

Hannah grinned and turned back to her checklist of tasks for the afternoon as a duet of male laughter rang through the office. She rather liked the idea of someone who knew what strings to pull to get Xander riled up. Tyler would be good for him. He was someone who didn't regard Xander as either a champion of justice or a troublemaker. Someone who didn't look up to him.

Maybe that's my problem. She felt as if a chill breeze had blown through the building and cleared her head. *I've been hero worshipping Xander and wishing he'd fall in love with me. Now that I see him as a real person with all his flaws, I can't believe him when he says he wants more between us.*

Of course, Xander hadn't said he was *in love* with her. He had only said he wanted to take their relationship deeper. She had assumed he intended love to be somewhere down the line. Hannah wondered if she had assumed a lot of things, and they were getting in the way.

She made a mental note to get Tyler alone somewhere and find out exactly what Xander had told his old college buddy about her.

~~~~~

Pure, sweet laughter rang out, bouncing off the ice coating the school playground. He stopped and leaned against the fence, dislodging snow from the chain links. He recognized that voice. It dragged him back to the happiest weeks of his life, the new boy in school meeting up with the new girl, talking about books, meeting in the library, walking home from school together after choir practice or football games. His angel had laughed like that.

She stood by the jungle gym, laughing with two other girls. They slipped and slid, deliberately skidding their feet on the slick, black ice that had collected under the climbing tower, holding onto the bars to keep themselves upright. She wore fluffy white earmuffs and her long, straight, dark hair swung in the gentle breeze. Her cheeks were red. Her dark eyes sparkled with life and purity and joy. That was his angel once more, come back to him looking just as she had when she left him.

The best part was, he knew exactly who she was, how to find her. No taking risks asking dangerous questions. No waiting outside her house or following her around town to learn her routine. He had been in her house
~~~~~

before. How could he not have seen that she was his angel, come back to him?

The other angels, the false angels, had distracted him. They deserved to die for that. But he had found her now. His angel.

Saturday, January 11

"Hannah?" Xander gaped, paralyzed in his own doorway. Despite his daydreams, he had never expected to see her standing on the front doorstep of his condo.

"Yes, me." She grinned, and mischief sparkled in her eyes. "Did you think I climbed into a storage locker on the weekends and slept until Monday morning?"

"Don't be silly. I mean, I see you in church." Xander sighed, rubbed his eyes, and wondered if ten in the morning was too early to get up on a Saturday. "I don't mean to sound rude, but what are you doing here?"

"Hey, leave my date alone," Tyler bellowed and emerged from the laundry room, via the kitchen. He tugged a Southeastern football jersey over his head and hurried to the front door. "Sorry, running late. We stayed up a little too late last night talking about the old days." He elbowed Xander aside. "She can come inside and wait, can't she?"

"Uh, yeah. Sure." Xander shook his head, hoping it would help. Maybe he would wake up and find out it was all a bad dream.

"Be right back."

"Take your time. I'm a little early," Hannah said. She nodded thanks as Xander stepped back and gestured for her to come in.

Tyler slid down the hall, his stocking feet turning the bare wood floor into an ice rink. It had been funny last night, Xander knew, but right now he envisioned his old buddy landing flat on his back.

"What's going on? What date?" Xander tried to remember if Tyler had mentioned Hannah coming over, but nothing sprang to mind.

"He's just being silly." She perched on the edge of the recliner and glanced around the stark living room.

Xander wondered what she thought of it. He never really cared what his condo looked like since he didn't spend much time there. The only times he thought about the interior, the furnishings or decorations, was when he thought about Hannah being here. He supposed there was something a little too Spartan about a recliner, a two-seater sofa, two bookshelves and the entertainment center holding his television and stereo system. No carpeting, nothing but basic blinds on the big picture window. The dining room was even more echoing empty, with his little bistro table and two filing cabinets. Tyler had laughed at him when

Xander showed him to his room that first night, neatly furnished with a mattress, a chest of drawers and a sheet hanging across the window. He hadn't thought anything of it, since Tyler's furniture was due to arrive by moving van on Monday. Maybe he had been living a little too simply?

"What are you two doing?" Xander bit his lip against asking if he could come along.

"Tyler asked me to give him a general tour of the area, that's all."

"I could do that. He didn't have to waste your time."

"It's not a waste. I like Tyler."

"But I live here—you live twenty miles away."

"Uh, huh. And how often do you get out and explore the area? I bet you know two grocery stores, the garage where you get your car fixed, and one bookstore. You know Padua better than Medina, because you spend most of your time there."

"Well... yeah. I guess."

"Do you even know where the Regal is in Medina?"

"The what?" Xander wished he could have taken back that question before it left his lips. Especially when Hannah grinned and shook her head, and her face reddened with repressed laughter.

"It's a theater."

"Hey, my favorite word," Tyler said, emerging from the hallway. He stopped short and tipped his head to one side, visibly studying them. "Something wrong?"

"Nope. Nothing." Xander hid his clenched fist behind his back. He didn't really want to deck his roommate. He didn't really want to shake Hannah and accuse her of playing the flirt to get his attention.

She wasn't that kind of girl. Although, whatever she was doing, she certainly had gotten his attention. Besides, Tyler had asked Hannah to give him a guided tour, she hadn't offered. Xander decided to have a little talk with Tyler when he got back and after Hannah had left.

Chapter Twenty-Three

"Where's your favorite place for carryout?" Tyler asked, as he shrugged into his brown leather bomber jacket.

"Why?"

"I thought we'd bring back some lunch. Unless you think we'll take longer than two or three hours?" he said, turning to Hannah.

"Nope. It won't take much longer than that. What do you want us to pick up?" Hannah widened her eyes in mock innocence, and Xander heard an echo of her words just moments before, accusing him of not knowing anything about the town where he lived.

"Why not surprise me?" he managed to say without growling.

"Sounds good." Tyler bowed and held out his arm to Hannah. She laughed and slid her arm into his. "See you in a while."

"Yeah, have fun."

"Why don't you come with us?" Hannah said as they headed for the door.

"Um... sorry." Tyler paused to open the door. "My 'Vette only seats two."

"You have a Corvette?" The awe in Hannah's voice made Xander's stomach twist.

"Amazing how a college professor can afford such an expensive car." Xander winced at the harsh note that crept into his voice.

"Not when I've had it ten years, and I inherited it," Tyler said with a grin and a shrug, as if he hadn't noticed the tone.

"Black?" Hannah asked.

"It's the only proper color for a Corvette. See you later, Xan."

Two seconds later, the door clicked shut behind them. Xander clenched both fists and fought the urge to race to the door and offer to drive them both around. He didn't want to look like an idiot, with Hannah having to give him directions around the city where he lived.

He didn't want to look like a jealous idiot.

~~~~~

"Sorry about that," Tyler said, after they had turned left onto Pearl Road and Hannah pointed out that it was a main thoroughfare through half a dozen cities.

"About what?" She studied the traffic ahead of them, already thick for so early in the morning, and oriented herself to where they were in
~~~~~

relation to all the major stores Tyler might need to locate.

"Using you to give Xander a hard time."

"You were?"

"The guy needs a good kick in the butt—and the head. He's like Superman most of the time, so busy saving the world he can't see Lois Lane standing right in front of him."

"And I'm Lois?" A startled chuckle escaped her. "Are you playing matchmaker?"

"Depends. Do you want me to? The guy's crazy about you, but he's a klutz when it comes to guy-girl things."

"Really?" Her face suddenly felt hot enough to cook an egg.

"Ever since he hired you, every single letter and phone call, he mentions you. If he was a normal guy, he'd never let me into the state, on the off chance I might try to steal you from him."

"But Xander isn't normal?" Hannah didn't know if that tight feeling in her chest was an urge to laugh, or to cry. Maybe she had finally found the right person to explain Xander to her.

"You have to understand, back in college, Xan got burned a couple times. He'd be crazy about a girl and she'd run away like he escaped from the Black Lagoon. She couldn't see past his face. Or the girl would play along, build his hopes up, meet for lunch and studying and whatever, and then as soon as he got his courage up to ask for a date, dump him hard enough you could hear his heart break. In public, with a big audience. After a while, Xander built up this wall. He'd like a girl, a lot. A really nice girl who was smart enough to see past his face and see the really great guy."

"The one out to save the world," she murmured.

"Exactly. But Xander wouldn't let it get any further than friendship. He learned to be a big brother to a lot of girls who would have been glad to get a lot closer."

"Best friends. Xander said we were best friends." Her throat tightened so much she couldn't swallow, as she thought about how she had stopped him cold when he said he wanted more than just a close, working friendship.

"Yeah, well, I figure he needs to get riled up enough to break through the wall. He can't see Lois Lane is just waiting for him to fly her to the moon."

"Probably because I've been just as galactically clueless as Lois Lane."

"Naaaaah." Tyler took his hand off the gearshift long enough to grab her hand and squeeze it. "You're something special, miles ahead of any of those half-wits in college, or Xander wouldn't have you on his mind so much."

"Thanks." Hannah scooted down to get more comfortable in the seat.

"Am I wrong to think Xander is the kind of guy who can't be hunted down and trapped?"

"You got that one dead center." Tyler spared her a grin before turning back to the snail's pace traffic in front of them. "Kind of makes things tough, doesn't it?"

Dead center, she thought.

Monday, January 13

"So, how did it go today?" Rene was in the kitchen when Hannah stumbled through the door of their apartment at the end of a very long, rough day.

"School was fine." She slung her portfolio case onto the table and dropped her purse on top of it, then dumped her plastic salad container from lunch in the sink.

"Not school, Xander." Rene pulled out her usual chair and sat down slowly at the table. "Did he say or do anything special when you got to work?"

"No. Business as usual."

"Hey, don't run away." Her laughter sounded a little too forced and bright. Rene patted the table opposite her. "We've both been so busy lately, we hardly talk."

For two seconds, Hannah wondered if her roommate was up to something. Then she shoved that thought away. Rene wasn't the kind of person to use tricks on anybody. Even someone she loathed.

"Xander?" She sighed as she peeled off her coat and settled into the chair on the other side of the table. "Business as usual, I guess." Hannah folded her coat into her lap and slouched until her head rested against the back of the chair.

"Is that good or bad?"

"I don't know. It was kind of nice, but kind of scary on Saturday, you know? I've waited so long for Xander to notice me, and now I'm just ruining everything. I should just be happy that things seem to be back to normal. I don't like it when he gets so tight and snippy. I thought for a minute he was going to hit Tyler. But I did kind of like the look on his face when I showed up at the door." A soft, tired chuckle escaped her. "Is it so wrong to want Xander to be jealous?"

"Does he have reason to be jealous? Are you interested in Tyler?"

"He's a nice guy, but... I don't know. I'm ready to give up on men in general, Xander Finley in particular."

"Are you in love with Xander?"

"If I knew that, I'd know what to do." Hannah closed her eyes and hugged her coat a little tighter against her chest, like a security blanket. "What's it like to be in love? Have you ever been in love?"

"I never got that far," Rene whispered.

"It was a guy who hurt you, wasn't it?"

"We're not talking about me." She forced a chuckle and reached across the table to slap Hannah's shoulder, startling her so she sat up and opened her eyes.

"I'm finding out that a lot of things I thought I wanted, I don't anymore."

"Xander isn't a thing, he's a person. Despite what the more radical feminists say about men in general," Rene added with a chuckle. "If you could have what you want, what would it be? The perfect life."

"Oh, I don't know."

"Yes, you do. If you could have it all, what would it be?"

"Oh... I'd have Montgomery leave me alone. I told him no last week, and he called both offices today, trying to track me down." Hannah shuddered in mixed anger and disgust. "I swear he's just doing it to rile Xander. He doesn't want me in particular, he's just chasing me to hurt Xander."

"Don't sell yourself short."

"Hmm. Maybe. If I could have what I wanted... I'd keep the office downstairs at the house and live upstairs. And have one big room just for books. And I'd have huge window boxes full of flowers. Maybe a few kids. I could run the office and have them right with me. And when they get older, I'd send them to the Mission for kindergarten. And by then our church would have its elementary school up and running."

"Would you adopt, or would you have a daddy for those kids?"

"Guess I'd have to adopt. The only guy I want... It's hopeless. I won't chase him down and trap him. Xander's the kind of guy who would resent it. He'd resent me. We're both a lot better off just leaving things the way they are. Why risk a good thing?"

"Who says it's a risk? Maybe you two were meant for each other?"

"You and Vic are meant for each other, too. I don't see you two getting all romantic," Hannah shot back.

"We're not talking about me. And we're certainly not talking about Vic." Rene stood abruptly and took two quick steps to the refrigerator. "What do you want to make for dinner?"

"Chocolate. Lots of it." She forced herself to laugh and got up to take her things to her room.

Class had been rough that morning. Hannah wondered if she just couldn't get her mind back into the student mode or there was something seriously wrong with her.

She had lied to Rene. Xander had been diffident when she finally got to the office in Padua that afternoon. Not chatty. He barely looked at her as he filled her in on the forms and briefs that needed attending to that afternoon.

On Tyler's advice, she had turned down Xander's invitation Sunday to go to a church league basketball tournament, saying she already had plans. When he asked what she had planned, she had given him what she hoped was a mysterious smile and walked away. Playing the mystery woman hadn't done any good, as far as she could tell. She didn't like playing games, and Xander only moved farther away instead of closer. Wasn't he supposed to chase her? When she got to the office after class, he hadn't been the slightest bit curious about her Sunday afternoon. She expected at least a question, a remark of some kind.

All things considered, things between her and Xander felt like that first week she worked for him, when he had been harassed and going in twenty different directions and she had no idea what to do. She had considered quitting three times in that first week, until she turned too quickly and sloshed stale coffee all over his white shirt and gray tie, and then minutes later, while drowning her sorrows in a jelly donut, she squirted blueberry all over her yellow shirt and matching pants. She and Xander surveyed the mess of each other's clothes and burst out laughing.

Hannah thought she had fallen for him in that moment. Maybe she *had* been miserable at times in the intervening years, despairing of ever getting Xander to notice her. Still, she had been too busy and proud of her contributions to Common Grounds to notice her misery. If only she could turn back the clock.

"I'm not going to run away, Lord," she whispered. "I don't know what I'm going to do, but I'm not going to make a bigger mess of things by running away. So what should I do?"

~~~~~

"Got time for a cup?" Vic said, leaning out of the Gold Tone Gym's office that evening.

"Anything to keep me awake on the drive home." Xander nodded, summoning up a half-hearted smile.

"How's it going with you and Hannah?"

"Same as always, I guess." He paused with his hand out for the cup. Did he really want to let Vic grill him about his non-existent love life, or offer more advice?

"Everything cleared up with the stalker and all that fallout?" Vic leaned forward, resting his elbows on the table.

"Yeah. Fine. Montgomery is still trying to steal her. He seems to think he can have anybody work for him just by snapping his fingers. Hannah's wishes don't mean a thing to an arrogant, self-righteous jerk like him."

"It's a good sign that she's staying with you, right?"
~~~~~

"I wish."

"Trouble in paradise?"

"If only it were that good." Xander sighed and copied Vic's posture; elbows on the table, cradling the oversized mug in both hands. "I tried to let things cool off for a while, but obviously not long enough. I thought, start out slow, quiet, take her to the youth tournament yesterday."

"That's quiet and slow?"

"I figured she wouldn't think I was pushing things. Just her and me and about a thousand screaming, sweaty teens. She turned me down, and she sure wasn't very talkative when she got to work today." He sighed and stared into his cup without seeing the contents.

"Maybe she was busy yesterday, and tired today."

"Yeah, and I need to step back about ten feet and give her room. She needs more cooling off time."

"I don't think that's smart. You let things cool off too long, Hannah will think she was completely right about you, and you've changed your mind about how you feel."

"Never."

"Convince her of that. Before she leaves."

"I have no idea how to do that."

"You're a lawyer — you're trained to persuade people."

"Yeah, that's easy. I've convinced a jury that a kid covered in blood and holding the butcher knife that killed his parents was ambushed and framed and didn't commit the murders. Convince the only lady for me that I'm serious? I can't seem to get my feet out of my mouth."

"And those are pretty big shoes you've got." Vic grinned when Xander glared at him.

Tuesday, January 14

"What brings you out here?" Hannah's face warmed. It was probably bright pink.

Xander stood in the doorway of her office in Tabor, giving her that bemused, crooked smile she loved. He shrugged, dislodging the fresh dusting of snow clinging to his hair and shoulders.

She wished she could sink into her chair and right through the floor. She had just finished talking to her mother, who wanted to know once again when she was going to bring Xander by for dinner. How could she explain to her mother that she had given up on Xander? She glanced at Bekka, busy with the first outgoing mailing for the office, who went on working as if she didn't hear what was going on.

"I thought you knew." He glanced over his shoulder as the bells over the door jangled and Vic and Rene walked in.

"Knew what?" Hannah stood. She caught her breath as suspicions leaped into her mind. "What are you two up to?"

"We need your opinion on a really big, touchy problem," Vic said. He hooked a thumb toward the conference room. "Okay if we close the door and take up about an hour of your time?"

"Do you know how much I charge by the hour?" Xander drawled.

Vic gave him a withering look and strode across the entry hall with Rene in tow. Xander turned to Hannah, asking with a glance if she understood. She shook her head.

"Hold all your calls?" Bekka asked.

Hannah nodded and followed Xander to the conference room. Just as she pulled the sliding doors closed, it struck her that Bekka sounded a little too innocent. Did she know what was going on?

"This is important," Rene said, and picked up one of the two tape players Vic had set on the table. "If you want to strangle us when this is finished, or never talk to either of us again, that's fine. All we ask is that you don't say anything until we're finished, all right?"

"Finished with what?" Xander said.

"Do you agree?" Vic pinned them both with his dark, steady gaze until Hannah wanted to squirm like a naughty toddler trapped in the middle of a temper tantrum.

"All right. We won't kill either of you until this is over," Xander said, nodding. He met Hannah's gaze, and she nodded agreement.

Rene pressed the 'play' button. Hannah gasped as she heard Rene speak and her own voice responded. It only took three seconds to realize her roommate had taped their conversation last night.

"Did he say or do anything special when you got to work?" Rene asked.

"No. Business as usual."

"Hey, don't run away." Rene laughed. "We've both been so busy lately, we hardly talk."

"You two haven't been talking much lately, either," Vic said, when Rene hit 'pause.'

"What's going on?" Xander demanded.

Hannah sat frozen, wanting to hide her face in her hands. She stared across the table, refusing to meet anyone's gaze. How could Rene do this to her? What would Xander think when he heard how she talked about him, about her dreams?

"Don't talk—listen," Vic said. He picked up the second tape player and pressed the play button.

"How's it going with you and Hannah?" his voice asked on the tape.

Hannah stifled a gasp as the picture came clear. Vic and Rene had set them both up.

"Same as always, I guess," Xander said on the tape.

"Everything cleared up with the stalker and all that fallout?"

"Yeah. Fine. Montgomery is still trying to steal her. He seems to think he can have anybody work for him, just by snapping his fingers. Hannah's wishes don't mean a thing to an arrogant, self-righteous jerk like him."

Xander actually sounded angry. Protective of her. Hannah had tried to find something amusing in Montgomery's persistence. Xander hadn't said anything, and until this moment she thought he was so sure of her loyalty he wasn't worried.

"It's a good sign that she's staying with you, right?" Vic asked.

"I wish."

"Trouble in paradise?"

"If only it were that good." On the tape, Xander sighed loudly enough for the machine to pick it up.

"You know, any court in the land would call this illegal," Xander began.

"Don't pull that with me." Vic gave him a fierce grin and paused his tape. "The law says as long as one of the parties being taped agrees to it, it's legal." He raised a hand, silencing Xander when he opened his mouth to protest, and nodded to Rene. She depressed the 'pause' button on her machine.

"Xander?" Hannah heard herself sigh just as loudly. "Business as usual, I guess."

"Is that good or bad?" Rene asked on the tape.

"I don't know. It was kind of nice, but kind of scary on Saturday, you know? I've waited so long for Xander to notice me, and now I'm just ruining everything. I should just be happy that things seem to be back to normal. I don't like it when he gets so tight and snippy. I thought for a minute he was going to hit Tyler. But I did kind of like the look on his face when I showed up at the door." She laughed, and Hannah thought she sounded tired enough on the tape to sleep for a year. Had yesterday really been that bad? "Is it so wrong to want Xander to be jealous?"

"Does he have reason to be jealous? Are you interested in Tyler?"

"Are you?" Vic asked, over Hannah's taped reply.

Chapter Twenty-Four

Hannah let the tape answer for her. She refused to look at Xander, because she could feel the intensity of his gaze on her.

"I'm ready to give up on men in general, Xander Finley in particular."

The tape players clicked, one pausing and the other resuming.

"I tried to let things cool off for a while," Xander said on the tape, "but it obviously wasn't long enough. I thought, start out slow, quiet, take her to the youth tournament yesterday."

"That's quiet and slow?" Vic asked, laughter in his taped voice.

"I figured she wouldn't think I was pushing things. Just her and me and about a thousand screaming, sweaty teens. She turned me down, and she sure wasn't very talkative when she got to work today."

Hannah squirmed. She thought the problem had all been on Xander's side. Why had she waited for him to make the first move? Talking to him wasn't chasing him, was it? Maybe she should just ignore what Tyler told her about Xander and his heartbreaking time in college.

"Maybe she was busy yesterday, and tired today."

"Yeah, and I need to step back about ten feet and give her room. She needs more cooling off time."

"I don't think that's smart. You let things cool off too long, Hannah will think she was completely right about you, and you've changed your mind about how you feel."

"Never."

"Are you listening?" Rene whispered, over the clicks as Vic's tape player stopped and hers started. "Are you in love with Xander?" she asked on the tape.

"If I knew that, I'd know what to do," Hannah heard herself respond. Had she really said that? "What's it like to be in love? Have you ever been in love?"

The tape player squealed and Hannah sat up, staring as Rene fast-forwarded through that portion of the tape. She wanted to protest that it wasn't fair to edit out the portions dealing with Rene. Then she thought of the hurt she had sensed in her friend.

"I'm finding out," Hannah heard herself say on the tape a moment later, "that a lot of things I thought I wanted, I don't anymore."

"Xander isn't a thing, he's a person. Despite what the more radical feminists say about men in general," Rene added with a chuckle. "If you could have what you want, what would it be? The perfect life."

"Oh, I don't know."

"Yes, you do. If you could have it all, what would it be?"

"Oh... I'd have Montgomery leave me alone. I told him no last week, and he called both offices, trying to track me down. I swear, he's just doing it to rile Xander. He doesn't want me in particular, just to hurt Xander."

"Don't sell yourself short."

"No, don't ever sell yourself short," Xander whispered. "Everything would fall apart without you."

Hannah couldn't look at him. She concentrated on her folded hands on the table and listened to the echoes of yesterday's conversation.

"Would you adopt, or would you have a daddy for those kids?" Rene asked.

Hannah hadn't heard the faint hunger in her roommate's voice yesterday, but she heard it now. Did Rene want to be a mother, to be passionately in love with the father of her children? She had confessed that she had wanted to be a missionary in college but had switched to business after her first year. She never told Hannah why, though Hannah suspected that was part of Rene's pain and the dark shadows in her past.

"Guess I'd have to adopt," Hannah heard herself say on the tape. Her voice sounded strained, trying to be humorous instead of full of tears. She hadn't realized she sounded that way last night. "The only guy I want...It's hopeless. I won't chase him down and trap him. Xander's the kind of guy who would resent it. He'd resent me. We're both a lot better off just leaving things the way they are. Why risk a good thing?"

"Who says it's a risk? Maybe you two were meant for each other?"

"Convince her of that," Vic said on the second tape. "Before she leaves."

"I have no idea how to do that." Xander's voice cracked. Hannah flinched, hearing pain and that strained laughter men used to cover fear and helplessness.

"You're a lawyer—you're trained to persuade people."

"Yeah, that's easy. I've convinced a jury that a kid covered in blood and holding the butcher knife that killed his parents was ambushed and framed and didn't commit the murders. Convince the only lady for me that I'm serious? I can't seem to get my feet out of my mouth."

"You're lawyers," Vic said in the silence that rang through the conference room after he turned off the tape player. "Talk for a change, would you?"

He slammed his chair back, gathered up his coat and stowed both tape players in the pockets. He and Rene kept silent as they hurried out of the conference room.

"Well." Xander sighed.

"Feel like a prize idiot?" Hannah ventured.

"Yeah." He scooted his chair around. She felt him watching her again, but she couldn't find the courage to face him. "It's not so bad being an idiot if you're one with me."

A snort of laughter surprised her. Hannah tipped her head up just enough to see that he smiled. She raised her gaze a little more. Laugh lines crinkled around his eyes, which glistened with a threat of tears. She swallowed hard, terrified she would burst into tears. What was there to cry about? Xander sounded like he was still serious about her, and now he knew she was serious about him.

The problem was that they couldn't seem to say that to each other, only to other people. What good was a relationship where they couldn't communicate?

"We have a lot of things to figure out." Xander rested his hand over hers on the table, his touch so slow and tentative, Hannah wondered if he feared she would resist. What kind of impression had she been giving him lately?

"We're a pretty pitiful couple."

"Partly right." He tried to chuckle. The sound seemed to catch in his throat. "You're the prettiest lady I've ever seen, and I'm kind of pitiful, and it'd be great if we really were a couple."

"Xander—" Hannah choked on a growl of complete frustration as tears filled her eyes. What was wrong with her?

"Sorry." Bekka shoved the sliding doors apart. "Emergency. I know Vic said he'd cancel my gym membership if I let anybody interrupt, but I think Chief Cooper has priority." She hooked a thumb over her shoulder, into the rest of the office.

Hannah was right on Xander's heels as they hurried from the conference room. Chief Cooper stood in the hallway, watching the girl who shivered and perched on the edge of Bekka's desk chair. Officer McGuire stood over her, hands protectively gripping her shoulders.

"Chief?" Xander asked.

A trembling sense of understanding moved through Hannah. The girl wore a blue plaid skirt with a white blouse, with her long black hair pulled back from her face in a simple ponytail. Hannah estimated she couldn't be more than twelve or thirteen. With her oval face, big doe-eyes and flawless skin untouched by makeup, she looked like a Madonna. Pure. Angelic.

She looked like those pictures of Toni's sister, Angel.

"White Rose number five?" she whispered.

Xander groaned. Chief Cooper nodded.

"Sheila, this is Xander Finley and Hannah Blake," McGuire said. "They know what it's like, and they'll help you." He looked from Xander to Hannah, and she saw the struggle for composure, the anger and fear in his eyes. "This is my niece, Sheila. She came to live with me and Nora just before school started."

"She got notes in her locker at school," Chief Cooper said. "She thought it was a boy in her class, until she found a white rose on her bed when she got home from school."

"He got into my house." McGuire's voice broke. "If I can't protect her in my own house, where can I? You were getting ready to help Annalee hide, right?"

"Arc will take good care of her," Hannah hurried to say. She finally got her legs moving and crossed the room to go down on one knee in front of the girl. "It's going to be okay, Sheila. You'll stay at my house, just next door, until we make the arrangements. It won't take long at all." She took the girl's hands in her own, and they were ice cold, trembling. Her thoughts raced, and she knew exactly what to do. "I'll drive her. If the White Rose sees her with another woman, he won't be suspicious right away. He won't think she's running away if her uncle stays in town."

"Good thinking," Chief Cooper murmured.

"Yeah. Good thinking," Xander echoed. When Hannah looked at him, his face was composed, stern, but his eyes held fear.

~~~~~

"You call me if you even suspect something," Xander half-growled.

He watched Hannah put on her coat, just moments away from walking Sheila out to her car and starting the long trip to Indiana and the Arc Foundation's battered women's shelter.

Vincent had driven up from Quarry Hall to follow and guard Hannah until she reached the state line, to make sure no one followed her and Sheila. He waited in his car around the corner to avoid suspicion. Vincent knew what he was doing. Despite knowing Hannah and Sheila were in good hands, Xander didn't feel any more secure. He was proud of Hannah, so quick on her feet, so ready to take personal responsibility for Sheila.

And he ached for her. Hannah had gone through something like this only a short time ago, fearing for her life, even when they were sure it was a copycat and not the real White Rose Killer stalking her. She had to be reliving those uneasy days. Combined with her concern and sympathy for the girl now in her care, Hannah had to be under far more strain than she showed.

"We'll be fine." Hannah paused in zipping up her coat to reach up and just touch his cheek with her gloved fingertips. "Bekka's already called the church, and the prayer chain is hard at work. With all the snow falling now, nobody could follow us if my car had a blinking neon light on the roof and a homing signal under the hood."
~~~~~

"Yeah, some consolation. And what if you get in a wreck halfway there, or halfway back?"

"I have my cell phone and my AAA membership, and a blanket and extra clothes in the back seat, and a shovel and bags of sand in the trunk. I'm used to Ohio winters, remember? Besides, do you think some lousy weather would dare interfere with Vincent on the job?" She rolled her eyes, and her exasperated tone was almost convincing.

Xander managed a grin, but feared it was a stiff grimace that didn't fool anyone. Least of all him.

"Yeah, you'll be fine. You don't need me watching out for you at all."

"Maybe. But I kind of like it when you do." She blinked back a sudden glistening in her eyes and turned to Sheila.

The girl had relaxed enough to devour the double cheeseburger, fries, shake and apple pie Xander had picked up for her. She watched them now, interest wiping away the wide-eyed, pale-faced terror she had worn when she first met them. She was a pretty girl. Xander could understand, just a little, how any man would be tempted to desperate measures to keep a girl like her for his very own.

He wasn't sick enough to use threats and to adore from a distance, though. What was wrong with a man to expect a girl to read his teeny, tiny mind and know exactly what he wanted, what he thought and felt? When this was all cleared up, he and Hannah were going to have that overdue talk. He'd been a coward and idiot for far too long.

"I'll always be worried about you." He wrapped his arms around her in a brief hug before he lost his nerve. "So you might as well relax and enjoy it."

"Is that so?" A bright blush darkened her cheeks. Hannah cleared her throat, licked her lips, and suddenly couldn't meet his gaze. "Lock up after me? Rene is working late tonight. Come on, Sheila. Your uncle should have your suitcase in my car by now." She flashed Xander a quick smile and snatched up her overnight bag from the table. In moments, she and the girl were out the door and heading down the fire escape.

"Is he your boyfriend or something?" Sheila asked.

Xander braced himself in the doorway, straining his ears for the answer.

"Boyfriend. Definitely. So hands off, understand?"

Sheila's answering giggle was the most beautiful sound Xander had heard in a long time.

Wednesday, January 15

"Miss Blake, you haven't returned any of my calls." Arthur

Montgomery's cold, affronted tones cut through the chatter in the front of the sanctuary as everyone found their places for Wednesday night Bible study.

Xander turned quickly enough to make his neck ache, searching the thickening crowd for Hannah. She had called from Indiana just before eleven that morning, with a six-hour drive ahead of her, and he hadn't heard from her since. She hadn't stopped in at either office when she got back to town, as she had promised. Maybe she hadn't reached town before he closed up and headed over to church?

He didn't care how silly his grin looked, when he spotted Hannah standing halfway up the right center aisle. He started across the front of the sanctuary to meet up with her. She looked tired, rumpled from hours of lonely driving, her coat over one arm and her purse and portfolio clutched in the other. Xander idly wondered if she had actually done any of the work she had brought with her, once she got Sheila settled into the shelter last night.

"What calls are those?" Hannah didn't back up one step though Montgomery moved up close enough to threaten her personal space.

His clique of supporters stood behind him, frowning at Hannah. Xander had a momentary image of a mob holding a rushed pretense of a trial before they strung up an innocent victim.

"I called both offices today. Several times. You've withdrawn from all your law classes, so I can't imagine you're too busy to respond. I certainly expected courtesy from you, at the very least."

"Wouldn't it be courteous to take someone's 'no' as their answer? Obviously, you don't think it rude to continuously badger people, ignoring their wishes and consistent refusal. I consider it rude to ignore people when they refuse you again and again, badgering them until they change their minds and give you what you want."

"Badger?" He chuckled, as if she had told a joke. "I do not badger anyone."

"Mr. Montgomery, I have told you eight times already that I do not want to work for you. Or are you one of those men who think that when a woman says 'no,' she really means 'yes'?"

"There's no need to be crude, Miss Blake." Montgomery drew back without actually moving a step.

Xander had an image of an affronted cobra, spreading its hood wide as it prepared to make the death strike.

"Hannah, dear, maybe you don't understand yet what a wonderful opportunity you're turning down?" Mrs. Guilfoil edged her way to the front of the little group.

Her sweet, persuasive tones never wavered — no matter the situation — in all the years Xander had known her. He hadn't realized until that moment that she was in Montgomery's camp. Her gentle, concerned mannerisms and her way of making every request and suggestion into a question suddenly turned sour in Xander's mind. She was one of those women, he realized, who tried to wrap everyone in guilt to make them do exactly what she wanted. That sweet, pillowy, cotton candy exterior hid a conniving, scheming old bat.

"I know what Mr. Montgomery is offering me. After a great deal of prayer and thinking, I'm convinced that it's better for me to stay at Common Grounds."

"You haven't prayed or thought long enough," a man snapped from the middle of the group. Xander couldn't see who it was from where he stood, five feet behind Hannah.

"Think of the advantages," Mrs. Guilfoil began.

"Money isn't everything," Hannah said with a light chuckle that sounded entirely convincing, despite her weariness. Xander wondered how much that effort cost her.

"Obviously not, if you accept the poverty-level wages Finley is paying you." Montgomery glanced past Hannah at that moment and his gaze locked with Xander's. For two seconds, he froze. His mouth tightened in displeasure.

"They're not poverty-level at all. The Arc Foundation doesn't starve the servants to feed the oxen."

"Maybe not, but if you were paid what you deserved, you wouldn't have had to drop all your law classes."

"That's none of your business. You had no right to access my records in the first place."

Xander heard the stress creeping into Hannah's voice. He stepped up and rested a hand on her shoulder, to let her know he was there. She glanced once at him, flashing him a tight smile before turning back to Montgomery.

"And in the second place, your information is inaccurate. I did not drop all my classes. Just the ones that don't interest me and won't benefit me. Although I don't owe you even that much explanation, because you have no right to look into my affairs."

"I have the right to check into the welfare of my employees. I was preparing to take over the burden of your education. Which you won't be able to continue if you remain with Mr. Finley, here."

"The Arc Foundation is providing Miss Blake with a full scholarship," Xander said. "I'm surprised your sources at the university didn't tell you that. Of course, someone handing out information against policy can't be too reliable to begin with."

"I'm not going to work for you, Mr. Montgomery. If you continue to harass me, I might need to tell these nice people exactly why someone in *your* office paid to have our new office set on fire, and then stalked me and pretended to be the White Rose. We don't want that to happen, do we?"

Xander heard a dozen distinct gasps. He swore the temperature around Montgomery's little coterie of supporters dropped twenty degrees in five seconds.

"Finley, talk some sense into the girl, will you?" Montgomery's mouth trembled as he tried and failed to conjure up a thin smile.

"First of all, she's a lady, not a 'girl'. She's *my* lady, to be exact."

Xander fought the grin that tried to take over his face when Montgomery flinched and several sets of widening eyes proved they understood exactly what he meant. Even more important to him, Hannah's mouth twitched as she fought a smile as well, and she didn't pull free of his proprietary grip on her arm.

"And second, I'd be an idiot to let my partner go to work for someone else." He allowed himself two seconds to savor the surprise and the shift of expressions on the faces surrounding him and Hannah. He released his grip on her shoulder and slid his arm around her back. "If you folks will excuse us, Hannah has been out of town attending to very important business for the Arc Foundation, and I need to discuss it with her immediately."

He took her coat and slung it over his arm and led Hannah around the dispersing roadblock of murmuring people to the front of the sanctuary. Xander liked the way it felt to keep Hannah close against him, safe in the curve of his arm. He also liked thinking about how that simple, protective gesture looked to other people. The news that he had claimed Hannah as 'his lady' was going to go around the church faster than ten prayer chains. He liked the idea.

It took another five seconds to gather up his Bible study materials and lead Hannah out the nearest door. She sagged against him a little as they escaped the thickest flow of traffic and neared the door leading to the main parking lot.

"Rough day, huh?"

"Actually, it was kind of nice, right up until I walked into the sanctuary. Don't those people understand what 'sanctuary' means?" Her voice cracked, sounding like she tried to laugh. "I had plenty of time to think and get my head straightened out."

"Why'd you quit your classes?"

Xander admitted he was a coward, working his way up to the really important questions. He wasn't ashamed of it; not with Hannah held close to his side, where he had wanted her for a long time.

"I don't want to be a lawyer."

"Why not?" He stopped them just two steps away from the doors. "You'd be a great lawyer. We need people like you."

"What I'm doing right now is just as important. Maybe more important, because everybody else in my position is just using it as a steppingstone to higher things. I like what I'm doing." She tipped her head back to meet his gaze. "Don't you think it's important?"

"Well, yeah. The way you handle people and get them to open up and you keep all of us in line and —"

Xander flinched when the doors slammed open and a gaggle of children raced through, obviously late for their activities at the other end of the church. He guided Hannah out of the way of the stampede, and then outside before the doors closed.

"I guess I was really looking forward to you passing the bar with flying colors and introducing you to everybody as my new partner." He shrugged, wondering if that odd, achy sensation in his chest was disappointment, a premonition of something going wrong, or he was just hungry. He hadn't been able to eat for worrying about Hannah and wondering where she was. "But you're already my partner, so what's the difference?"

"Maybe it wouldn't look so weird to date another lawyer, rather than just your paralegal and office manager. Even if she was your partner." Hannah nodded and looked across the parking lot. Xander couldn't see her face clearly enough in the shadows to guess what she might be thinking or feeling.

"Do *you* think it would look wrong if I dated a lowly paralegal?" He tried to laugh. "Or maybe even married her?"

"Wow," she murmured. "You actually let the 'M' word past your lips. You must have really been worried about me today."

"What's it going to take to convince you that I care about you all the time, not just when you're in danger?"

"You're a fantastic lawyer, Xander Finley. I'm sure you'll think of a way to convince me."

"I don't want to battle you, like another lawyer." He sighed. "And I don't see you as someone I need to defend, either. There are a lot of different ways to be partners, Hannah. We're partners in the office, even if you never become a lawyer. I hope someday, we'll be partners in the rest of our lives, too."

"Sounds like a workable proposal."

"Proposal, huh?" He released her once they reached his car, to unlock the door for her. "I like that word."

"Not so fast, counselor." Hannah smirked at him, mischief sparkling in her eyes. Xander didn't realize how much he had missed that look until that moment. "I did a lot of thinking on my drive back here."

"Am I in trouble?" He walked around to his side of the car.

"No." She rested her crossed hands on the roof of the car and her chin on her hands. "I think we should take it slowly."

"How slowly?" Xander paused in unlocking his door.

"Six months of dating."

"Six months?" He didn't know whether to be upset or delighted. Dating was a step forward. Six months could be forever, but it would be a lot of fun. "Exclusive access rights?"

"I'm a one-man woman. Or haven't you noticed that?"

"Yeah. Finally, I noticed." He nodded and finished unlocking his door. "Why six months? Why not three?"

"We need to get to know each other better."

"Hannah, we've been spending nine, ten hours a day together, five days a week, for the last four years!"

"That's work. Our private, personal lives are different." She turned and got into the car. "Take it or leave it," she said, when he dropped into the driver's seat and slammed the door shut.

"Different, huh?" Xander considered that for a moment, and decided she was very right. There was a lot he didn't know about Hannah. He had ignored far too much in the pursuit of defending the innocent and downtrodden. "Okay. This could be fun."

"Oh, I think it could be a lot of fun."

"Deal." He held out his hand. Hannah gave hers into his grasp. Xander held onto it after they shook to seal the deal.

Where would they be in six months? He had a very good idea, and it was better than anything he had ever dared hope for. He looked into her eyes and remembered something else he had been hoping for.

"Make it official?" He tugged her closer, leaned down, and forgot to breathe when Hannah smiled and tipped her head up, meeting him halfway in their first kiss.

The End

THANK YOU!

Thank you for reading this book from Mt. Zion Ridge Press.

If you enjoyed the experience, learned something, gained a new perspective, or made new friends through story, could you do us a favor and write a review on Goodreads or wherever you bought the book?

Thanks! We and our authors appreciate it.

We invite you to visit our website, MtZionRidgePress.com, and explore other titles in fiction and non-fiction. We always have something coming up that's new and off the beaten path.

And please check out our podcast, **Books on the Ridge,** where we chat with our authors and give them a chance to share what was in their hearts while they wrote their book, as well as fun anecdotes and glimpses into their lives and experiences and the writing process. And we always discuss a very important topic: *Tea!*

You can listen to the podcast on our website or find it at most of the usual places where podcasts are available online. Please subscribe so you don't miss a single episode!

Thanks for reading. We hope to see you again soon!

About the Author

On the road to publication, Michelle fell into fandom in college and has 40+ stories in various SF and fantasy universes. She has a bunch of useless degrees in theater, English, film/communication, and writing. Even worse, she has over 100 books and novellas with multiple small presses, in science fiction and fantasy, YA, suspense, women's fiction, and sub-genres of romance.

Her official launch into publishing came with winning first place in the Writers of the Future contest in 1990. She was a finalist in the EPIC Awards competition multiple times, winning with *Lorien* in 2006 and *The Meruk Episodes, I-V,* in 2010, and was a finalist in the Realm Awards competition, in conjunction with the Realm Makers convention.

Her training includes the Institute for Children's Literature; proofreading at an advertising agency; and working at a community newspaper. She is a tea snob and freelance edits for a living (MichelleLevigne@gmail.com for info/rates), but only enough to give her time to write. Her newest crime against the literary world is to be co-managing editor at Mt. Zion Ridge Press and launching the publishing co-op, Ye Olde Dragon Books. Be afraid … be very afraid.

And please check out her newest venture: Ye Olde Dragon's Library, the storytelling podcast. Each week, listeners are invited to join Michelle on her blog to ask questions and give feedback and suggestions. Interspersed between the chapters will be interviews with authors of fantastical fiction. Listen to the podcast on your favorite podcast app or listen on the website: www.YeOldeDragonBooks.com, and click on the Ye Olde Dragon's Library link. Then go to her blog to interact: www.MichelleLevigne.blogspot.com

www.Mlevigne.com

www.MichelleLevigne.blogspot.com
www.YeOldeDragonBooks.com
www.MtZionRidgePress.com

Look for Michelle's Goodreads groups:
Guardians of Neighborlee
Voyages of the AFV Defender

NEWSLETTER:
Want to learn about upcoming books, book launch parties, inside
information, and cover reveals?
Go to Michelle's website or blog to sign up.

Thanks for reading!
**If you enjoyed this book, would you help Michelle by posting a
review on Goodreads?**

**Are you a member of Book Bub? If so, please follow Michelle
on Book Bub, and you'll get alerts when new books are coming
out.**

**As a way of saying thanks, Michelle invites you to the Goodies
page on her website. It will change regularly, offering you a
free short story, a sample audiobook chapter, sneak peeks at
new cover art, inside information on discounts and new release
dates, etc.**

Please go to: Mlevigne.com/good-stuff.html

Also by Michelle L. Levigne

Guardians of the Time Stream: 4-book Steampunk series
The Match Girls: Humorous inspirational romance series starting
with **A Match (Not) Made in Heaven**
Sarai's Journey: A 2-book biblical fiction series
Tabor Heights: 18-book inspirational small town romance series.
Quarry Hall: 11-book women's fiction/suspense series

For Sale: Wedding Dress. Never Used: inspirational romance
Crooked Creek: Fun Fables About Critters and Kids: Children's short stories.
Do Yourself a Favor: Tips and Quips on the Writing Life. A book of writing advice.
To Eternity (and beyond): *Writing Spec Fic Good for Your Soul.* A book defending speculative fiction.
Killing His Alter-Ego: contemporary romance/suspense, taking place in fandom.
The Commonwealth Universe: SF series, 25 books and growing
The Hunt: 5-book YA fantasy series
Faxinor: Fantasy series, 4 books and growing
Wildvine: Fantasy series, 14 books when all released
Neighborlee: Humorous fantasy series
Zygradon: 5-book Arthurian fantasy series
AFV Defender: SF adventure series
Young Defenders: Middle Grade SF series, spin-off of *AFV Defender*
Magic to Spare: Fantasy series
Book & Mug Mysteries: cozy mystery series
Quest for the Crescent Moon: fantasy series starting in 2023
Steward's World: fantasy series reboot and expansion
The Enchanted Castle Archives: fantasy series